# OUR SECRET BETTER LIVES

## MATTHEW AMSTER-BURTON

Nakano
Books

Published by Nakano Books
ISBN 978-0-9984698-0-5 (pbk.)

Cover by CL Smith
The Laundry Room logo by Denise Sakaki
Book design by Matthew Amster-Burton
Text is set in Alda and CF PunkRockShow

# OUR SECRET BETTER LIVES

*To Scott Miller*

# FALL

*September 1994*

The scent of rain drew Katy out of her room. She pulled on her University of Oregon sweatshirt, stepped through the open door, and glanced back at her roommate. "I'm going to the record store. Want to come with?"

Alicia was lying on her stomach on the top bunk with a high-lighter and an open copy of *Campbell Biology*, her feet almost touching the ceiling. "Hmm? I need to finish this before I head out to the party in Weller. You sure you don't want to come? I'll wait for you."

"No thanks."

Alicia sighed. "You should consider it for once. Lot of senior hotties in that dorm."

Katy headed downstairs and out the double doors of Mitchell Hall. Hands in her pockets, she walked down College Way and turned onto Eagle Rock Boulevard. The sun was on its way down, and it wasn't raining yet, just threatening, that pre-rain static crackling in the air like a sneeze refusing to happen. She passed small shops plastered with signs for *aguas frescas* and *tortas,* and a pile of limes outside one store, ten for a dollar.

The Rhombus Records sign came into view. Posters for upcoming releases and shows covered the front window, and a couple of milk crates out front were filled with 99-cent LPs. When Katy pushed open the door, a bell jingled.

Saturday night, and the store was full of people flipping through CDs and standing at listening stations, wearing oversize headphones, nodding to various beats. She found the new Lush album and turned it over to look at the track list.

"It's not punk, it's pop." The declaration came from the next aisle over. Katy looked up to see if the guy was talking to her, and smiled when she realized he wasn't. It was exactly the same kind of record-store argument she and her friends used to get into back in Salem.

"Who gives a shit?" said a female voice. "I'm not asking if they misfiled it, I want to know if I should get it." The woman held a CD out over the divider and waved it in front of Katy's face. Bad Religion, *Stranger Than Fiction.* "This guy is no help. Should I get this?"

"I've only heard some of their stuff," said Katy. "But 'American Jesus' is pretty good."

Katy had been wrestling with the thorny vocabulary issue of whether female college students should be referred to as "girls"— they shouldn't, Katy had concluded, but she still couldn't stop saying it. This person, however, was obviously on the "woman" side of the line. Tall, black leather jacket that made her light skin look even paler, silver stud earrings.

"See, Travis," said the woman. "'It's pretty good.' That's all you had to say."

"I was getting there," said Travis. "Pop is not a bad thing. I approve." He was Asian, skinny, with a gray hooded sweatshirt zipped up to his chin. Katy recognized him from the other side of her dorm. First-years lived on the west side of Mitchell, also known as Mitchell I. Over in Mitchell II, an assortment of sophomores and upperclassmen lived the sweet life in singles, roommate-free.

Leather Jacket turned back to Katy. "You go to Atwood, right?" Katy nodded. "Megan. Senior. From Spokane. That's Travis. Sophomore. Seattle."

"Katy. First-year. Salem. Um, Oregon, not Massachusetts."

"Yeah, no shit," said Megan.

"The sweatshirt?"

"That, and the fact that you went out when it's obviously going to rain." Megan headed off toward the local music section, leaving Katy and Travis behind in Pop/Rock/Soul A through L.

Katy kept flipping through CDs. Travis watched over her shoulder, scrutinizing, and several times it seemed like he was about to say something about the album she'd paused on. She sighed and turned around. "Travis, right?" The guy nodded. "What's it like, living in Seattle? Rock bands and espresso, twenty-four-seven?" *Great. Katy Blundell, brilliant conversationalist, maintains her perfect record of saying the most awkward thing.*

"We've moved beyond espresso," said Travis. "A new place called Just the Foam opened last summer. They only serve steamed milk, but in a hundred flavors."

"Really?"

"No."

Before Katy could figure out how to respond to this, Megan wandered back over. "Let me guess, Oregon Girl. Smartest kid in your high school, then you show up here and everyone else is just as smart as you, and now you don't know what the fuck is going on."

"How'd you know?" asked Katy.

"Because that was me, three years ago."

"And now?"

"Applying to med school. If I get in, great, I get to go be the dumbest chick in med school. If I don't, who knows? I know how to make forty-seven different coffee drinks, including steamed milk, so I should be employable."

"Megan thinks angst makes her more sophisticated," said Travis.

Katy turned to him. "So what's your story?"

"I don't think he actually applied," said Megan. "I hear he wandered onto campus, outsmarted some professors, and they begged him to study civil engineering."

"Chemical," said Travis. He reached for Katy's CD without asking. "Shoegaze with pop hooks. Strong female vocals. I approve."

"You know Lush?" said Katy.

"Mostly from *120 Minutes*."

"I saw them at Lollapalooza '92 in Tacoma. Did you go?"

Travis snorted. "Yeah, right. My mom told me it was the dream of all overprotective Korean parents to have their son spend the day in a field doing ecstasy, having group sex, and watching the Chili Peppers put socks on their dicks."

"She said that?"

"I think maybe she was also worried about sunburn. So did she nail the Lollapalooza atmosphere?"

"Pretty much. I read an interview where Eddie Vedder said he was going to be in the crowd hanging out with the kids when he wasn't on stage, so I brought the insert from my *Ten* CD and a Sharpie in case I ran into him."

Megan's lips curled up into a smile. "I'm sure that happened as soon as you got there and now you and Eddie are like this." She held up her crossed fingers.

"I call him Uncle Eddie," said Katy. "Actually, my CD insert got all crumpled, and now it doesn't fit into the jewel case anymore."

It was dark out now, and the first raindrops splashed against the window. Three guys who were about to leave turned around and went back to comparing DJ headphones, and a store employee rushed out to rescue the crates of LPs.

Megan turned to Travis. "Should we head? I want to see Californians freaking out." She and Katy brought their purchases up to the front. The clerk glanced at the rain-slicked window and slipped each CD into a plastic bag.

Katy followed them out into the rain. It was coming down hard now, but the temperature remained stubbornly at seventy-five, and she felt like a poached egg. She wiped her glasses with her shirttail, but it was useless. By the time they crossed College Way, she was soaked through to her underwear.

"Well, I'm up north in Broad," said Megan. "Catch you next time it rains, I guess." She turned onto the North Campus path and broke into a run.

Travis and Katy continued on toward Mitchell. "You want me to tape this CD for you if it's any good?" said Katy.

"Nah," said Travis. "I'm trying to wean myself off cassettes."

# 2

Katy returned to an empty room. She put on the Lush CD and turned it up as loud as she thought she could get away with at 10 p.m. Yeah, the single hadn't led her astray: This album was going to be all right. As she toweled off her hair and got into bed, her eyes fell on the row of photographs on her roommate's side of the desk.

Alicia wearing a HOMECOMING QUEEN sash, next to a grinning king who looked like what you'd get if you could order "Southern California White Guy" from a catalog. Alicia with three friends, each on horseback, on the beach in Costa Rica. *I wouldn't want those things even if I could have them. Right?*

She fell asleep in the arms of Lush's swirling guitars and was awakened by the creak of the ladder when Alicia got back from the party. "Hey, how was it?" Katy asked.

"Sorry I woke you up." Alicia climbed the rest of the way into the top bunk and settled into bed. "The DJ was good. Lot of white guys trying to impress me with what they thought were hot urban dance moves. They didn't play any of your music, though. How was the record store?"

"Oh, they had a bunch of good stuff on the listening stations. Veruca Salt. Sebadoh." She was about to go on, but caught herself. Over the course of a month, Katy and Alicia had found two albums to agree on: Bell Biv Devoe's *Poison* and Tori Amos's *Under the Pink*. And Katy was starting to get tired of "Cornflake Girl," something she wouldn't have thought was possible. "It was fun. I met some cool people." *Definitely too cool to be friends with me.* "Do you know a guy named Travis? I think maybe he lives in our dorm."

"What does he look like?"

"Skinny Asian kid," said Katy. "Wears a sweatshirt a lot."

"You just described basically everybody," said Alicia. She took a breath in the darkness. "Can I ask you something?" When Katy didn't respond, she went on. "How come you never want to do stuff with me or the rest of the hall? I mean, we've been here over a month and I'm trying to be a good roommate, but I can't figure out what your deal is. Are you just shy? Or super-religious? I mean, you didn't even come to the frozen yogurt place last week."

Katy laughed. "Yeah, I'm a member of an anti-froyo cult." She looked over at her alarm clock, but couldn't make out the digits without her glasses. "Seriously, it's just... my family doesn't have a lot of money, and I'm not from California. You and Quan and Bianca and Derek, and everyone else in our hall, it's like you were all best friends and had your shit figured out before you even got here."

Alicia laughed. "Would you look around, please? Notice any other black people in our hall?"

"No, but—"

"Maybe you're not the only one who feels like the little circle outside the Venn diagram."

*Oh.* "Sorry."

"Why'd you want to come here, anyway?"

"Because I didn't get into Brown."

"Oh, that's brilliant," said Alicia. Her voice sounded like an eye-roll. "At Brown you'd *never* have to deal with rich kids who think they know everything. Hey, tell you what." She hopped down off the top bunk and turned on the light.

"Hey!" said Katy. She squinted against the brightness and reached for her glasses.

Alicia pulled her keys out of her purse, and slipped a fingernail between the layers of the metal keyring. "You can borrow my car. Anytime. No questions asked. Just bring it back in one piece, and don't leave the radio on the alternative station."

Katy sat up and accepted the key. "You're trying to buy my friendship with your car?"

"Pretty much," said Alicia. "There's a lot of cool stuff to do around here that requires a car. Now you have one, too."

Katy mimed inserting the key into the ignition and starting the car. She smiled. "Thanks."

"And now that we're friends, we've got some important stuff to figure out. Like, what code word do we put on the whiteboard if we have a guy over?"

"Good point," said Katy. "Also, how do I avoid torturing you with my weird music?"

"Easy," said Alicia. She smiled, pulled out a pair of headphones, and plugged them into the boom box.

•

Katy ticked the boxes for green peppers, cheddar, and mushrooms on the order slip and handed it to the ancient woman who ran the omelet station. Katy had often made scrambled eggs for solo breakfasts, but never an omelet. The Omelet Lady made it look easy. She slid the finished omelet onto a plate, folding it as it slipped out of the pan. "Mushroom, green pepper, cheddar cheese, mm-hmm."

Katy and her omelet walked into the dining room, looked around for a familiar face, and saw the guy she'd met at the record store a few days earlier. Travis. He was sitting alone at a table, staring into a bowl of cereal. Honestly, she'd been hoping to run into him or Megan, but now that she'd located half of the Rhombus gang, she wasn't sure what to say. Or maybe he was about to leave? That was the worst, having someone rise to their feet just as you sat down. Even if they legitimately had to run to class, it still made Katy feel like a disease.

Finally, she approached the table. "You mind if I sit here?"

"Sorry, everyone from N.W.A is going to join me so I can help them work out their differences. But you can take Eazy's seat until they get here." Katy sat down, and while she was putting the first perfect bite of omelet into her mouth, Travis said, "Look at this. It's B.S."

"What are you talking about?"

"The cereal. Did they think we wouldn't notice?"

Katy studied the cereal bowl. "I give up. Looks like Froot Loops to me. It's a nutritional crime, but I'm guessing that's not what you mean."

"It's not Froot Loops," said Travis. "Froot Loops come in six colors. These have four colors."

"So maybe some cereal-obsessed weirdo combed through the

Froot Loops and picked out their two favorite colors," said Katy.

"Also, I saw them refilling the container from a big bag labeled Fruit Circus."

"You maybe could have started off with that point. But who cares?"

"These taste like cardboard," said Travis. He looked at Katy. "And before you say it, yes, they taste more like cardboard than real Froot Loops. Hang on a second, I'll be back." He stormed off, leaving Katy alone for a few peaceful seconds with her perfect omelet, then returned with a new bowl of dry cereal. "This is even worse."

"It's eight o'clock on a Wednesday morning, dude. Too early to play cereal detective," said Katy. "Actually, I'm pretty sure I never want to play cereal detective."

Travis picked through the bowl of cereal. "Lucky Charms, right?"

"I guess."

"Wrong! Look at these marshmallows. Where are the pink hearts? And what is this supposed to be?"

Katy sighed. "I don't know."

"Me neither," said Travis, "but it looks like a green penis."

"Jesus Christ, Travis. I'm going to eat this omelet now." She looked up and saw Megan walking toward them with a bowl of yogurt and granola. She was wearing her leather jacket over a pajama shirt, and her bangs were roughly trimmed.

Megan sat down. "Hello, young people. Looks like some intense political debate for stupid o'clock in the morning."

Katy laughed nervously. *Don't say anything weird.* "Travis is convinced that evildoers have replaced his regular cereals with inferior generic equivalents."

"Capgras Syndrome," said Megan. "It's where you believe everyone you know has been replaced by an impostor. Sounds like you have that, but with cereal. Hey, look at me—signing up for abnormal psych on Wednesday mornings paid off. Can I bring you to class with me?"

"What does this look like to you?" asked Travis, holding up the offending marshmallow.

Megan looked. "Where'd you get a dick-shaped marshmallow?"

"Is there a mental disorder that makes you believe misshapen marshmallows look like genitalia?" asked Katy.

"If there is, I don't want to be cured," said Travis. "I just want genuine Lucky Charms, like my ancestors enjoyed in the Old Country."

"Now you're talking," said Megan. "You want to fix something around here? Easy." She pulled a sheet of paper out of her bag and started writing. "The administration believes students should participate in the political process. You want something done? Write a petition. As long as it's something completely trivial, you'll probably win."

"Breakfast isn't trivial," said Travis. "I mean, it's the only meal that comes with a platitude about how it's nontrivial."

"The way you eat it, it's trivial," said Megan. "Here, how's this?"

*While we understand the need to minimize expenses, generic cereals are inferior in quality and appearance to their name-brand equivalents, and feature offensive marshmallows. We, the undersigned, request that the Atwood dining hall bring back name-brand cereals immediately.*

"You sound like a corporate goon," said Katy.

"It's a petition. It's supposed to sound like that," said Megan.

Travis grabbed Megan's pen. "Am I going to get in trouble for signing this?"

Megan snorted. "Yeah, you're really fucking shit up here. Katy?"

"Fine," said Katy, scrawling her signature below Travis's. Megan signed the paper and walked it around to a few tables, earning signatures from bleary-eyed freshmen. Meanwhile, Katy finished her omelet, trying to ignore the way Travis was noisily scarfing his knockoff Lucky Charms, without milk.

"If those are so terrible, why are you eating them?" she asked.

"We learned the word in my freshman seminar..." said Travis. He scratched his head. "Oh yeah. Self-abnegation."

"You know what I wish they had at breakfast?" said Megan. She set the signed petition onto the table and plopped back into her chair. "Pie. I don't even really have a sweet tooth, but I'm telling you, even the shittiest pie is the ultimate breakfast. Especially lemon meringue or key lime. It's healthy, even, because of vitamin C and shit."

"*Key Lime Pie*," said Travis. "Camper Van Beethoven, 1990. Not sure whether it wants to be a folky violin album or a California stoner rock album, but I approve."

Megan pushed her chair back like she was about to stand up. "Travis, first of all, what do you know about stoner anything? And second, *everybody in the world knows that album.* It's like, 'Hey, guys, don't be intimidated by my encyclopedic knowledge of music history, but have you ever heard of this album *Sgt. Pepper*?'"

Katy, who'd been concentrating on finishing her omelet while Travis and Megan did their thing, found herself raising her hand. "So, maybe I'm stupid," she said, "but I've never heard of that album. Not *Sgt. Pepper.* The other one."

Travis and Megan turned to look at her with precisely the shocked expressions Katy had anticipated. "What are you doing after class?" asked Megan.

"Going to the library, I think."

"WRONG. You're coming to my room to listen to *Key Lime Pie* in its entirety. And then you're going to thank me like I taught you that orgasms exist. You do know orgasms exist, right?"

Katy looked around helplessly, her eyes alighting on Travis's face. He looked equal parts embarrassed and intrigued. "I, uh–"

"I'll take that as a yes," said Megan. "See you in an hour."

If there was one thing every first-year at Atwood could bond over, it was the outrage of requiring everyone to register for a freshman seminar that met every weekday at 8:30 a.m. The purpose of the seminar system, as far as Katy could tell, was to reassure parents that their children would be up at a reasonable hour, discussing philosophy or literature, maybe even eating a breakfast that wasn't seventy-five percent marshmallows. Your seminar professor was also supposedly your faculty liaison, a term that Katy thought was hilarious, given that first-years had also received an excruciating and euphemistic lecture about not sleeping with their professors.

Katy didn't love waking up at 7:48, which she and Alicia had jointly determined was the latest they could set the alarm, but she found she actually enjoyed the class. Her first choice of seminar, "Super Mario Soul Sisters: Race, Gender, and Identity in Electronic Games," had been full, so she ended up in "Celluloid City: Los Angeles on Film."

Professor Gill was a fiftyish white woman with curly gray hair and oversized glasses. She had a New York accent but seemed to know everything about L.A. "Los Angeles is the entertainment capital of the world," she told the class. "People in every country know what L.A. looks like through the camera's lens, and people come here from every country to tell stories. There is no Hollywood without the immigrant experience." She paused for emphasis. "This city is your home now. Don't let the fact that you're living in a leafy corner of the map prevent you from learning more about its history, its peoples, and its cultures."

Even though Professor Gill was a compelling lecturer, this morning Katy's mind kept wandering to her conversation with Megan at breakfast. *She wasn't serious about me coming over to hang out and listen to music with her, right?* Katy imagined herself knocking on Megan's door and getting an annoyed, "What are *you* doing here?"

Celluloid City students were expected to watch the movies on their own time at multimedia stations in the library. So far she had watched *Boyz N the Hood* and *Sunset Boulevard,* and she was looking forward to *Chinatown* and *The Decline of Western Civilization.* In high school, Katy and her friends watched terrible movies for fun, and she'd gotten the idea that L.A. was full of vacuous people making disposable entertainment. She hated rethinking her assumptions, especially at 8:45 in the morning. After class, she stopped at the Java Cave for coffee and headed to the library to watch *Blade Runner.*

●

That night, Katy was listening to *Definitely Maybe* and working on a French assignment when the phone rang. She raised her eyes just enough to make sure Alicia was there to answer it. Alicia was on the phone constantly. She could talk with a friend and do homework at the same time, which drove Katy crazy, since Katy not only couldn't manage this, but couldn't concentrate on homework while listening to Alicia's half of the conversation. Thank god for headphones—although Liam Gallagher's voice could be similarly distracting.

Alicia tapped Katy on the shoulder. "It's for you."

"Oh. Okay, thanks." The only people who ever called Katy were her mother and her friend Christina, who went to University of Oregon. She pulled the headphones off and pressed the receiver to her ear. "Hello?"

"You stood me up," said a stern female voice.

"What? Who is this?"

"You were supposed to come to my room after class. *Key Lime Pie*, remember?"

"Megan? I thought you were being, you know, rhetorical."

"I'm never rhetorical. What are you doing right now?"

"Homework."

"Great, I'll be there in ten minutes."

"It's eleven o'clock at night." *Shit, I sound like my mom.*

"Oh, fuck yes. The Midnight Special is on. I'll call in the order."

"Okay, I guess. My room is—"

"I already looked you up in the directory." *Click.*

Katy put away her French textbook. "Um, a friend of mine wants to come over and listen to music. You want some pizza?"

"Yeah, I heard. No thanks." Alicia threw a textbook into her backpack. "I'm going to the library anyway."

Megan showed up a few minutes later. "Nice place. How's your roommate?"

"Alicia? Very... cheerful," said Katy. Every room in the dorm had a whiteboard on its door, and earlier in the evening Alicia had written STUDYING!!! on theirs and drawn a big smiley face. "She's from around here somewhere... Palos Verdes Estates?" Katy didn't know whether that was a city, a neighborhood, or just a collection of mansions surrounded by a moat.

Megan went for the closet without asking. "Holy shit, does she have enough shoes? I'm a girl too, but seriously."

"How do you know they're not my shoes?"

Megan held up a red slingback sandal and rolled her eyes. "Please. It's a compliment." She put her hand on a battered acoustic guitar case and said. "This hers or yours?"

"Mine. But I don't really know how to play it."

"Then why'd you bring it?"

"Beats me. I learned just enough to play camp songs when I was a Girl Scout camp counselor. I guess I figured college would be sort of like camp. Which it's not, by the way."

"I love camp songs," said Megan. "'Barges'? 'Ob-La-Di, Ob-La-Da'? 'This Land is Your Land'?"

"Pretty much," said Katy. She couldn't tell whether Megan was being sarcastic. "You know, we learned 'Ob-La-Di, Ob-La-Da' in music class in elementary school, but the teacher changed it from 'Life goes on, bra' to 'Life goes on, la' because she didn't think we could handle the word 'bra.' So then when I taught it to my campers, I wasn't sure what to do. La or bra?"

The phone rang again, and Katy buzzed the Pizza Hut delivery guy in. She and Megan dug through their pockets for crumpled dollar bills, and they started in on the half-veggie, half-pepperoni. "We're going to need help with this," said Megan. She dialed four numbers on the phone and said, "Hey, Travis. We got pizza. Room 207." She hung up. "So, what did you decide? La or bra?"

"La. I chickened out."

Travis appeared in Katy's doorway. She invited him in, and he sat on the floor and took a pepperoni slice. "You know the Midnight Special is a conspiracy, right?" He gestured with the slice, dripping sauce on the floor.

Megan slurped her soda. "Here we go." She applied a napkin to the sauce spots.

"Think about it," Travis continued. "The dining hall serves dinner from five to six. Who eats dinner at five?"

"I can answer that," said Katy. "My grandparents, in Arizona."

"Precisely. So everyone shows up for dinner at five, and dinner sucks."

"Says the guy who always goes back for thirds," said Megan.

"I'm a growing boy. That's the majesty of nature, that I can take the sludge they serve up with ice cream scoops and turn it into this statuesque form." He patted his chest. "So ten o'clock hits, boom, everyone on campus gets hypoglycemia. They call Pizza Hut and fork over ten dollars for pizza and sugar water. Speaking of which, can I get some of that?" He looked at Katy's drink, and she handed it over.

"Ding!" said Megan. "That sound means I can't listen to any more of this theory."

Travis started flipping through the contents of the CD rack. Katy felt like she was undergoing an invasive exam, but she smiled and said, "Can you tell which shelf is mine?"

"Let's see," said Travis. "Ace of Base. Boyz II Men. Madonna. Janet Jackson. That's got to be you."

Megan picked up the framed photo on Katy's desk and started singing the chorus of "All That She Wants." Travis covered his ears ostentatiously. "This your family?" asked Megan. "Younger sister?"

"Yeah, Julie, a.k.a. the pretty one." The photo had been taken on a trip to Portland the previous spring. Katy's brown hair couldn't make up its mind between straight and wavy, and she was three inches shorter than Julie, and her sweatshirt—the same one she was wearing now, in fact—made her look shapeless. "You have any siblings?"

"No," Megan said quickly. "Oh, shit, I almost forgot why I'm here." She slipped a CD into the player and turned it up loud.

Katy had no idea what to expect from *Key Lime Pie*, but she certainly hadn't expected it to lead off with a slow instrumental track with a dissonant lead violin part. But Travis and Megan were both nodding along happily, so she wasn't about to betray her dorkiness by saying, "What the hell is this?"

"Classic," said Travis. He turned to Megan. "But don't you find the drumming simplistic?"

"Yes, Travis, we drummers all agree that a record can't be good unless it has 96-bar drum solos. Let's turn this shit off and put on *2112*."

"You play drums?" asked Katy. "Are you in a band?"

"I was last year, but our singer and guitar player graduated," Megan went on, "and that leaves me and Keith, the bassist. We've gotten together to jam a couple of times, but we're not really into experimental drum and bass music." She wiped her mouth with a napkin and gave Katy a thoughtful look. "You have a guitar. If Keith's around tomorrow, you should come by and play with us."

"Me? Yeah, I don't think so," said Katy. "My musical skills are barely good enough to entertain a bunch of ten-year-old girls trying not to burn their marshmallows." The CD had moved on to a more guitar-driven track.

"How many chords do you know?"

"Um. I don't know, six or seven?"

"That's plenty," said Megan. "I'm not asking you to go on tour, just kick around and sing along with a couple of Def Leppard and Guns n' Roses songs that I'd bet my long-lost virginity you know all the words to anyway." Megan clicked ahead to the next track. "Now shut up, this is my favorite song."

Katy listened to the pleasant, unthreatening melody and could not begin to fathom how this could be Megan's favorite song. You couldn't headbang to this song; the best you could do was nod along. So she lied. "Great song."

"No talking during 'Sweethearts'!" Megan turned up the volume and let the music spill out into the hall, and they all sat and listened. When the song was over, Megan reached for a slice of pizza, but the box was empty. "What the fuck, Travis? How many slices have you eaten?"

"Five. Like I said, statuesque form."

When Katy woke up at eight, Alicia had already left for seminar. Megan and Travis had hung around until at least 2 a.m. At one point, Travis had fallen asleep in the hall, splayed out against the wall in a crime-scene contortion.

Katy raised her groggy head. She stopped at the dining hall for a quick bowl of cereal—corn flakes, which had no telltale food dyes or marshmallows to distinguish generic from name-brand— and found herself whistling a song on the way back. It was melodic and strange and very much the soundtrack to walking across a suspiciously green California lawn. *Oh, it's one of those songs Megan played for me. Camper Van Beethoven.*

And just like that, Katy understood why "Sweethearts" was Megan's favorite song. How did that work, anyway? How could a song sneak over from "it's okay, I guess" to "we will be together forever" when you're not paying attention? Katy didn't know, but she went straight to Rhombus after seminar to pick up a copy of *Key Lime Pie*. She stopped at the computer lab on the way back, and there was an email from mdougherty@atwood.edu. Subject line: *Saturday. 2pm. Rock. Be there.* She included her room number in Broad Hall.

Katy held her breath and wrote back: *OK.*

•

Katy set her guitar down outside Travis's door and knocked.

"What do you want?"

"It's Katy. Can I come in?" The door swung open a crack. Katy tried to push it open, and the door heaved against crumpled printouts, discarded t-shirts and jeans and boxer shorts, and a few Ziploc bags of Fruit Circus and Lucky Stars. "Jesus, you could hide a dead body under here," said Katy. "Or a family of rats."

"Unlikely," said Travis, staring at his monitor. On one corner of his desk was a framed photo of himself with a pretty blonde girl, her arm around his shoulders. "Rats, that is. I've been careful about crumbs."

"Is it always like this in here, or are you having a breakdown or something?"

"I'm working," said Travis.

"Homework?"

"Or something." He closed a window on his desktop—some audio waveform—and swiveled his chair towards Katy. He handed her the jewel case for *Nevermind,* with its baby-penis cover. "It's like this. These CDs, they're just bits, right?"

"What do you mean, bits?"

Travis groaned. "A CD is just ones and zeros etched into plastic. The CD player shoots a laser at the CD and converts the bits into sound."

"Yeah, I know how a CD player works. What's your point?"

"Okay, so Nirvana goes into the studio to record a song. They beat on guitars and drums and sing for a few days, and a recording engineer sets up microphones and sits behind a mixing console. Everything they're doing, the whole point, is to get the track burned to a CD, and then it's just bits."

"Is that a bad thing?" asked Katy.

"No, it's not a bad thing, it's an amazing thing. Think about it. Every three-minute song is just a different series of bits. 'Smells Like Teen Spirit?' Bits. 'Heart Shaped Box?' Bits. That Ace of Base song that's trying to kill me by boring a hole through my skull from the inside? Bits, bits, bits." Travis grabbed the CD back from Katy and peered at her through the hole in the disc. "It's not guitars or synthesizers or vocals anymore. It's just ones and zeroes. So if I generate a random string of ones and zeros and tell the computer to run it through the sound card, like it's a CD..."

"You're trying to create the next Nirvana song."

"I'm trying to create the next Nirvana *album*."

"How's it going so far?"

"Not very well." Travis handed Katy a pair of Sony headphones, and she slipped them over her ears. He clicked his mouse a couple of times, and Katy was rewarded with an onslaught of white noise, TV test pattern, the wind rattling a plastic tarp. She struggled to tease out any hint of aggressive chords or drum hits.

Katy took off the headphones. "How many combinations do you need to try?"

"Well, a three-minute song is 254 million bits."

"So you have to try 254 million combinations?"

"I wish," said Travis. "It's two to the 254-millionth power. So it'll take longer than the age of the universe. *Much* longer. But

I can't think of any other way I want to spend my free time, so."
He shrugged. "If I had more computing power I might be able to
write a filter to automatically throw out files that don't have anything musical in them. Hey, is brunch still on? Could you bring
me a bagel?"

"Seriously?"

The phone rang. Travis hit a function key and his PC generat-
ed a new waveform. The phone rang again. "Are you going to get
that?" asked Katy.

"Wasn't planning on it," said Travis.

His answering machine picked up. "This is Travis. When you
hear the 1000 Hz tone, leave a message."

*Beep.* "Travis, this is your mother speaking. Call home tonight
so we can talk about your chemistry class." *Click.*

"Does your mom leave messages like that?" asked Travis.

"I'm not taking chemistry," said Katy. "And my parents are
more the hands-off hippie type."

"Lucky. If the school allowed it, my mom would be living next
door to keep an eye on me. Actually, that wouldn't be close enough
for her. She'd be my roommate."

Katy straightened a pile of incomprehensible printouts. "That
would probably do a lot for the decor." She bit her lip. "Hey, will
you come to Megan's with me? For the jam session thing?"

Travis eyed the guitar case. "Oh, that's a relief. I thought maybe
you had an M-16 in there." He pressed a few keys and frowned at
the monitor. "I don't know anything about that stuff."

"Me neither, but—" *But I'm kind of desperate to have Megan be my
friend and I'm too nervous to go over there by myself.* "Tell you what, I'll
get you that bagel and you come with me to Megan's."

Travis looked at the ceiling. "Two," he said. "Not two halves.

Four halves. Be sure and put the peanut butter on when they're right out of the toaster so it gets a little melted."

Megan's single in Broad Hall had the same *Boys Don't Cry* and *London Calling* posters Katy had seen in plenty of other dorm rooms, but these were actually hung level, without wads of blue tacky adhesive oozing out at the corners. A sparkle-blue Ludwig drum set stood in the middle of the room. "Welcome to my rock and roll dungeon," said Megan. She nodded at Travis. "You brought a roadie?" Travis grunted and flexed his biceps. Megan laughed. "Never do that again. But feel free to stick around, as long as you don't interrupt the songs with any cogent observations."

"I would never." He pulled a candy bar out of the pocket of his sweatshirt and started eating it.

Katy rolled her eyes. Was it too late to un-invite Travis? *Say something.* "Nice drum kit."

"Thanks. I don't actually know how to play. I just got them so if I invite a dude over, he'll trip on a floor tom and fall face-first into my lap."

"Shut up."

"Sweet comeback. No, I've been playing since I was eleven. But they haven't gotten a lot of action this year, so thanks for coming by."

Katy looked around for a place to sit. Travis had claimed the desk chair, and Megan was seated on the little stool behind the drum set, so Katy sat on the floor, unsheathed her guitar, and set it across her lap.

"Hey, Megan," said Travis. "Did you ever tell Katy the name of your band?"

"My *ex*-band," said Megan. "Oh, here we go. We were called Slag, and we did mostly hard rock and metal covers. Def Leppard, Mötley Crüe, that sort of thing. Our singer was good at that stuff, so as long as our guitarist could download the chords off the Nevada archive, we'd play it. And before you say it, yes, I know metal isn't cool, but it was 1993, dude. It was a different time, before everyone simultaneously decided guitar solos and songs about girls were 'unsophisticated.' We added a few alternative songs last year."

Before Megan could continue, in walked the most beautiful human being Katy had ever seen. He was at least six feet tall, with shoulder-length blond hair, his ethnicity intriguingly indeterminate. His blue t-shirt fit so well, it made Katy realize that all of her own t-shirts, even her favorites, didn't quite fit right. *Can you get a t-shirt tailored? That would be weird, right? Or are shirts just manufactured to fit that guy?* "Katy, this is Keith Lopez, my old Slag-mate. Keith, you know Travis, right?"

Keith nodded. Katy stood up awkwardly and leaned the guitar against the wall, then had to steady it so it wouldn't fall over. She reached for Keith's hand and shook it. His skin was smoother than she expected, but she could feel the callused pads on the ends of his fingers, and when he took out his bass and started gently plucking the strings and adjusting the tuning pegs, she was jealous of the instrument.

"Nice to meet you," said Keith. His voice was, well, bassy.

Katy turned to Megan. *So, are you and Keith...?* she wanted to ask, but instead she said, "So what are we playing?"

"What are you in the mood for?"

"Well, what was a crowd favorite when you guys played last year?" Katy asked.

Megan laughed. "Let's see. Keith, what did we do for our encore at the Tacoma Dome?"

"Ah, the Dome," said Keith. His fingers walked up and down a scale on the neck of the bass, and Katy shivered a little. "I'm pretty sure we closed it out with 'Livin' on a Prayer.'"

"Ooh, let's do that," said Katy. She pulled her guitar out of its case.

Keith scribbled some letters down on a sheet of loose-leaf paper and passed it to Katy. "Here, I think this'll do it."

Katy accepted the paper and set it in her guitar case. Keith had written LIVIN' at the top, and underneath was a chord progression. E-minor, A-minor... *Fine, I know all of these chords.* "You bring a strap?" said Megan. Katy shook her head.

"Hey, are you allowed to play drums in your room?" asked Travis.

"Absolutely not," said Megan. "So I'm using these." She held up a brush-like implement and whacked the snare drum. It was still pretty loud. "And if campus security comes by, we all play dumb. 'Why, officer, I had no idea.'"

"Does that work?" said Katy.

"Hot college girls can talk their way out of anything," said Megan. "It's totally unfair and sexist and awesome. Now let's do this.

Two-three-four!"

Katy sat and listened while Megan slapped the drums and Keith played the "oo-wow-oo-wow" intro on the bass. She watched Keith's fingers—not an unpleasant way to spend her time—and tried to follow along. Her gaze shifted back and forth between Keith and his handwritten cheat sheet, but the chord changes were fast, and Katy had never played anything more rocking than "Kumbaya."

If she played quietly, at least, Megan would mostly drown her out. She and Keith and Megan all started singing sloppily, and by the time they got to the chorus, she was almost relaxed. When she looked over at Travis, he was flipping through Megan's CDs but bobbing his head in time to the steady drumbeat.

"Phew," said Megan, when they finished out the song. "That was rough. Katy, A-minor on the verse. Not A-major."

Katy grimaced. *How had she even noticed that?* "I should probably go." Sure enough, this had been a bad idea. She couldn't keep up with the music, and Travis's fidgety presence was making her even more nervous. She felt oddly maternal, like she needed to get him home for his nap. At the same time, she wanted to press herself up against Keith Lopez until not a molecule of air separated them.

She hoped, not for the first time, that there was no such thing as ESP.

"Come on," said Megan. "Stick around for a couple more songs. This isn't a job interview. I don't give a shit if you suck."

Well, there it was. *You suck.* Katy wanted to get out of there, *now*, but at the same time she wanted a chance to prove to Megan that she deserved at least a D-minus, not an F. "Okay, can we do that one again? Travis, you gonna join in this time?"

"Maybe," said Travis. He fiddled with the zipper of his jacket. "Hey, Megan, can I borrow your Pixies import?"

"Not a chance," said Megan. "And I agree with Katy, if you're going to hang around, at least sing the song. Or have you not heard this one before?" Even Travis laughed at that. "And Katy, play louder. We're not at camp."

Megan counted off, and they started the song again. Katy followed Keith's chord sheet and everything seemed okay, although she was concentrating so hard on keeping up with the changes that she gave up on trying to sing at the same time. Halfway through the first verse, however, it became clear that something weird was going on. The song sounded full and fleshy, completely different from their last attempt. It couldn't possibly be due to her guitar playing. She looked over to see if Travis had somehow put on the Bon Jovi CD as a prank, but no, he was just singing along like everyone else.

Or maybe not *quite* like everyone else. Megan caught Katy's eye and tilted her head toward Travis, like, *are you getting this?* Keith had stopped singing, too, and even over the drums and amplified bass and Katy's enthusiastic strumming, Travis's voice filled the room, a faithful likeness of the original. They got to the final chorus, where the pitch modulates up three steps and millions of kids singing along to the radio shake their heads and give up, and Travis sailed right through it like it was no harder than singing "Happy Birthday."

"What the *fuck*." Megan's eyes were huge.

Travis held up the Pixies CD he'd been eyeing earlier. "I swear I'll just rip it and bring it right back."

Katy jabbed a thumb in Travis's direction. "Megan, you're telling me you didn't know about this?"

"Not at all," said Megan. "Never heard him sing. Never came up."

"Wait, are you guys talking about me?" said Travis.

"Of course we are," said Katy. "How did you learn to sing like that?"

"And please don't say you didn't know you could sing, or I *will* kill you," Megan added.

"Oh, I figured I was pretty good," said Travis.

"Wait, I think I want to kill you anyway."

Travis put the CD back on the shelf. "It's like this. You know the stereotype that all Asian parents force their kids to play violin or flute or whatever? Well, my parents don't buy into that Mozart Effect stuff. According to my mom, music is a distraction."

"Isn't music good for your college applications?" Katy asked.

"Thanks for the painful flashback. 'You know what is good for college applications? Your grades and your SAT scores.' It's fine. I didn't want to play violin anyway. I asked for guitar lessons, and they said no, so I picked an instrument they couldn't confiscate. My mom used to bang on the door and tell me to keep it down, but beyond that, what could she do?"

"We should play another song," said Keith. "What do you guys like?"

"You know any Nirvana?" said Travis.

6

*So this was what they meant by "academically rigorous."*

Katy's professors started piling on assignments so abruptly, it was like an ambush. Katy imagined the college president cackling and pressing a big red button. *These freshmen have had it easy long enough. Let's see who really belongs here.*

A biology test to study for. A paper on Sartre—in French. A personal essay for English composition. A ten-page paper on post-apocalyptic images of L.A. for seminar. Falling asleep with the corner of a textbook digging into your arm. Late nights breathing ozone fumes in the computer lab.

Katy didn't see Travis or Megan at breakfast, or anywhere else, all week. At first she was too busy to miss them. By Saturday, however, she had started wondering whether they were caught in the same academic meat grinder, or whether they'd decided she hadn't made the cut. Maybe while Katy was sprawled on the floor of her room, studying to the beat of a Pet Shop Boys song—not one of Alicia's worst musical offenses, Katy had to admit—they were at Rhombus Records, shopping for a new friend.

She headed to Travis's room to investigate. "Hey," she said, knocking on the frame of his open door. "You busy?"

"Extremely." Travis was playing a video game where all you could see of the protagonist was a hand holding an absurdly large gun. Katy had never seen anything like it, and it was mesmerizing, watching him vaporize aliens, or soldiers, or alien soldiers, with realistic spurts of gore.

"Have you talked to Megan recently?"

Travis didn't look away from the screen. "Yeah, she called and asked if I wanted to come sing with them this week. Why?"

"Wait, are you fucking serious?"

"Okay," said Travis. He turned off the screen and did a one-eighty in his swivel chair. "I get the sense that I did something wrong, but I have no idea what it was." He held his hands palms-up and spread his fingers, like he was waiting for Katy to hand something over.

"No, it's just..." *That she didn't call* me. "What did you tell her?"

"I said no. I mean, it was sort of fun, but I have other stuff to do."

"Like what?"

"Studying. Playing Doom. Agitating for better cereals."

Katy felt her forehead growing hot. "You should go. You're really good."

"Maybe. I don't know. But who cares? If I was really good at archery, I wouldn't go around shooting arrows all the time, although now that I say that, it sounds pretty awesome, right? Huh, I wonder if this game has a bow-and-arrow mod." He turned the screen on and started typing. "Besides, come on, you were there. People like you and me, we're not rock band material. But, I mean, you should go. If you want."

"Apparently I'm not invited."

"Oh. Well, wanna shoot some stuff?"

●

It was one of the most peculiar aspects of Katy's college experience thus far: Suddenly everybody is talking about a thing you've never heard of.

"Are you going to Fall Fest?" asked Bianca one day on the way to lunch.

"I don't know," said Katy. The image that came to mind was kids jumping into a pile of leaves. On the bulletin board at the dining hall, however, was a new flyer offering key information about the annual campus festival:

**FALL FEST**
OCTOBER 27
FITZ FIELD
TWO STAGES
NUMEROUS BANDS
BEER (21+)

Judging by the hyperventilation that accompanied any discussion of Fall Fest, Katy developed a mental list of major American gatherings, ranked in order of historical importance:

3. The Boston Tea Party
2. The March on Washington
1. Woodstock/Fall Fest (tie)

"Can you explain Fall Fest to me?" Katy asked Travis at lunch.

"It's a music festival," he began. By now, Travis had come to understand when Katy's glare meant *you're taking the question too literally.* "Well, it's one of the few things that happens around here that's not boring."

"Okay, but why am I supposed to get excited about a bunch of bands I've never heard of?"

Travis laughed. "For once, you're the weird one, not me. I agree with you, but most people here don't need to have it explained why they should get excited about standing around in the sun drinking beer and listening to music."

"So you're going to go?"

"No way. I went last year. It was a bunch of people standing around in the sun drinking beer and listening to music."

"What's wrong with that?"

"Nothing," said Travis. "Except it was all jam bands. Perfect music for people who hate music."

"Remember when you said to tell you when you're being a jerk?" said Katy.

"I never said that."

"Well, you should. I'm volunteering. We can sign the contract while listening to my Grateful Dead CDs."

Katy looked at Travis to see if he was formulating a response to this, and noticed Megan walking into the dining hall carrying a tray. Katy tried to send a mind-beam in her direction: *Please skip the nerd table and sit somewhere else.*

She hadn't spoken to Megan since the jam session, or band practice, or whatever you wanted to call that unbearable afternoon when Megan had upbraided Katy for her lousy guitar skills in front of the best-looking guy on campus. Katy was dealing with this by avoiding Megan and Keith as much as possible. Like playing the guitar, this proved to be sort of easy and sort of impossible. The two-chord basics were simple: Walk around the back of Megan's dorm on the way to biology, and sit in the dim back corner of the dining hall at breakfast. Keith lived in the same dorm as Megan—Katy had looked him up in the directory. This made them easier to avoid as a package deal, although Katy spent way too much time thinking about what Keith's room might be like and whether she'd ever score an invitation.

But Atwood was smaller than Katy's high school. What was her long-term Megan-avoidance plan, exactly? Dart behind pillars? Plastic surgery? She resigned herself to the inevitable "we used to be friends" nod popular with broken-up couples and former roommates who never got along.

It didn't work. Megan sat down with a salad topped with three chicken strips. "Fall Fest," she said. "Who's going?"

"Hey, I haven't seen you in forever," said Katy. "Travis says he's going to skip it."

"Man of the people," said Megan.

"Ah, must be America's most popular holiday," said Travis. "Gang-up-on-me day. Weird, it feels like we were celebrating it just yesterday."

"An argument? Ooh, this sounds juicy," said Megan. "Give me the facts. I'll judge. Wait, this isn't cereal-related, is it?"

"I thought you were going to med school," said Katy. "Is it law school now?"

"No, but I've watched a ton of *People's Court*." Megan chopped her chicken strips into crouton-sized pieces and stirred them into her salad.

"Travis says jam bands aren't real music," said Katy.

"No, I said they're music for people who hate music," said Travis. "It's like this. When you write a song, you're trying to build this perfect thing. It's like sculpture. You chip stuff away until there's nothing left but the essence. The Grateful Dead have some good songs, but when they play a twenty-seven-minute version, it's like pouring chocolate sauce on Michelangelo's *David* and calling it an improvement. Everyone likes chocolate and guitar solos, right?"

"You're talking about music like everyone has to enjoy it exactly the same way you do," replied Katy. "I think a good jam is more about making people feel a certain way. Don't you ever just want to zone out for a while?"

"Not really."

"Shocker."

"Order!" said Megan. "Katy, your argument is lame, so the judge is stepping in. Travis, which band wrote the best songs?"

"That's easy. The Beatles."

"You are so predictable. And I agree. You want a perfect song, you turn to Lennon-fucking-McCartney. But what about 'Revolution 9'?"

"What about it?" said Travis. "If you're arguing that 'Revolution 9' is a prototypical Phish song or something, you're crazy."

"I'm saying even your musical heroes understood that not every sound has to be a three-minute pop song. I listened to the *White Album* a million times when I was a kid, and mostly I turned it off when 'Revolution 9' came on—"

"My point exactly," said Travis.

"You're in contempt of court," said Megan, smirking. "But sometimes it was just what I needed. I'd get *fucked up* on that song."

Katy tried to think of something intelligent to inject into the conversation, but Travis had already started in again. "You're arguing that any sound that makes you feel a certain way is by definition good music. Like, if I zone out to the hum of my refrigerator, credit Kenmore with writing a brilliant song."

"That's kind of what Brian Eno says about ambient music," said Megan.

"Then Brian Eno can bite me. Except he also produced *The Joshua Tree*. Hmm, is that guy going to heaven or hell?"

"Both of you shut up," said Katy. Dammit, Megan was too much fun to hate. "I've never been to Fall Fest and I want to go. Are you two coming with me or what?"

"Absolutely," said Megan.

"Travis?"

"Yeah, okay," he said. "Just so I can say I told you so."

•

On the stage, five white guys in an assortment of plaid and paisley noodled their way through a fifteen-minute opus. The singer, unkempt hair cascading over the shoulders of his flannel, mumbled something like "every day is like every day" into the microphone before blasting a few notes on his harmonica.

"Okay, this is the worst thing I've ever heard," said Katy. "What band is this?"

"Nabisco Session," said Megan, who was pressed up against Katy's left side at the back of the swaying crowd. Travis took her other flank. "Local talent. Rumor has it they're signing to Tentpole Records."

"They're from around here?"

Megan sighed. "You really are new here, huh? Harmonica Boy up there is Nick Dimmett, Atwood College senior and number one crush object on campus. For reasons I can't understand."

"I don't think his charms are working on me, either," said Katy. Someone exhaled nearby, and she screwed up her face at the cloud of marijuana smoke.

"Well, the song's not even half over," said Megan. "Check with me when they reach the thirty-minute mark and tell me if your panties are still on." Katy laughed. "Seriously, though, these guys may be toked-out couch jockeys, but they fucking *practice*."

"So they're using their power for evil," said Travis.

"Oh my god," said Megan. "You are the only thing more tedious than this song."

A vision of flowing blond hair wandered over with a plastic cup of beer in one hand. Keith Lopez. "This is awesome!" he proclaimed, nodding his head in time with the beat. "Megan, I didn't expect to see you here."

"Yeah, neither did I."

"The bass player is amazing," Keith went on. "Close your eyes and listen to what he's doing." Katy tried, but couldn't really distinguish the bass from the rest of the music.

"Keith," said Megan, "you realize the only people who ever get excited about bass playing are bass players or people going out with a bass player."

"Bass man, at your service," said Keith. He gave an ironic bow, making his hair sway like a pendulum. A sexy, sexy pendulum.

"It sounds like you're speaking from experience there, Megan," said Katy.

"Dating a bass player? God, no." *Well, that was something.* "But

I've been in enough bands to know that bass players are their own species."

"Compliment accepted," said Keith. He really did look like an organism endemic to California, *Surfia sixpackensis*. Katy tried to give him a flirty look without doing the thing she always did, waggling her eyebrows like Groucho Marx. But he didn't notice anyway.

"I didn't mean it like that," said Megan. "I mean, I'm a drummer. If we're dealing in stereotypes, I'm the dumbest one in the band, the biggest flake, the one with no musical skills who just wants to bang on shit. How can you tell when the stage is level? The drool comes from both sides of the drummer's mouth." Katy laughed. "It's not funny," said Megan, pouting. "Just kidding, I can take it. Anyway, the bass player can't be too full of himself because nobody gives a shit about bass-playing unless we're talking about Flea or Geddy Lee. Nobody notices if the bass player is good, only if he's bad. This sound familiar?"

"You have a lot of theories," said Keith. "I just show up and play. Who needs a beer?" When no one responded, he shrugged and wandered off.

"On the other hand," said Megan, "every bass player I know gets laid consistently."

*Sure, if they look like that guy*, thought Katy.

The lull in the conversation was punctuated by a tepid swell of feedback from the stage. The guitarist stepped back from his amp, played a lazy, drawn-out riff, and grinned.

"I'm thinking of taking up harmonica," said Travis. "Megan, got any unsupportable theories on harmonica players?"

"Yeah," said Megan, nodding toward the stage, where "Every

Day" was reaching a crescendo. "But I think the evidence speaks for itself."

Katy's financial aid package required her to take a work-study job, and she got an interview at the library. "Do you have any library experience?" asked the librarian.

"I've checked out a lot of books," Katy replied.

"Good. You know about the Library of Congress system, right? We don't use the Dewey Decimal here." She made it sound like the Dewey Decimal System was the equivalent of baby food.

Katy knew the system well enough, apparently, because she got the job—three hours a week at $6.50 an hour. Sometimes she sat at the desk and answered questions, which mostly took two forms: "Where do I find ML3795?" and "Where do you keep the books about Russian history?" Both of these questions could be answered by looking at the library maps kept under a thick plastic overlay on the desk, but students always seemed vaguely impressed when she gave them the answer.

Most of her shift, though, was spent shelving books and running her fingers along the spines of already-shelved books, looking for anything filed in the wrong place. *So that's why the library's full of signs saying* PLEASE DON'T RESHELVE BOOKS. For her first few shifts, every time Katy found, say, a book about herpetology shelved among physics texts, she frowned and thought, *Some idiot doesn't understand the Library of Congress system.* How could a job be both infuriating *and* boring?

Everything changed the day Katy realized nobody cared if she listened to her Discman while working in the stacks. One day she found herself descending the spiral staircase to the B1 level while listening to *The Downward Spiral,* and laughed. The basement level featured a row of massive bookcases on rails, with hand-cranked gears to slide a pair of shelves apart to get to the books trapped within. Sometimes Katy turned off the music here, just in case someone tried—through negligence or malice—to squish her between two bookcases like the trash compactor in *Star Wars.*

Today, however, she had finished the Nine Inch Nails album and was rocking out to Fugazi's *Steady Diet of Nothing* when someone tapped her on the shoulder. "Shit!" she yelled, banging into the cart and sending half a dozen books about Catholicism onto the floor.

"Sorry," said Travis. He grinned. "Just saying hi. Hey, where can I find books about surfing?"

"What are you talking about?"

"I figure it's time to embrace this California thing, so I'm taking up surfing."

Katy paused the Discman and hung her headphones around her neck. "You're not serious, right?"

"I don't know. It looks fun. My parents would hate it, which is a plus. I guess the ocean is kind of far from here, huh?"

"If you're going to bug me at work, at least help me pick this shit up," said Katy. Travis smirked and picked the books up off the floor. "No, don't shelve them. Hey, can I ask you a question?"

"Is it about surfing? It's all about applying the right amount of surf wax. When I'm dropping into the curl—"

"It's about guitar playing."

"Oh, perfect," said Travis. "Another thing I'm an expert on."

"Do you remember when Megan mentioned something about a Nevada archive? I assume she wasn't saying she went to study at, like, a guitar ashram in Nevada. Do you have any idea what she was talking about?"

"It's probably an FTP site," said Travis. "Let's go, we can probably figure it out."

"I'm literally in the middle of work."

"Oh. Then come by later. I'll be around."

●

When Katy got to his room, Travis was lying on his bed, eating Froot Loops (Fruit Circus?) out of a large Ziploc bag and listening to music on his headphones. The pile of dirty clothes had grown to the point that the door would only open partway. "Jesus, Travis," she said. "Before you invite a girl back to your room, at least do the bare minimum." When he didn't respond, she went over and touched him on the shoulder. Travis sat up quickly, scattering cereal, and pulled the headphones off. Katy could hear loud guitars spilling from the earpieces. "Now we're even," she said.

Travis was eternally unperturbed. "What's up?"

"You were going to tell me about this FTP thing."

"Oh, sure," said Travis. "It's a data repository. You transfer files between your machine and the site with a command-line utility."

"Can you show me how it works? Like, how do we get to Nevada?"

"Well, let's see." Travis sat down at his computer, crushing a lone Froot Loop under the wheel of his chair. Katy held her tongue. She was hoping to score a single in next year's room draw, but what if this was the natural state of nineteen-year-old humans with a room of their own? "Nevada is probably University of Nevada. Let's try nevada.edu."

```
% ftp nevada.edu
Connect
ftp> ls
200 PORT command successful.
150 ASCII data connection for /bin/ls (0 bytes)
a/
b/
c/
...
```

"The letters are probably for names of artists or songs," said Travis. "Give me a band name."

"The Pixies," said Katy.

```
ftp> cd p
ftp> ls
```

A long list of band names flew by on the screen. The Police. Pulp. Presidents of the United States of America. Travis scrolled up, and there it was.

```
ftp> cd pixies
ftp> ls
200 PORT command successful.
150 ASCII data connection for /bin/ls (0 bytes)
cecilia_ann.tab
gigantic.tab
```

```
here_comes_your_man.tab
where_is_my_mind.tab
```

"Does that mean they have the music for those?" asked Katy. "How do we get it?"

"Like this," said Travis.

```
ftp> get where_is_my_mind.tab
```

He opened the document, and Katy saw that it included the lyrics for the song and a bunch of dashes and numbers that looked like machine code. "I don't understand this guitar notation," said Travis. "But I assume you do. Want me to print it?"

"Sure," said Katy. Travis's Epson sprang to life, the print head dancing and chattering from side to side. When it finished printing, he tore off the sheet, removed the perforated tractor-feed strips from each side, and handed it to Katy.

Back in her room, Katy found that she didn't understand the guitar notation, either:

```
|-----4-----4-|----4-----4-|-----4-----4-|-0--0----0--
|--5-----5----|-5-----5----|--4-----4----|-5--5p4--5--
|-------------|------------|-------------|------------
|-------------|------------|-------------|------------
|-------------|------------|-------------|------------
|-------------|------------|-------------|------------
```

Were the numbers different types of notes, like quarter-notes and half-notes? But there was no such thing as fifth-notes. Megan knew how to decipher this, but Katy didn't want to ask.

Suddenly, Katy realized that the music on the printout didn't have the five lines of a musical staff. It had six lines. Like the six strings of the guitar. What if the numbers weren't types of notes, but instructions for where to place her fingers on the fretboard?

Alicia was sitting at the desk, studying. "Will it bug you if I play a little guitar?" Katy asked.

"Will it make any difference if I say yes? Hey, don't give me that look, I'm kidding." Alicia slipped her headphones on and turned back to her textbook.

Katy retreated into the back corner of her bed. It was such a tight squeeze that she felt like she was inviting the guitar for a make-out session. When she plucked the notes on the tablature, however, it sounded nothing like "Where Is My Mind?" She was about to give up and put the guitar away when she was struck with another thought: Maybe the top line of the chart represented the highest string on the guitar rather than the lowest?

Now the melody was familiar, a song she'd heard a hundred times before. When she hit a bum note, it came as a surprise, because she'd somehow forgotten that she was playing the song.

Katy left her guitar on the bed, slipped her shoes on, and ran down the hall, ignoring Alicia's call of, "Are you okay?" She ran across the quad to the computer lab, logged into a PC, and tried to remember the commands Travis had used to communicate with the server in Nevada. Over the next hour, she blew through half a ream of paper. She printed the guitar tabs for "Mayonaise," "Fuck and Run," "Miss World," and thirty-eight other songs.

Grinning, Katy went up to the desk to retrieve her printout. She ran back to Mitchell with the stack of paper under her arm. She heard a voice yell, "Hey, Katy!" as she crossed the quad, and saw Keith Lopez, resplendent in a royal blue Henley and a Dodgers cap. She swallowed the urge to run over to him and say, "Hey, look, I'm learning to play guitar. We can hang out!" Instead, she gripped the stack and waved awkwardly with her left hand, but a couple of sheets slipped free, and she cursed, dropping to one knee to pick them up.

When she got back to her room, Alicia was gone. Katy looked at the clock. It was 2:55 p.m., five minutes until English composition. She liked English comp. Dr. Watson was a black woman in her thirties who headed off the Sherlock Holmes jokes by cracking plenty of them herself. She gave open-ended assignments like, "Write about a learning experience." Katy had written about learning to drive her car, an ancient Datsun rusting in her parents' driveway, and how learning to shift gears was like trying to train a squirrel. Dr. Watson had circled that with a red pen: "Choose an analogy we can relate to. Unless you actually have squirrel training experience, in which case, WRITE ABOUT THAT."

Katy felt guilty about skipping Dr. Watson's class, but once she had her headphones back on and the guitar in her hands, the feeling evaporated. *Everything* evaporated. The pile of cryptic Nevada printouts was a ring of keys. Each one enabled Katy to unlock a favorite song and climb inside it.

Some songs resisted her attempts to invite herself in. Smashing Pumpkins songs were especially challenging, and she imagined Billy Corgan sneering at her and saying, "Nice try." Beatles songs were a real tease: What sounded simple on the LP would turn out to require ten acrobatic changes. Those were the tough nuts, though. A lot of songs just leaped off the page and into her fingers. "Here Comes Your Man" was a particular delight.

When Katy checked the clock again, it was 5:45. She'd been playing for almost three hours, and there were fifteen precious minutes until the end of dinner.

By the time she got to the dining hall, the line stretched from the counter nearly to the entrance. Travis passed her on his way out. She punched him on the shoulder, harder than she'd intended. "Why didn't you get me for dinner?" she asked.

"I don't know, your door was closed," he said. "I figured you weren't there."

"You could have knocked," said Katy, pouting. But he was only obeying one of the unwritten laws of Atwood student life: A closed door meant DO NOT DISTURB. Up and down the corridors of Mitchell Hall on any given evening, you'd find students in their rooms, doors wide open. *Please, help me procrastinate.* It reminded Katy of the street she'd grown up on in Salem, where after elementary school she'd just wander over to Christina's house, and Christina would always be there, ready to play.

Katy rejected the baked chicken in favor of the Indian spiced potato and cauliflower. Aloo gobi, as it was called, had become a cult favorite among vegetarians and carnivores alike: The name was fun to say, and it actually tasted like something.

Stepping solo into the dining hall at dinner was a bad high school lunchroom flashback. The tables were mostly full, and she stood in the corner with her tray, searching for anyone she knew. The room was filled with the noise of a hundred aimless conversations. Alicia was sitting with some of her friends from the track team, identifiable by their matching sweats. One of them was Keith Lopez.

"Can I squeeze in?" Katy asked.

"Sure," said Alicia, making room. "How's the music going?"

Katy looked around at the table. She felt like the new recruit in a benign cult based around matching outfits and vegetarian Indian food. "I feel like a baby learning to talk."

"You've been playing?" said Keith. "Cool."

"Just practicing in my room, annoying my poor roommate." *Did he mean cool as in, "You're a cool person and I want to get to know you better"? Or cool as in, "Cute, maybe in ten years you can come hang out with us again"? Only one way to find out.* "Are you guys still look-ing for band members?"

"We had this one guy come in, but he was sort of... bad vibes, I guess."

"Could I come by and play again?"

"With Travis?"

"He's not into it, I don't think." She swallowed a big bite of aloo gobi.

"Too bad. That guy can sing. Anyway, you'd have to talk to Me-gan. She's really the woman in charge."

For some reason, whenever Katy was about to get a cold, her ear-
lobes got hot and tender. She squeezed one. Ouch. Also, her throat
was prickly.

Every family has its own cold remedies, and Katy had grown
up with two: long showers and Licorice Spice tea with honey. Because it was afternoon, far from the morning and evening shower
rush, she allowed herself a long, wasteful shower. *Mucus, go to hell.*
"Anyone in here?" she called out.

No response. She was clear to sing. Katy loved singing in the
shower, and hated the idea that anyone else might hear her. Of all
the little differences between living at home and living in a dorm,
losing the privacy to sing in the shower was among the most unexpected. She cleared her throat and sang the little snippet that
had been stuck in her head since she woke up. It must have been
something Megan had played her, with a chorus that went:

*Summer on, summer on*
*We will all summer on*


Was that from *Key Lime Pie?* She mentally clicked through the track list but didn't find a match. The style didn't seem to fit, anyway. Maybe one of Alicia's pop confections? She didn't think so. It felt like the notes of the song were tickling her brain the same way the cold was irritating her throat. If only there were something like a song encyclopedia.

*Oh, of course.*

Katy toweled off, threw on her clothes, and grabbed her guitar from its stand at the end of the closet, knocking down one of Alicia's sundresses. She left the dress on the floor and spent a couple of minutes picking out the chords to the song. In high school, she'd occasionally tried to figure out songs from the radio, but it was too hard; every chord sounded wrong, and she had wondered whether professional musicians were issued a book of secret chords. Now, after a few days of Nevada-inspired obsession, the chords came easily.

She headed over to Travis's room, guitar in hand. He was lying on his bed, wearing bulky headphones over the hood of his sweatshirt, and when the body of her guitar accidentally thunked against his desk, Travis's eyes popped open.

"Huh?" He pulled one side of the headphones off his ear. "Oh, hey, it's you."

"How can listening like that possibly sound good?"

Travis pulled the hood off. "It gives early eighties records a little more bass. The poor man's EQ." He looked at his watch. "Is the dining hall open? Could you grab me a burger or something?"

"Travis, this thing where my job is to bring you food, it's only in your weird brain. Which, incidentally, I need."

"Great, I'll put it in a jar for you. Just bring it back before finals."

Katy suddenly realized that if she wanted the answer to this gnawing question, she was going to have to sing in front of Travis. Her stomach knotted at the prospect, but she pressed on. "I only need the part of your brain that knows too many songs. So I can get out the scalpel, or you can just tell me what band sings this song."

"Hit me."

She cleared her throat, put the guitar across her lap, and sang the twelve-note melody, watching Travis's face for any sign of recognition. Did she want to see any, or not?

When she was finished, Travis shook his head. "Never heard it."

"You sure?"

He rolled his eyes. Stupid question. "Did a campus radio DJ accidentally play a good indie song at three a.m.? That's cheating."

"I think I made it up," said Katy.

"Seriously? Huh." Travis fiddled the strings of his sweatshirt, tightening and loosening the hood. Katy had never seen Travis involved in any kind of exercise, but the guy was in constant low-intensity motion. Was this enough to explain why he was so skinny? "How'd you do that?" he asked.

"No idea," said Katy. "I always get weird when I have a cold."

"Well, thanks for being my local disease vector. Hmm, I may retract my food order. Do you have any latex gloves handy?"

Katy imagined herself in white latex gloves, carrying a plate of food from the dining hall to Mitchell. "Travis, I can think of at least six reasons that's not going to happen. Hey, you sing it, and then we're going to dinner."

"Okay, demo it one more time," said Travis. Katy played the

song, or the tiny nub of the song, again. She didn't feel any more confident this time. "Keep the music going." She went back to the beginning of the four-chord sequence, and Travis took over. He delivered the lines with a throaty, masculine edge quite unlike his speaking voice. And he was *loud*. She strummed the guitar harder to keep up.

Travis stopped singing abruptly. "Wait, what about this for a verse?" He paused to think for a moment, then started singing *a cappella*:

*Pacific state of mind*
*Green linoleum memories*
*Westward tides*
*Elemental energies*

His voice had gone from sandpaper to freshly Windexed glass. Katy closed her eyes and got lost in the melody, which was different from her "summer on" chorus but somehow complementary, and was then immediately tossed back into the reality of Travis's room when he stopped singing.

"That's good," said Katy. "Let me figure out the chords. Oh, hey, it starts on C, the world's most boring chord."

"Is that bad?"

"I don't know, I've never done this before. I like the tune, but is it okay if I mess with the lyrics?"

Travis looked offended. "You mean the gibberish I just came up with? How dare you?"

Katy groaned and strummed a C chord. "Give me a minute. 'Pacific state of mind' gives me an idea." She hummed Travis's melody to herself and walked through a few chords, and she could almost hear an audible *thunk* as the next few measures clicked. "How's this?"

*I can't be myself here*
*The light is always shining*
*Devastating air*
*There can be no denying*

"You can't say that," said Travis. "That's a Led Zeppelin lyric."

"Can they trademark one line?" asked Katy. She started to launch a counterargument: Surely Zeppelin wasn't the first to use that line, and anyway who cares? But in the end, she realized Travis was right. Zeppelin was the most beloved band on campus; Katy was no small fan herself, and now she could only hear the line to the tune of "The Rover." She tried again.

*The sun shines every day*
*The devastating air*
*The color of the sky—*

"That's a line from a 10,000 Maniacs song," said Travis.

"You actually know every song, don't you?"

"Of course not. I tried to figure out how many songs I know, and it's definitely less than eight thousand."

"Good for you, but if you keep stopping me every time I say anything that's ever appeared in any other song, I'm going to kill you. Do you want to tell me which death metal songs contain the lyric 'I'm going to kill you' so you can get it out of your system?"

Travis considered this. "No, I'm okay."

*The sun shines every day*
*But the air is devastating*
*What kind of life is living here*
*What future is awaiting*
*Summer on summer on*
*We will all summer on*

She repeated the lines, tweaking a note here and there, and added an unlikely chord leading into the chorus. It was like watching the song shimmer into existence. After a couple of refrains, Travis joined in, and they sang in unison, their voices blending into a tone so clear and unexpected that Katy actually looked around to see if there was a third person in the room.

"Uptempo, strong hook, culturally appropriate level of angst," said Travis. "I approve." He rubbed his temples. "Crap, this is worse than I expected."

"What? I thought we sounded pretty good," said Katy.

"We did," said Travis. "That's what I was afraid of."

No experience since arriving at college gave Katy a headier sense of adult responsibility than operating the waffle iron. Unlike the omelet bar, this was a self-service device consisting of a hot cast-iron waffle chamber on a rotary mount so you could flip the waffle halfway through for even cooking. The thing was just sitting there, plugged into a 220-volt outlet, with a pitcher of batter sitting alongside. The outside surface was hot enough to raise welts. The cooking surface... well, better not to think about the kind of damage it could do.

Just another entry for her secret shame diary: *Making my own waffles kind of turns me on.*

While carrying the finished waffle to the dining room, Katy stopped to take a peek at the suggestion board. A nameless official had written a reply to the generic cereals petition: BRAND-NAME CEREALS WILL BE BACK WHEN WE FINISH THE PRESENT STOCK. IN THE MEANTIME, PLEASE ENJOY THE FLAVOR OF FRUIT CIRCUS.

Katy and her waffle sat down next to Travis. "Hey, did you see we won?" She drowned her waffle in celebratory syrup.

"Hmm?" said Travis. He was eating a bowl of corn flakes and studying a paper table tent from the Jewish Student Union. "Which do you think would piss my parents off more?" he asked. "If I majored in art history or converted to Judaism?"

"Earth to Travis. Generic cereals. We won."

"Seriously?"

"Yeah, check the board," said Katy. "We just need to eat ten pounds of green penises, or however much they have left. Also, what happened to surfing?" She pushed a piece of waffle around on the plate, stalling. "Hey, I've been thinking about the song. Do you want to try playing it with Megan and Keith?"

Travis snorted. "What's the point? So they can make fun of our song? We'd probably have better luck with surfing or Judaism." He gestured with his cereal spoon, flinging a spray of milk droplets across the table.

Katy tried to imagine what Megan would say to this. She came up with, "So the hell what? I'm not saying we should try to join their band. Just... don't you want to hear what the song would sound like with drums and everything?"

"It's a waste of time. Guys like Nick whatshisface are in bands. Guys like me study too hard and play video games."

Katy finished her waffle. "Well, if you change your mind, the offer stands. You can be the harmonica player."

Travis's lower lip quivered oddly. It wasn't until she was on her way back to her room that Katy realized he'd been laughing.

●

Katy had a problem. Or rather, *elle avait un problème.*

In high school, Katy's best subject had been French. While her classmates struggled with verb conjugations, she found them secretly thrilling: a complex system of rules and exceptions that could, with enough study, be thoroughly mastered. And her mouth instinctively curled itself around the clipped and throaty syllables of the language. She sometimes imagined herself in the foreign service, serving in Paris or on the Côte d'Azur. She became obsessed with the educational video series they used in class, *French in Action,* and its sexy costars, Robert and Mireille.

On her second day at Atwood, she'd taken a French placement test. She breezed through the written portion (*"Décrivez votre famille"*), then sat down with a French professor and chatted about the weather, food, and Jordy the Singing Baby. "You've only been studying for four years? Really?" the professor asked in French. Katy blushed, not realizing the depth of the hole she was digging.

Because she'd aced the placement test, Katy found herself in French 301 under the tutelage of the stereotypically stylish Professor Régine Chabert. Her classmates were juniors and seniors. All that was fine. The curriculum, however, focused on detailed analysis of classic works of French literature: Colette, Voltaire, Flaubert, Zola. She excelled at this sort of thing in English class, but doing it in French was like swimming laps in a trenchcoat.

Hell, said Sartre, is writing a ten-page French paper in the fluorescent pallor of a windowless computer lab. But that was where Katy found herself after dinner, trying to remember which key combinations would produce accented characters on the PC keyboard. *"L'éssence de l'humanité, c'est..."* she began. The essence of humanity is what? Apparently a bunch of dead French guys had a lot to say on the matter.

Katy played around with different fonts on the computer,

looking for something that could subtly make one paragraph fill ten pages.

"That looks terrible," said Travis's voice. He sat down next to her. "Of the system fonts, I think Book Antiqua is probably the best, but they've installed a lot of Adobe stuff here. Check it out." He reached over, grabbed Katy's mouse, and started selecting text and applying type styles.

"Travis, get your hands off my shit," said Katy, smacking him on the wrist. "Seriously. Do you want something, or are you just here to torture me?"

"Come on, you're not really working on this," he said, gesturing at the screen. "I was thinking about what you said. Could we still try out our song with them?"

Katy turned the question over and over like a coin in her pocket. Her paper was due tomorrow. French was her best subject. "I don't know," she said, closing the window without saving her work. "I haven't talked to Megan about it. Let me see if I can get her on *talk*."

•

Email had come into Katy's life at freshman orientation. She'd heard the word before as something her dad used at work, and filed it away along with memos, performance reviews, and grant applications in the category of "things I hope I never have to care about."

Then, in her orientation packet, she'd found a single sheet of paper sprinkled with a few mostly unintelligible pieces of information:

**Name:** Katherine Blundell
**Username:** kblundell
**Address:** kblundell@atwood.edu
**Initial password:** HEjqfRU2g9

This page had ended up sandwiched in a pile until the first time a professor said, "I'll add you all to the email list." Katy dug out the paper, hiked to the computer lab, logged into the VAX system for the first time, and found to her surprise that she'd been accumulating emails not only from professors, but also from classmates and even friends at other colleges.

Email, it turned out, was amazing. Katy could send a message to Christina at University of Oregon and it would arrive literally seconds later.

This was astonishing enough. But then Alicia taught her how to *talk*.

*talk* was a real-time chat application. You typed *talk ckim@oregon.edu*, and the screen would split in two horizontally. If Christina was logged in, she'd accept Katy's talk request and they'd type at each other for hours. Unlike a long-distance call, it cost nothing, but Katy soon realized that a *talk* talk was very different from being on the phone or chatting in person. She and Christina talked about subjects they'd never gotten into at home. Loneliness. Death. The surprising dearth of masturbation opportunities at college.

It was also the perfect medium for asking Megan a hard question.

•

Megan accepted Katy's *talk* request.

> **Katy:** Hey, got a minute?
> **Megan:** What's up?
> **Katy:** Travis and I wrote a song.

At this point there was a long pause. Even though a pause during a *talk* session was as likely to be caused by a network time-out as an actual lull in the conversation, Katy's stomach lurched.

> **Megan:** Is it any good?
> **Katy:** Maybe. I don't know.
> **Megan:** You want my help with something or are you just confessing? Forgive me Megan, for I have sinned. Instead of studying, I wrote a song.

Megan typed really fast. Katy felt oddly jealous of this.

> **Katy:** I know I'm not going to be in your band, but we kind of want to hear how it would sound with drums and stuff.
> **Megan:** Always nice to be lumped in with "and stuff."
> **Katy:** Sorry.
> **Megan:** I'm fucking with you. Okay, on two conditions. Number one, you help carry drums. If we're going to do the full-band treatment, we should do it at the music building. We had a late-night time slot there last year. We can be loud without the campus rent-a-cops throwing all our gear in the reservoir.
> **Katy:** What's the other condition?
> **Megan:** Convince Travis to sing.

**Katy:** He's right here. He just said "rock and roll" and gave an exaggerated thumbs-up. I think that means yes.

**Megan:** Great, then I'll see your powerful arms and his lungs Friday at midnight.

Megan's half of the screen went dark, and Katy turned to Travis. "Now get out of here so I can get some work done."

"Right-o," said Travis.

•

Katy reloaded the empty document that was nominally her French paper. The clock on the screen read 6:58 p.m. Existentialism, Katy's high school English teacher had explained once, wasn't as complicated or as much of a bummer as it was made out to be. The way Katy remembered it, the Existentialists said: *Life is absurd and we're all going to die, so in the meantime let's be our true selves and revel in the absurdity.* It seemed like as good a philosophy as any, although the more Katy thought about it, the more the corollary seemed to be: *Don't waste your life writing this stupid French paper.*

Katy closed the Microsoft Word window and zoned out, scanning the icons that dotted the Windows desktop. Word. Excel. The Telnet program that offered access to email and talk. And an icon that Katy had noticed but never bothered with, assuming it was a jargon-infested computer science tool for hardcore nerds: NCSA Mosaic. With nothing better to do, Katy double-clicked the icon.

The window opened onto something called the NCSA What's New Page. It looked a bit like a word processor, but the text wasn't editable. Instead, some of the words were underlined and in blue. Katy found that clicking on one of these words would change the text in the window.

She clicked on a link called "Cute Puppy Pics." An S-shaped graphic in one corner of the window sprang to life, spinning and pulsating like it was hooked up to a car battery. The screen slowly reconfigured itself until Katy was looking at a collage of puppy photos. She found herself saying "awwww" involuntarily, then clicked back to the previous screen. Most of the links were to university math and science departments—and, oddly, they were departments at other universities, not Atwood. She scrolled through the What's New page a bit more. *Oxford University Humanities Department. Middlebury College Juggling Club. DARK TOWER: Since 1982, Houston's Original Metal Band!* Well, that sounded interesting.

This one—*what are these things called, anyway?* Aha: "Welcome to DARK TOWER's website! Under construction." Except for the puppies, all the other websites Katy had visited were just small text on a gray background. This was more like a page from a magazine, with carefully arranged photos of the members of Dark Tower, brooding and scowling as heavy metal musicians are legally obligated to do. The photos had blue borders around them, and when she clicked one, it expanded to fill the window. You could see the lead singer's stubble. Katy wished there was some way to hear what Dark Tower sounded like, although she had a pretty good idea.

Weird. There was no reason a computer at Atwood should contain information about a metal band over a thousand miles away. Had Katy somehow caused her PC to reach out over the wires and scoop up high-resolution photos of Texan headbangers?

The on-screen clock read 10:15. Katy had spent three hours in this electronic Narnia without doing anything resembling actual work. She reluctantly closed NCSA Mosaic, ejected her disc, and went out into the night.

Katy poked her head into Travis's room. "Want to work on the song?"

Without removing his headphones, he stabbed a pile of notebooks with his finger. "O-chem!"

Fine. She needed the practice a lot more than he did, but she couldn't think of a place where to practice without driving Alicia crazy.

Finally, she thought of the study rooms on the second floor of the library. Judging from the time she'd opened the door to one and interrupted a surprisingly loud and heated discussion about 19th century poetry, they were pretty soundproof. So Wednesday night, she grabbed her guitar and a notebook and started to head out. At the last minute she called to Alicia, "Hey, want to walk me to the library?"

"Sure thing."

On the way, Katy and Alicia passed a grove of trees that carried a dank and uncanny odor. Katy had never given plants the slightest bit of thought, but here everything was some kind of palm tree or weird cactus-like thing, and these smelled like, well, semen. Katy was tempted to elbow Alicia and say, "Hey, that totally smells like what I think it smells like, right?" But she refrained. *No sense proving to her that I'm even weirder than she thinks.*

Alicia pulled a fruit-flavored lip balm out of her purse and applied it liberally. "What's wrong? Boy trouble?"

"Not really." Katy filled her in on the plan for Friday night, leaving out the "Katy plays so well that Keith Lopez wants to keep it rolling with a hands-on, one-on-one practice session" fantasy segment.

"Why is this so important to you?" said Alicia.

"It's not."

Alicia laughed. "Wow, you're a terrible liar. It's like you were squeezing your legs together and hopping around saying, 'I don't need to pee, really.'"

"Thanks, now I totally need to pee," said Katy. "It's just, everybody here has a thing, and maybe this could be mine, but I'm terrible at it."

"What's my thing, then?"

"Jesus, Alicia, *everything* is your thing. You dress great, you get along with everybody, you take these hard academic classes in your first semester, you know what do at a party other than stand around and pretend you're having a good time."

Alicia shook her head. "Yeah, it's *so* easy being me."

They passed groups of students talking about boyfriends and girlfriends and TV shows and last night's parties, with a sprinkle of philosophy and politics. The path wound between a pair of hedges, and then it was quiet again—just another Wednesday night in the dullest corner of L.A.

"So, I don't know what to do," Katy said. "I guess I want to play with them again, but I don't want to assume they're all into it if they're not, and I don't want to embarrass myself in front of them, but I really don't know how to play. I should probably just call it off. This sucks."

"Do you want my advice or do you just want me to listen to you work this all out?" asked Alicia.

"I don't know."

"You know what I think? You spend too much time worrying about what other people think of you. It really doesn't fit with your whole grunge thing."

"What grunge thing?"

"The flannels, the hooded sweatshirts, the ripped jeans, the music. I figured that was your personal style."

Katy laughed. "No, that's called being from Oregon. So you mean you *don't* care what people think of you?"

"I played that game all through high school," said Alicia. "All I wanted was to be a popular kid, and then I drove myself crazy making sure I *stayed* popular. And being one of the few black kids in that school didn't make it any easier."

"If it was so hard, why'd you do it?"

Alicia shook her head. "Because it was high school and I was stupid! Weren't you? Anyway, you're obviously into this band thing. What's the worst that could happen? Somebody tells you you're not—I don't know, Eddie Vedder? Eric Clapton? Who cares?"

"Eddie Vedder doesn't play guitar," said Katy. Alicia's advice made a lot of sense, and Katy wasn't about to admit it, not for a million dollars and private guitar lessons with Mike McCready. So she changed the subject. "Hey, look, someone added some new stuff to the Fuck Tornado."

"Excuse me?"

"Over there, next to the Led Zeppelin symbols." Katy pointed to the three-foot-tall wall demarcating one side of the quad. A whitewashed retaining wall in an urban area attracts graffiti. On a college campus, it attracts semi-intelligent graffiti. Years ago, the administration had decided to stop painting it over, and the Wall of Free Expression was born. Katy was fond of the more erudite efforts, like *Postmodernists don't know whether they do it better, because reality is a social construction,* but she also had a spot for the simply weird.

"Oh, that thing," said Alicia. One morning in early September, the Wall had sprouted an artistic nest of obscenities whirling around each other in assorted typefaces. It looked like the brain of a Tourette's sufferer with a degree in graphic design. Fans called it the Fuck Tornado.

"If you were going to paint something on the Wall," asked Katy, "what would it be?"

"I'm not really the graffiti type."

The four columns of the library's facade came into view. They were illuminated at night, and it was beautiful and a little spooky. Katy felt taunted, like the night itself was telling her to cheer up, and she refused to give in. Instead, she turned to Alicia. "Why do you put up with me when I'm such a lousy roommate?"

Alicia put her hands on her hips. "Now that's just not true."

"Oh, shut up. I play annoying music, I'm always moping around when you probably want time to yourself, I—"

"You give me as much closet space as I want," said Alicia, and she walked off.

The Atwood campus was a mishmash of three architectural styles:

1. Old buildings that looked like they'd been imported from Oxford, but with Spanish tile roofs, like British business-people coming back from vacation sporting international hats.

2. New buildings, like the computer science building, made of steel and glass, presumably designed by hip architects wearing skinny glasses.

3. Unadorned mounds of gray concrete from the sixties and seventies.

The music building was one of the latter. Why was everything built around the time of Katy's birth so ugly, anyway? She only knew it was the music building because she always heard the sounds of bassoon and percussion practice when she walked past it on the way to English comp.

Katy set Megan's floor tom on the doorstep of the music building and swiped her ID card. In her mind, her intended maneuver was balletic: Pull the door open wide, spin around, grab the drum, and step backwards into the building just before the door slams shut. Like Indiana Jones, if he were a roadie. Instead, the heavy door smacked her in the side, and she dropped the drum. One of its extensible legs retracted on impact, and the drum listed like it was doubled over in pain.

"Travis, get the fuck over here," Katy yelled.

"How is this my fault?" said Travis, clattering up behind her, cradling an array of chrome drum hardware in his arms.

"Sorry. Just, a little help here, please."

Megan walked up behind them. "Next time we are borrowing your roommate's car," she said, setting down the bass drum. "Or you carry everything and I'll be at the Stoop drinking a milkshake until twelve-thirty."

"Why do drums have to have so many... drums?" asked Katy.

"I hate you," said Megan. "Keith! Where the hell are you? Katy, what did you do to my floor tom?"

Katy carried the drum down a corridor lined with practice rooms on both sides. She put her face up to the small window in one door and was surprised to see a girl holding a violin up to her chin, eyes closed, pulling the bow across the strings. Katy moved on before she was revealed as a peeping tom with musical tendencies.

Finally, they got all the gear into the alcove outside the large practice room. The room was occupied, and some familiar aimless sounds seeped under the door. "Fuck me," said Megan. "I put us on the board for midnight. Today *is* October twenty-ninth, right? I'm not losing it?"

"Yeah, I think so." Katy checked her watch. Twelve-ten, and the jams were still rolling. "Is this—wait, what are they called? Oreo Sunday?"

"Nabisco Session," said Travis. "The greatest band in the world."

"I guess there's no way to tell if this song is almost over, huh?" said Katy. No one laughed. She walked back down the hall and stepped outside into the night. She put her hands in the pocket of her jeans. This felt a lot like a bad date. With all the drum-hauling, in fact, it was like she'd agreed to help her date move into a new apartment.

When Katy got back inside, however, the prospects looked a lot better. The members of Nabisco Session were carrying their gear out, and Megan showed Katy that her drum wasn't broken, just a little out of whack. Nick Dimmett stepped into the hall carrying an acoustic guitar case plastered with stickers, mostly for his own band. He looked directly at Katy. "Ladies. Gentlemen. Sorry we ran late. Just got lost in the groove, you know?"

Katy nodded, afraid of what might come out of her mouth if she opened it.

"Hey, look, it's my old friend Megan," said Nick. "How've you been? Putting Slag back together?" Megan's eyes narrowed to slits. He turned to Katy. "Nick Dimmett," he said, extending his hand. Katy took it, and he gave her some kind of hybrid hippie/soul handshake that involved his palm sliding against hers. She laughed and introduced herself, then stepped into the practice room.

An upright piano stood on one side of the room, and the rest of the floor was littered with sheet music stands, some standing

74

and some knocked over like they'd been in a fight. It reminded her of Travis's room. Several tall piles of music books teetered in a corner, all the classical pieces for oboe and clarinet and viola you could ever need. A grid was drawn on a large rolling green chalkboard. A few of the squares had names in them, but those could have been music students. The only obvious band name was Nabisco Session, which had signed up for Monday, Wednesday, and Friday from ten to midnight. Beneath that, on Friday, Megan had written MEGAN D.

While Katy tuned her acoustic, Megan set up microphones for Travis and Katy to sing into, and plugged them into the PA system. Travis leaned in toward the mic. "Check, one-two. Wow, I've always wanted to say that."

Katy tuned her guitar and attached the vinyl strap she'd bought at Rhombus. She paced around, testing its weight. "This feels weird," she said. "I've never done it standing up before." Everyone fell into hysterics, even Katy. "I mean the guitar!" she screamed, but her voice was lost in the slap of Megan's drum warmup.

"Okay," said Megan, tightening a wing nut atop a cymbal. "Now, did you guys bring a song or what?"

"Yeah, uh, it's here." Katy pulled a couple of folded sheets of printer paper out of her pocket. On each one she'd handwritten the lyrics to "Summer On," along with capital letters indicating the chord changes. "I don't know if I used the right notation or anything." She handed out copies to Keith and Megan. "Travis?" she said, extending one in his direction.

"I don't need it," said Travis.

"Okay, you guys play it through once and I'll listen," said Megan. "Keith, come in whenever."

"You got it."

Megan looked at Katy like she was trying to decide something. "Can we mic your guitar? It's going to be too quiet otherwise."

Katy had no idea how to mic a guitar, but she was grateful for the momentary reprieve. Anyone could tune a guitar and fumble with a strap and hand out sheets of paper. It was like the part where the nurse is chatting and swabbing your arm before you get a shot, and then suddenly you realize, *wait, the preliminaries are done. This is gonna hurt.*

Megan set up another microphone and pointed it at the sound hole of Katy's acoustic. "Give me a chord." Katy played a C chord and was rewarded with a painful blast of feedback. "Shit," said Megan. She turned a couple of knobs on the PA. Now there was no feedback, but no amplification, either. "Well, fuck it. I'll use brushes, otherwise we won't be able to hear you."

"Is that bad?" said Katy.

"It's not good."

Katy waited until Megan took her seat back behind the drums. She closed her eyes, held her breath, and played the intro to the song. "The sun shines every day," sang Travis, and then Katy joined him on the chorus, just like they'd done in his room. *This is working.*

"Stop a second," said Megan. "Katy, you should sing harmony there. Unison sounds dumb."

"I don't even know what that means," said Katy.

"It means instead of singing the same note he's singing, sing a third up. Here, I'll show you. Travis, take it from the chorus, okay? Katy, don't sing, just play the chords."

Katy put her head down and strummed the chords. As Travis began singing, Megan added her voice, ragged and heavy, on a higher note that melded with Travis's into a seamless package.

The sound was so beautiful and so maddening. "I have no idea what you're doing," said Katy.

"Okay, play it again and listen to me. Travis, be quiet this time." At least Megan was telling someone else to shut up. Katy's fingers found the first chord. Megan sang the chorus, and it sounded similar to the way Katy had sung it, but higher in pitch. "Just sing that. I'll keep going."

Katy ran through the chords again and sang along with Megan. "Now, Travis, come back in," said Megan. His baritone rejoined the effort, and the sound grew rich and full. "Keep going!" yelled Megan, and they sang through the chorus two more times.

"See, that's all I meant," said Megan.

"Yeah, but I was just singing along with you," said Katy.

"No you weren't. I stopped once you nailed it."

"Really? Oh." Katy wasn't sure if she believed this.

"Okay, take it from the top," said Megan. "I have a couple ideas. Two-three-four!"

Katy played the intro again, and this time, Megan's drums slammed in just before Travis sang the first line. One minute earlier, "Summer On" was Travis and Katy fooling around on guitars. Now, with a few kicks and snares and cymbals, it was something almost like a *song*. She looked at Keith and realized, no, it wasn't just the drums: Keith's bassline was gluing the whole thing together.

Katy realized that the chorus was coming up, and she was supposed to sing the notes Megan had just taught her. On the first pass through the chorus, she blew it and went back to singing along with Travis's part—unison, Megan had called it. Megan glared at Katy. Then, on the second chorus, Katy opened her mouth, and she was singing harmony. Slightly off-key, but it was there. Her tongue relaxed, and the two notes locked together. If Katy were asked to write an essay for Dr. Watson's class explaining how to sing harmony, she'd have to write: *You just do it.*

Megan finished off the song with five tight slaps of the snare. "Not bad," she said. "Want to take it again?"

Megan counted off, and Katy laid into the guitar strings with her pick.

By the second verse, Katy was relaxed enough to listen to Travis sing. He looked the same as ever: the too-small sweatshirt, hands in his pockets, a little hunched. But his voice, amplified through the PA, was *massive.* He'd inched away from his usual Cobain impersonation, Katy noticed, and had introduced a few quirks into his vocals that reminded her of the way he spoke, plain-vanilla Seattle English with a twangy snarl on certain vowels, like the I's in "what kind of life."

The chorus rolled around again, and Katy brought her lips to the mic. She'd been listening so closely that she came in late, lost the timing, and said, "Wait, sorry, stop."

Megan glared at her and kept playing, eighth-note flourishes on the hat and snare. Katy tamped down the panic and came back in on the second half of the chorus. Her voice locked in with Travis's, and they finished out the song without further incident.

"Katy, rule number one," said Megan. "If you fuck up, figure out how to keep going."

"It's just practice," said Katy.

"Exactly, and if you don't practice recovering from a mistake, you'll never do it right on stage. Trust me, the audience won't even notice, unless you stop the song and apologize, and then you'll lose them, fast."

That seemed reasonable to Katy, but somehow it hadn't occurred to her until just now that she might ever find herself "on stage" in front of "the audience." She felt a little sick thinking about it, and noticed that she was probably developing a bruise on her right hip where the door had clipped it.

"One more time?" asked Megan. But Katy's legs were suddenly so unsteady that she had to sit down on the floor. She pushed her hair out of her eyes, prodded the bruise on her hip, and stifled the urge to fling off her guitar and run—or else to hug everyone in the room.

She rose slowly to her feet with an idea. "Hey, do you guys know 'Where Is My Mind?'"

"The Pixies song?" said Travis. "Of course."

"Classic," said Megan.

"I don't know it," said Keith, "but I can probably follow along."

"I've been messing around with it," said Katy. "Want to give it a try?"

"Stop," said Travis.

"What'd I do?"

"The first word of the song. 'Stop.'"

She laughed. "Oh, right. Say it again."

Travis stepped up to the mic. "STOP."

Katy strummed the intro to the song, and Megan came in with the beat. Kick, snare, kick-kick, snare. Travis sang, a spot-on recreation of Black Francis. Keith picked up the song right away, and Katy sang Kim Deal's high, wailing backup part.

"That one needs some work," said Megan. "Should we call it a night?"

"Absolutely," said Katy.

"Trick question," said Megan. "No one goes home until this fuck-ton of drums is back in my room."

# 12

Saturday afternoon Katy lay on her bed, staring at the bottom of Alicia's bunk, picking out designs in the faux woodgrain slats like a Rorschach test. Her left hand was sore from gripping the neck of the guitar. Her stomach ached. She felt like she'd lost her virginity again.

Tenth grade. She'd been going out with Chad for a couple of months, and they both wanted to do it. Chad was considerate, gentle, and reassuringly fumbling, but Katy was surprised by how much it hurt and how little they had to talk about afterwards. She was glad to get it over with and, after a couple of days, interested in doing it again—but not particularly with Chad. They broke up a week later.

Now, here she was again, lying in bed with weird aches and a swarm of conflicting emotions. She closed her eyes and tried to work through some irregular French verbs, but her mind kept drifting back to Megan's room.

Was that band practice? Were they now a band? Probably not.

Megan had treated Katy like a child. Keith played like he was working a highly competent shift at the Gap. Travis? Aloof, as usual. Katy didn't know how to sing harmony and only knew about ten chords on the guitar—and the guitar she owned was absolutely the wrong kind for rock music. She wasn't sure if she'd even enjoyed the experience, but then she thought about how, for a few seconds at a time, she'd nailed that harmony. Katy had sung plenty of songs, but this was the first time she'd been *inside* one. Had she discovered a secret hiding place only musicians knew about?

She put on the Offspring's *Smash* and sang along with "Self Esteem" while she got dressed. On the way out, she doodled a stick-figure with long hair and a guitar on the whiteboard before walking over to Travis's room. His whiteboard had a list of assignments and due dates. O-CHEM LAB REPORT 11/23. ENGLISH PAPER 11/25. She knocked.

"Just a minute." Travis eased the door open. "What's going on?" Through the cracked door, Katy could see that he was wearing a T-shirt and boxer shorts.

"Sorry, I can come back later," said Katy.

"Nah, come in. I have pants around here somewhere." Normally Katy would ask herself a few questions before entering the dorm room of a pantsless boy, but this was Travis. She sat on the floor while he pulled on a pair of pleated slacks, realizing that she didn't really have a working definition of the word "slacks" beyond "unfashionable pants your parents would wear to work," which was exactly what Travis was wearing. Still, it was an improvement over no slacks.

"Did you have fun yesterday?" asked Katy.

"You mean our rock and roll moment?" said Travis. "I guess."

"What does that mean?"

"Well, nothing really sounded right, did it? Like, what's worse than banging on an acoustic guitar and calling it rock and roll? And those brushes. We sounded like a jazz combo or something."

"Travis, the jerk alarm is going off right now," said Katy.

"What? What did I say?"

"What about the Nirvana *Unplugged* show? Are you saying that's not rock?"

"That was a good show," Travis admitted. "But do you think they would have gotten famous playing acoustic?"

"Probably not. Dinner?"

"What time is it?"

"Six."

Travis looked stricken. "The place is going to be ravaged. Let's go."

It was steak night at the dining hall, and as Katy slid her tray along the metal runners, she considered her options. Accept the extruded slab of gray flesh they were calling a steak? Or go for the perfunctory vegetarian option, a casserole of canned beans, mushy rice, and probably ketchup? In Katy's mind, ketchup abuse was one of the dining hall's most serious offenses. On pasta night, the spaghetti sauce gave off a suspicious aroma of sugar and cheap vinegar. Estella, her favorite dining hall server, was working, and Katy asked for steak, with the gluey mashed potatoes and the army-fatigue green beans.

Travis asked for two steaks. "You eat one, then you come back for seconds," said Estella.

"Estella, you know me," said Travis. "I'll be back up here in six minutes for another steak, and then you'll have to do twice as much work."

"Or you could follow the rules and keep the line moving," said

Estella, laughing. She heaped two steaks onto a plate with a pair of tongs, passed it to Travis, and waved them on. "Now, I don't want to see you again before tomorrow, okay?"

Katy frowned and tried to think of something clever to add. All she could come up with was, "Is Estella your favorite lunch lady, too?"

"Sure," said Travis. "Did you know that in England they call them dinner ladies?"

"Seriously?"

They found a table in the courtyard, under a trellis. The Atwood campus was trying so hard to be a Mediterranean village, and this particular corner wasn't doing a terrible job.

"Do you want to know the secret of surviving on dining hall food?" asked Travis.

"Steal cereal?" said Katy.

"I'm serious," said Travis. "You should listen to me. I'm older and wiser than you, and it's my duty to transmit my wisdom to the next generation." He pulled a small glass bottle out of his pocket.

"Aha, your secret cyanide capsule."

Travis opened the bottle, shook it vigorously over his plate, and passed it to Katy.

"You know, they have Tabasco at the condiment bar," said Katy. "What is this stuff?"

"Tabasco is for freshmen and other amateurs," said Travis. "You're better than that."

Katy looked at the bottle. A busty cartoon woman holding a DANGER sign winked at her from the label, which read MELISSA'S XXX HABANERO. "Thanks, but I'll pass," she said.

"Just try it," said Travis. "First dose is free."

"Fine." Katy dispensed two drops of Melissa's XXX onto her steak and took a bite. The meat was still leathery and overcooked, but the sauce brought a lively heat. Despite the threatening label, the sauce wasn't really that spicy. Katy dotted the rest of her steak with hot sauce and handed it back to Travis.

"See?" he said.

"Shut up," said Katy.

Keith Lopez sat down with his tray of vegetarian casserole. "Travis, nice to see you made bail," he said. "Got any three-X on you?"

"Oh no, he's got you hooked on it, too?" said Katy.

"This stuff is amazing," said Keith, uncapping the bottle. "I think it's made from red peppers, MSG, and crack."

"I have more in my room if you want to buy some," said Travis. "Five bucks a bottle."

"What would your parents say if they knew you were running an illegal hot sauce business out of your room?" asked Katy.

"I told them," said Travis. "They were happy I was showing interest in entrepreneurship. I buy it by the case at Vons and mark it up."

"You are so weird," said Katy.

"Call me names all you want," said Travis. "But when you're stuck in a flavor-free wasteland of your own making, and you come crawling back to me for the cure, it'll be ten dollars."

Keith laughed. "Hey, so are we going to get together and play again? Or was that a one-time deal?"

Oh, shit. Katy's cheeks were turning bright red. She faked a sneeze to try and cover it up, then turned to Keith and said, "Um, yeah, we should do that. Do you think Megan's interested, though? She seemed kind of annoyed with the whole thing."

"That's just how Megan is," said Keith. "I think she had a good time, but I agree it's sort of hard to tell with her."

Katy felt a happy glow settle around her eyes, but maybe it was just the hot sauce.

# 13

On top of an astronomical amount of homework, Katy gave herself two personal assignments to complete that weekend: *Get in touch with Megan to ask if she wants to practice again,* and *Call Keith and ask him out.*

Through a lens of academic detachment, Katy could see that neither of these tasks amounted to a Promethean feat. Here in her own body, though, they were more daunting than a hundred pages of French. Which, incidentally, she still hadn't finished even one page of.

*Also, how do you even ask someone out in college?* In high school there were school dances, an official scenic make-out point, parents' cars to borrow. Maybe she should just ask if he wanted to meet up and study. That would be innocent enough, and Katy imagined cuddling up next to Keith on the floor of his room with textbooks splayed open around them. That wasn't how it would really go, though, right? Keith was good-looking, popular, a senior, and a nice guy, too. Katy didn't think she was bad-looking, but she was a first-year who apparently dressed like a Northwestern street kid. She calculated the odds of pulling off a date—or even a successful hangout—with Keith, and it looked negligible.

Besides, if she asked Keith out, it would probably make things weird at the next practice. She decided to shelve the Keith question for now, and focus on determining whether there would *be* a next practice. If anything, though, calling Megan was even more intimidating, and Katy was just as convinced she'd get a "thanks, but..." response.

So Katy ended up going to seminar and then French class on Monday morning without having made either call. Sitting in French, she opened her sketchbook and doodled a logo, something like the Fuck Tornado, but with "Katy's Band" emerging from the maelstrom. Her Sartre paper, due today, was one paragraph, striped in ones and zeroes on the floppy disk at the bottom of her backpack. She added a guitar, stretched out and spiraling into the funnel of the tornado, then erased the whole thing in a shower of Pink Pearl shavings.

"Mademoiselle Blundell? Votre réponse?" said the professor.

"Um. Sorry, I have to go." She dropped the notebook into her backpack and walked out of class. Katy had never skipped a class in her life. Her heart was racing as if she'd just told her professor to go fuck herself. But no one ran after her. No klaxons went off; no armed guards drew their weapons. Atwood College shrugged.

The sun was out—welcome to California—but the air was so pregnant with ozone and particulates and NO2 that it threatened to precipitate a brown film onto every surface—welcome to Los Angeles. Katy had showered that morning before class, but she wanted to shower again, and she realized with some surprise that there was no reason she couldn't. She slung her backpack onto the floor next to her bed and took her towel to the bathroom. She spent ten blissful minutes wasting water, and by the end of her shower, she had a plan for the rest of the morning.

She dried her hair and called Megan. "Can we go shopping? I need your help."

Ten minutes later, Katy and Megan were sitting in Alicia's minivan. "Let's go to the Guitar Center on Sunset," said Megan. She spun the radio dial until it landed on KROQ-FM, at the top of the chorus of Bad Religion's "Infected." Katy gripped the steering wheel with one hand and turned the credit card over and over in the other.

Most of Katy's classmates had a credit card. They came in two varieties:

1. The bottomless well. Take it to the mall, clean out the Hot Topic, Gap, or Wet Seal, and Mom and Dad pay the bill, because whatever you bought is a rounding error.

2. The emergency card. *Honey, take this credit card with you. Feel free to use it whenever you need to, as long as your life is in imminent danger and your kidnappers accept Visa. Love you!*

Katy's emergency card had sat in the back corner of her underwear drawer since the first day of orientation. When she slipped it into her pocket along with Alicia's car keys, she hated herself. But she didn't put it back, either.

"This is literally the cleanest car I've ever been in," said Megan. "So, care to explain why we're Thelma and Louise-ing this morning? You want to have The Conversation, right?"

"What conversation?"

"The 'define the relationship' conversation. I've been here before, dude. We got together and played a song. So, basically, we made out. Now you want to know what it all means. Are we going steady? Are we a band?"

"How did you know I was thinking all that?" asked Katy.

"Because everyone does. It's just like dating someone, but worse, because there are more of you. It's like standing up after the orgy and saying, 'So, are you and me and that uncircumcised guy and that lady over there, are we going out or what?'"

Katy laughed. "So, are we?"

"I've got to be honest with you," said Megan. "I'm a senior, and med school applications are not a joke. And we both know your guitar playing needs a ton of work, and unless you and Travis are sitting on a trove of fucking platinum hits, we have three-quarters of one song. Which would make a shitty setlist."

"Okay, I get it," said Katy. Her eyes stung, and not from the NO2. "Should we just head back?"

"Jesus, let me finish. On the other hand, that song has fucking *potential.*"

"Megan, everything I *do* has potential. It just never seems to pan out."

Megan shook her head. "Travis's voice and that song? I want to be in that band. Besides, you guys wrote one song, you can probably write another one. It's not magic."

*Sure it is.* It wasn't that Katy literally attributed the song to miracles, or God, or tapping into the elemental vibrations of the universe (though she could imagine Nick Dimmett putting it that way). But she had absolutely no idea how it *had* happened and was pretty sure that it wasn't going to happen again.

She pulled the minivan into the Guitar Center parking lot. Two massive walls of the store were lined with guitars, enough guitars to power a hundred bands. If the Big One hit now, she wondered, would she be killed by an avalanche of Fenders and Gibsons and Kramers?

A guy in a leather jacket with a dark mustache and hoop earrings came over. "Can I help you lovely ladies find anything today?" he said. "Keyboard room is that way."

"Just looking around," said Megan. She ushered Katy away from the sales guy and whispered, "Welcome to Misogyny Center."

"What's the deal with that?" asked Katy.

"Let's see, women can't be in bands, because we get PMS, and our fingers are too delicate to play chords, and our boobs distract the real musicians, and we don't have any life experiences worth singing about. And above all, when we're around, dudes don't feel comfortable talking about all the chicks they're banging. We should get out of here before I get the vapors."

"People don't actually believe that stuff, do they?"

Megan groaned. "Come on, let's get you something you can rock out with."

"Where do we even start?"

"With the most popular guitar in the world. Try this." Megan pulled a Fender Stratocaster off the wall and handed it to Katy. It was black and shiny like patent-leather shoes, and Katy ran her hand along the glossy back of its neck. "Let's plug you in," said Megan.

"In front of everyone?" said Katy. "Can't I just, like, strum it and see how it feels?"

"Yeah, and next we'll head over to the Toyota dealership and sit in the car and play with the steering wheel, pretend we're driving like grownups. Come on." Megan found a braided guitar cable, plugged one end into a small amplifier, and tossed the other end to Katy. She caught it and snapped it into the jack with a satisfying thunk. Megan flipped on the amplifier.

Katy had never played an electric guitar before, or even touched one—and she was positive that Megan knew this, knew that Katy was a poor pathetic guitar virgin. She sat on top of the amp and fingered a few chords, then pulled a pick out of a nearby dish and tentatively strummed a C, the first chord of "Summer On." The sound was huge, shimmery, clean. Megan turned a couple of knobs on the amp and said, "Now hit it again." This time, Katy's chord crashed in like it was wearing the world's itchiest sweater, but she could still distinguish each note ringing through the dirty fog. It was the greatest sound Katy had ever made, and she strummed the chord over and over.

"This is really different from an acoustic. Compared to my guitar, it sort of plays itself."

"Well put," said Megan. "And if you're suggesting that electric guitar players are pussies whose baby fingers are too soft and delicate to play an acoustic, sure, I know a lot of guitar players like that. Want to see something cool? Hand me the guitar." Katy reluctantly handed it over. "You're fingering the chords like this." Megan mimicked the way Katy had just played the C chord, with three fingers.

"What's wrong with that?"

"Nothing. But try it like this." She slipped her hand a couple of frets up the neck and played. Now the chord sounded muscular, and she recognized the sound from half the CDs on her shelf. "It's a power chord," Megan explained. "There's nothing to it."

Katy studied Megan's fingers, then gave it a try. Each chord came out of the amp like a side of beef. Her fingers hopped around the fretboard, and no matter what order she played the chords in, it sounded almost like a song.

"Killer," said Megan. She held out her hands, and Katy handed over the guitar again. Megan played a couple of scales up and down the fretboard. An employee who had been approaching them made a surprised face and headed back the other way.

Katy laughed, but when Megan passed the guitar back, she turned off the amp, leaned the guitar against it, and put her head in her hands. "This is stupid," she said. "You're ten times better at guitar than I am. And you're the *drummer.* I'm wasting your time."

Megan sighed. "If you're looking for a heart-to-heart pep talk, I am *not* your girl," she said. "So let me say this. Your attitude is fucking obnoxious."

"Sorry," Katy whispered.

"You want to skip over the part where you suck and go straight to being awesome, right? Well, you and me and everyone else."

"In high school, everything was so much easier. I just assumed—"

"Yeah, you know why that shit was easy? Because it *wasn't worth doing.* Jesus Christ, I sound like a fucking televangelist."

"I'd watch a foulmouthed televangelist." Megan laughed. "I know I need to practice to get good," Katy continued. "It's just... you're already good. Why do you want to waste time messing around with me and Travis?"

"You are so dumb," said Megan. "Because I like you guys. You're weirdos who go out in the rain. Look, I've played with a lot of good musicians. Most of them are guys, and most of them think with their dicks most of the time. It gets really old."

"Well, I've never been accused of thinking with my dick," said Katy.

"That doesn't mean I'm giving you a license to suck. If all you ever do is play power chords, I will murder you. And if you do write a bunch of hits, you have to promise to tell Rolling Stone I taught you everything. Come on, let's get you a guitar and get the hell out of this toilet before some guy comes over and tries to make our panties fly off by playing Def Leppard riffs."

Katy picked up the blue guitar. "Should I just get this one?"

"No, because that one's nine hundred dollars," said Megan. "Try this." She reached for an identical-looking guitar.

"Can I try the red one?" asked Katy.

"Now we're talking." Katy unplugged the blue guitar, forgetting that the amp was still on, and the speaker gave an offended pop. She shook her head and turned down the volume before swapping in the red guitar. She ran through the same chord progression she'd been playing with earlier, and it sounded the same. "This one's made in Mexico and it's two hundred bucks," said Megan. "And if you don't think too hard about the labor conditions, it's going to be fine."

"Sold," said Katy. "What about an amp?"

"You can borrow my little Silvertone," said Megan. "Confiscated it from my old guitarist. But you should get a headphone amp for practice."

Katy bought the red guitar, the headphone amp, a soft zipper case, a cable, and an electronic tuner. The mustache guy threw in an extra pack of strings and another lecherous smile. When he swiped Katy's Visa card, she almost expected her parents to walk through the door with disappointed looks. But the $297 charge went through with a polite beep. "I'll pay my parents back when we sign our first contract," said Katy. She wasn't sure whether she was being facetious.

"Tell it to your mom," said Megan. "Let's get lunch at In-N-Out."

"What's that? It sounds like a porn theater."

"You've never been to In-N-Out? Oh my god, I am your best friend ever. Pull into the drive-thru. We're going to *ruin* this car."

They ordered Double-Doubles and fries. "Would you like a bag or a box?" asked the metallic voice of the drive-thru speaker.

Megan leaned across Katy's lap and yelled, "The box." They crammed the cardboard box of cheeseburgers and fries between their seats and ate messily on the freeway at sixty miles per hour. "This is it," said Megan. "The ultimate California experience. Sunshine, a new guitar, the freeway, greasy fingers. The only thing missing is sawing the top off this mom van."

It was the best burger Katy had ever eaten. When their exit sign came into view, she felt a pang of disappointment. "Do you mind if we stop at Vons? I need a couple of things."

"You're the driver. But bring the guitar in with you. Leaving instruments in a car is like having a vanity plate that says ROB ME."

Katy felt like a badass walking down the condiment aisle with the new guitar strapped to her back. On the top shelf, above the pickles and mayonnaise, was row of hot sauce bottles. Nestled between Tabasco and Tapatio was Melissa's XXX. As Katy reached for it, however, she noticed that not all the bottles were the same. "NEW!" screamed the label. "Melissa's XXXX: 2 Hot 4 U." The red hue of the sauce was a little deeper, as was the cleavage. She bought two bottles.

"Travis has you hooked on that stuff too, huh?" asked Megan.

"Yep. So what do I do now? With the guitar, I mean."

"You practice."

Ten minutes later, they pulled up in front of Megan's dorm. "So

94

what's next on your schedule of truancy and debauchery?"

"Uh, I need to go to the administration building."

Megan hopped out of the van. "Wow, the fun never stops with you."

Katy parked behind Mitchell but didn't go inside. With the guitar on her back, she walked to the registrar's office. She lowered her head and said to the woman behind the counter, "Can you tell me how to drop a class?"

"Is that new?" said Alicia. Katy pulled the red guitar the rest of the way out of its case. "Oh, wow, that's the real thing, huh?"

"I guess so," said Katy.

"Well, put it on, show me."

"Right now?"

"Come on, I don't make you wait before I model new shoes, and I know how much you appreciate it."

Katy laughed. "A guitar isn't a fashion accessory."

"That's for me to decide," said Alicia. "Put it on." Katy shrugged. She hoisted the guitar strap over her shoulder and tried to strike a defiant pose, but couldn't stop giggling. "Well, the sweatshirt's gotta go, but damn, the rest of us girls are in trouble. That thing fits you like a good pair of shoes."

"Oh, shut up." Before setting the guitar aside, Katy strummed a chord with her fingers, and jerked with surprise. Unplugged, an electric guitar was the quietest of all instruments. "Oh, hey, I need to get to my shift at the library." She sheathed the guitar and then, at the last minute, decided to bring it along. A ten-minute break was enough to play "Summer On" two or three times.

On the path to the library, Katy saw a familiar figure. Nick Dimmett, alone and walking through campus, could still project an air of *I'm a celebrity and I know it.* He was wearing a denim jacket and scuffed brown corduroys, and his full beard seemed carefully ungroomed. A considerable percentage of the guys at Atwood tried growing a beard sooner or later. Most of them failed. She'd seen patchy beards, blond beards that looked like cereal stuck to someone's face, and beards sculpted into unwise configurations. A successful beard like Nick Dimmett's made its inadvisable brethren look that much more ridiculous.

Katy wasn't sure whether to say hello, but as they passed, Nick looked at her and said, "Oh, hey, I know you. Megan's band. Casey, right?"

"Katy."

"Katy, yeah, I'm terrible with names, you know? How was practice?"

"Fine, I guess. So, do you guys have any shows lined up? Gigs? I'm not even sure what to call them. Can you tell I'm new to this?"

"Don't worry about it," said Nick. He pulled a pack of cigarettes out of the pocket of his jean jacket, looked at Katy's face, and reconsidered. "When the Session started it was just me and Steve screwing around."

"And now?"

"Us screwing around in front of a whole lot of happy people. We're playing at this place in Pomona next week. It's not a big venue, but it's really..." He searched for the word. "Authentic. Hey, if we're going to get to know each other, we should have a seat, right?"

Katy looked at her watch. Her shift had started two minutes ago. "Sure." They sat on a bench alongside the path, underneath a tree that was shedding oddly knife-shaped leaves. A faint smell of pot smoke clung to Nick's clothes. "So are there other bands on campus? Or is it just you guys and... Megan's band?"

Nick laughed. "Oh, there have been a couple of others, but not, like, actual bands that play out." The way he said it made "not playing out" sound like an embarrassing personal problem. "It's about commitment, right? This place sometimes it makes it hard to know what's important in life."

Katy nodded and looked up at the people crossing the quad, behind the row of trees. "I don't know if I fit in with these people at all."

"Us musicians, we're kind of a weird species, you know?" said Nick. "So let's hear what you've got."

"Huh?"

"Play me something. You guys working on originals?"

"A little bit," said Katy.

"So? That's a guitar you've got there, isn't it?"

"I can't sing," said Katy, but she was unzipping the case. She put the guitar on her lap and strummed as hard as she could so the thing would make a little noise. When she started to sing, Nick closed his eyes and tilted his head back a little, which was at least an improvement over him staring at her. Somehow she made it through a rough solo rendition of "Summer On" without any botched chords or voice cracks.

"Wow," said Nick. "A beautiful girl singing a beautiful song. Good day to be alive." He nodded, stood up, and pulled out a cigarette. This time, he lit it. He started toward the quad, then looked back at Katy. "If you ever want to sit on one of our practices, let me know. Open invitation, me to you."

•

"Megan, this is the amp you're lending me?" said Katy. "Seriously?" The thing was a gray block the size of a shoebox set on its end, with a ratty power cable and frayed cloth over the speaker. It looked like a junkyard television.

"Trust me," said Megan. "A small amp turned up sounds better than a big-ass amp. We can mic it if we need to."

Katy strapped the guitar on, plugged in, and strummed a G major, which had always struck her as the most joyous chord. Megan was right: With its volume knob cranked up to nine, the tiny amp sounded like a monster.

"Woohoo!" said Keith.

"Am I going to be electrocuted, though?" She was a little out of tune, and paused to plug into her electronic tuner. Katy enjoyed tuning. Unlike playing a song, it was possible to get it almost exactly right every time. Once the needle told her she was in tune, she tried to catch Travis's eye, but he'd pulled his hood up over his head and was clutching the microphone in its stand. "Travis! You ready?"

"You're the captain."

"*I'm* the captain," said Megan. She held her drumsticks aloft. "Jesus Christ, I was getting sick of brushes." She clicked the sticks together three times.

Katy realized too late that Megan was counting off the song, and screamed a panicked "Wait!" into the microphone.

To her relief, Megan laughed. "My fault. Four-count." Click, click, click, click.

Katy played the two-bar intro. It was still novel, the way the strings on the electric were so slim and easy to press against the frets compared to playing acoustic. When Megan came in on the drums (kick-snare-kick!) and Travis started singing, it was hard to imagine the sound could be contained by the four walls of the music room. While she sang the chorus, Katy looked over at Keith, the way his fingers moved effortlessly up and down the neck of the bass. *I'm going to call that guy*, she thought. *Soon.*

The song was over a lot faster than Katy had expected. "How was that?" asked Megan.

"You tell me," said Katy. "But it sounded like the way I imagined in my head. Maybe louder."

"It was a decent start. Hey, feeling good, boys?" Keith and Travis nodded. Megan reached into her bag and pulled out a small plastic case. For a second, Katy wondered if she'd brought some kind of drugs. When she opened the case, however, it was full of blue foam earplugs. "Put these on," she said. "I wanted you to hear how we sounded without them, but let's not be idiots."

Keith tapped his ear and nodded: He was already wearing plugs. Katy squished a pair between her fingers and inserted them into her ear canals. It tickled, and as the foam expanded, the room went silent. Travis's lips were moving. Katy plucked out one earplug. "Huh?"

"I said, these things are heavy-duty," said Travis. "Like, probably thirty dee-bees of attenuation."

Katy laughed. She reinserted the earplug and tried a chord. It sounded thin and muffled, and her own voice rattled inside her head like a penny in a tin can.

"Again!" shouted Megan. Katy watched her count off, and they played the song again. This time it was choppier, as everyone got used to the earplugs. Katy could easily hear Keith's bassline, and she keyed off this, trying to ignore the claustrophobic sound of her vocals during the chorus.

"Guys, that is what we call a good fucking song," said Megan. Katy felt herself turning red. "Can we try something? The verse needs to breathe a little, I think. Let's add four bars at the top of each verse, and Katy, give us a riff to go over it."

"I have no idea how to do that," said Katy. Without thinking, she'd said it into the microphone, and her pronouncement echoed off the walls.

"Just finger the chords and pick around until you find something," said Megan. "Everyone, let's just vamp on the verse pattern while she works on that."

"What am I supposed to do?" asked Travis.

"I don't know. Time to bust out the harmonica."

Travis stepped away from the mic stand and wandered around the music room while Keith and Megan played through the four-chord progression. Katy pressed her fingers against the fretboard and plucked a few individual strings in turn. To her surprise, it didn't sound like total garbage. "Can you slow down a little?" she said into the mic. Megan nodded and eased into a more laid-back tempo. Katy tweaked the pattern and extended it across the remaining chords. "Okay, pause. Travis, Get over here! What do you think?"

"I wasn't paying attention," he said. "Play it again?"

"You remind me of my cat," said Katy. "Let's try it at normal speed."

Megan counted off, and Katy played the riff. She flubbed a couple of notes, but remembered Megan's advice and kept going. By the third time through, she could almost play it fluidly. "Oh man, that is great," said Travis. Katy turned away so he wouldn't see how hard she was grinning.

"Great, let's put it all together," said Megan. They played "Summer On," with the new riff, and the power chords, and the harmonies, and Katy marveled at how it sounded like several invisible musicians had joined them, like little empty corners of the song had been filled in by... well, as much as she hated the word *magic*, *teamwork* was even worse.

"Anyone in the mood for Top Thai?" asked Keith.

Katy was suddenly starving. She smiled at Keith. "Always."

Katy thought nothing could extinguish the thrill buzzing through her body after practice, but carrying drums managed to douse it. She dropped her guitar and amp off at Mitchell and met up with the rest of the band (*her band!*) in the quad.

Atwood was an oasis in the midst of a dangerous area, or so the story went. Katy had often heard students talk about a trip to a taqueria like they'd survived a tour in Iraq, or reminisce about how the 1992 riots had come within a few blocks of campus.

Top Thai was the best and only Thai restaurant in the neighborhood, open every night until 4 a.m. "Are you sure it's safe to go out this late?" Katy asked.

"Oh, don't tell me you buy into that racist bullshit," said Megan, pressing the crosswalk button. "People go into town, see a couple of Latino kids, they think they've walked into an Eazy-E song."

"She has a point," said Keith. "Look at us. An Asian guy, a Hispanic guy, a girl with a studded leather jacket. We're the scary people we're supposed to watch out for."

"Wait, I'm not scary?" said Katy.

"I think you're scary," said Travis. "You're always showing up at my room and making me do stuff. Plus, you can handle Melissa's."

Katy laughed. "Okay, if we run into any rival gangs, I'll dribble hot sauce on them."

Top Thai had once been a 24-hour diner. When it converted to a Thai restaurant, the decor stayed the same, but some of the old couples moved on to make way for students looking for their second dinner. Tough-looking middle-aged Thai women shuttled efficiently between tables.

They settled into a corner booth and ordered noodles and red curry and Thai iced coffee. Katy watched the tendrils of condensed milk swirl into the black coffee for a while before ruining the effect with her spoon. She bit her lip. "Okay, I hate to say this," she began, "but I have to ask something."

"You can't borrow my Pixies import," said Megan.

"Megan, shut up a minute. I'm just going to put this out there. I want us to be a band. Are we?"

Megan laughed. "Of course, stupid. We're all thinking it, right?"

"Really?"

"I was thinking maybe I should have ordered the drunken noodles instead of the pad Thai," said Travis, "but yeah."

"I just assumed," said Keith.

Katy hid her grin with a big slurp of iced coffee. A waitress delivered their food, and Katy piled her plate with noodles, rice, and chicken curry. Katy pulled the bottle of Melissa's XXXX out of her bag and set it on the table without saying anything.

Travis glanced at the bottle. "Wait, *Four*-X? I thought this stuff was an urban legend. Oh, wow, we have to try this right now." He spooned out four lumps of steamed rice and shook a couple of drops of sauce onto each. Katy looked around, wondering if they were going to get busted for bringing in outside food, and swallowed her mouthful of rice.

"This isn't so—oh, shit," she said as her mouth ignited. Panting, she took a gulp of water, which made it worse. "You are so stupid."

Megan's face had gone bright red. Keith tried to say something, but it came out like the hiss of a deflating balloon.

Travis seemed unaffected. "Well, that was an experience," he said. "So what's next? Band-wise, I mean. I don't need to know what the next level of hot sauce is."

"I'm not sure which of you to murder," said Megan, when she could speak again. "Have you seen *The Doors?*" Everyone had. "You remember that scene on the beach, where Jim Morrison sings a couple of lines, and Kyle MacLachlan says, 'Those are great fucking lyrics, man,' and then ten seconds later they're playing 'Light My Fire'?"

"And then he takes his penis out on stage in Miami?" said Travis. "I'd have to check with them, but my parents would probably be opposed to that."

"Killjoys," said Keith.

"Do you think we could get our song on KROQ?" asked Katy.

"Hit the brakes, Camaro. What I was going to say is, that's not how it works. We've got one original and one cover, and they both need work. If we add a couple more covers, we could probably play open mic night at the Java Cave. Also..." Megan added a packet of sugar to her iced coffee and stirred. "I hesitate to bring this up, because we'll never get to sleep, but The Doors had something we don't. Besides buckets of LSD."

"What's that?" asked Katy.

"A band name."

That was a good point. Katy had gotten so attached to the idea of being in MEGAN'S BAND that she'd lost sight of the fact that it was not, in fact, a workable band name.

"What, we're not still called Slag?" said Travis. "I wanted to be in Slag." He mimed holding a phone to his ear. "Hello, Mom? Guess what? I joined Slag!"

"Slag's dead, baby," said Megan. "How about Fuck Tornado?"

"Like the one someone painted on the Wall?" said Keith.

"I do not approve," said Travis. "Don't get me wrong, Megan, you're a genius and I love you, but let's not pick a name that forces us to be an underground punk outfit that can only play in illegal clubs. Because that's maybe not my scene."

"How about we soften it to, I dunno, Friend Tornado?" said Katy.

"That is literally the worst thing I've ever heard," said Megan. "Guys, did you hear about Katy? She was killed by a friend tornado. So many hugs."

"The Ketones," said Travis. "It's a type of organic compound."

"Sounds like a lounge band from the 70s," said Katy.

"Short and snappy is good," said Megan. "Bush. Blur. Helmet. Rancid. Pixies. Easy to spell, easy to remember. No one's going to get it wrong on a marquee."

"Makes sense," said Katy. "How about, I don't know, Fire?"

"Nice," said Keith.

"I don't like it," said Travis. "Too R&B. I mean, not that there's anything wrong with R&B. We're just not it. Also, there are probably fifty bands named Fire. Are you all seeing the beauty of Slag yet? We could call our first album *Heap*. Get it?"

They shot names around until the platters were empty. "Let's table the motion," said Megan. "Next Friday, same time, same orchestra pit?"

"Works for me," said Katy.

"In the meantime, how about you and McCartney over there write us a new song?"

Travis looked at Katy and said, "Gold records, all the way."

●

Keith and Megan split off to North Campus, and Travis and Katy headed back to Mitchell. Katy slipped into the bottom bunk. Her head was buzzing from music and caffeine. Alicia's digital clock read 3:45.

Katy got out of bed. What to do? She found her slippers, pulled the laundry bag out of the closet, tossed a book in on top of the dirty clothes, and stepped into the hall. She'd never seen the hallway empty before. Prowling the dorm at this hour enabled her to neatly sidestep a key existential question: *How put-together do you need to be before exiting your room?*

This was not a simple question. Well, it was a simple question if you had a mismatched set of sex chromosomes, apparently, because she'd seen every guy on her floor in his underwear—crossing the hall to the bathroom, doing laundry, hanging out (sometimes literally). Alicia's approach was full makeup, except when heading to the shower, although in that case she would still dress smartly for the eight-foot journey across the hall to the bathroom. Meanwhile, Bianca, who never missed an opportunity to mentioned that she had done "a few magazine shoots," had spent so much time walking down the hall in a t-shirt and panties that even the guys were bored of it. Katy settled on a philosophy of "something that looks like clothes, except when dashing to the shower." Tonight, however, the best she could do was her Happy Mondays t-shirt, pajama shorts, and fuzzy slippers.

The laundry room was on the first floor. Katy walked down the grand staircase into the lobby and turned into the back hall. She flipped the switch, and the laundry room was bathed in a clinical light.

A person could walk through Mitchell Hall at 2 a.m. and find the full range of student pursuits: deep discussions around a congealed Midnight Special, studying, indiscreet make-out sessions. Two hours later and Katy was the last woman on earth, the star of one of her apocalyptic seminar films. Early morning was confusing: scary or dull? Sleepy or secretly thrilling? Katy shrugged and emptied her clothes into one of the front-loading washers. As usual, someone had left an open box of off-brand powdered detergent on the table, and Katy scooped some up without guilt. *I play guitar in a band and I steal soap*, she thought.

Katy watched her clothes tumble for a while, then sat on the table and opened *The Book of Three*. When the spin cycle started, she remembered a high school rumor that sitting on a washing machine would give you an orgasm. It couldn't be true. Right? While she was eyeing the quivering machine, the door opened and Travis walked in. Katy jumped. At 4 a.m., it took her a moment to realize that he couldn't actually see her dirty mind.

"Hey, what are you doing here?" he said.

Travis was holding a mesh bag of clothes and a jug of Tide. "Same as you, obviously," said Katy. "Couldn't sleep?"

"Nope." He stuffed his clothes into the adjacent machine, pressed the start button, and leaned against the column of dryers.

"But I'm up a lot. I start thinking about something and my brain won't turn off. Tonight it was acid-base reactions."

"Me too," said Katy. "In general, I mean, not chemistry. So, you think we can write another song?"

"Right now?" said Travis.

"Why not? Hey, I just thought of something. You know that hidden track on the *No Alternative* CD?"

"The Nirvana song? Sure. 'You're in a laundry room...'" He laughed. "Okay, I see why you thought of it."

"That's it. The Laundry Room. What do you think?"

Travis looked around. "Uh, it seems fine to me. What are we talking about?"

"As a band name, silly. The Laundry Room. It's easy to remember. It's kind of mysterious. It's a Nirvana reference, but you really have to know your shit."

"Okay, that's really good," he said. "Maybe even better than Slag. I don't know how Megan's going to feel about it, though. She'll probably say something like, 'Give me a fucking break. Why don't we just call ourselves The Men's Room and get it over with?'"

"Actually, The Men's Room is kind of great, too," said Katy. "But I think it would have to be an all-girl band."

"The Laundry Room," said Travis. "Huh." He sat down on the table next to Katy.

"You know something?" said Katy. "If any parent in the world came in here, they'd tell us not to sit on the table because we're going to break it. Is that what being an adult is about? Getting to do all the stuff our parents told us not to?"

"I don't know," said Travis. "Maybe it's when we realize they were right about that stuff. God, I hope that's not it."

They spent the next hour talking about music. Katy told Travis how she'd skipped lunch one day to drive to the record store to buy *Automatic for the People*. Travis remembered watching the "Smells Like Teen Spirit" premiere on *120 Minutes*. "At first I laughed because it sounded so much like a 'Louie, Louie' knock-off. But then..." He flung his arm out for emphasis, and his hand brushed Katy's shoulder. "I wished there was some way to rewind it and watch it again, but then they started showing all day, anyway."

"I think I saw the premiere too," said Katy. "But it didn't really make an impression the first time."

Travis snorted.

"Hey, question," said Katy. "Do you know how to make a web site?"

"No," said Travis, "but I assume it's not very hard. I've seen some pretty stupid websites."

Email and *talk* became as much a part of Katy's life as lunch and dinner. The main computer lab was just five minutes from Mitchell, and Katy started to drift over there more and more often. She'd open her inbox to a note from Christina, or a dirty joke forwarded from Megan. At first it seemed weird to carry on an email conversation with someone she saw every day at school, but she couldn't argue with the pleasure of an endless thread of favorite eighties songs batted back and forth with Travis (tlee3@atwood.edu).

"Why the '3'?" Katy asked. "Are you Travis Lee the Third, or something?"

"I wish," wrote Travis. "I think there were just a couple of T. Lees who got accounts before me. Teddy Lee. Terminator Lee. Those guys."

This exchange was buried in a jungle of angle brackets, the vestiges of reply after reply, "Billie Jean" parried with Billy Idol, "Personal Jesus" versus "American Jesus."

"'American Jesus' wasn't the eighties!" Travis protested. "That was like last year!"

"Great, I guess I'm disqualified."

None of this, of course, could replace the ritual of visiting the mailboxes which lined two walls of the Mitchell office. Every day, the student employee working the afternoon shift grumbled through a couple of hours of sorting and distributing campus and U.S. mail into the grid of four-inch cells. Nothing made Katy happier than receiving a handwritten postcard from Christina, who had bought a shoebox of blank tourist postcards from a yard sale during the summer and was now sending them out to friends with fabricated tales of globetrotting. ("Darling, Monte Carlo is beautiful, but the palace staff are giving me *fits*.")

Packages were left in a haphazard pile in the back of the office, and when you received one, a slip of orange paper in your mailbox would alert you. Katy had received one care package from home already, featuring a box of her favorite cheesy crackers and a Costco-sized plastic tub of red licorice. When she set it down in the hall and yelled, "Who wants Red Vines?" it was like throwing blood-red chum to a pack of sharks.

As Katy passed the office this afternoon, she saw a telltale orange slip curled up in her mailbox. She smiled. Even if it wasn't another care package, she'd have the pleasure of telling Alicia she'd received a pair of mail-order shoes. Alicia got more excited about her twentieth pair of nearly identical catalog shoes than Katy could imagine ever getting about a single pair.

When Katy retrieved the slip of paper, however, it wasn't a package notification at all.

**To:** KATHERINE BLUNDELL, CLASS OF 1998
**From:** Prof. Deborah Gill

*Dear Katherine:*

*Please call 5804 to make an appointment with me at your earliest convenience.*

The note didn't have a pair of boxes labeled GOOD NEWS and BAD NEWS, but Katy was pretty sure she wasn't being asked to accept the Student of the Year award. She'd call Professor Gill soon. For now, she stuffed the note into the back pocket of her jeans and headed off for a little extracurricular research.

•

Making a website was harder, and then easier, than Katy expected.

First, she went to the campus bookstore to ask if they had any books about creating websites. Nobody had the slightest idea what she was talking about. "Web-what? Is this for an entomology class?" asked one employee.

So she went to the computer lab. The guy working the help desk was sporting an unfortunate Vandyke that didn't make him look any less like a nervous sixteen-year-old. She asked him for help despite knowing that he was almost certainly going to give her the look that meant, *great, another girl who doesn't understand computers.*

He gave her the look. But he also opened a file drawer and removed a two-page handout entitled BEGINNING HTML. "If you get stuck," he said, "just go to a page you like and hit View Source."

Katy sat in front of a PC and read it over twice. She was expecting something as incomprehensible as French existentialism, but HTML was surprisingly simple. She logged into the VAX like she was going to check email, launched a text editor, and had made her first web page five minutes later.

*Your URL will be http://www.atwood.edu/~username,* said the handout. Katy browsed to that address, and there was her "Hello, my name is Katy!" page. She emailed Christina to say, "Hey, check this out!"

Katy found her way back to the Dark Tower website and viewed the source. At first glance, it was a prickly fog of angle brackets and cryptic uppercase words. <HEAD> and <A HREF...> and <H1>. She resisted the urge to close the window and design a business card instead. After reading through the code a second time, it started to make sense. It was a lot like the way Dr. Watson would mark up an English comp paper.

Katy printed the Dark Tower HTML code, thanked the guy at the desk, and walked over to the Stoop. She bought a chocolate milkshake and ate it with a spoon while studying the code. She opened her notebook to a fresh page, clicked her mechanical pencil twice, and began writing out the code for the Laundry Room website by hand.

When she looked up, Megan was at the counter. "Hey!" called Katy.

Megan sat down with her quesadilla, and Katy told her about the name. To her surprise, Megan loved it. "That's some indie shit," she said. "Can I do the logo?"

Megan started sketching laundry-inspired graphics on a napkin between bites of quesadilla. "Hey, have you ever heard the Geraldine Fibbers?" she asked. Katy hadn't. "They're playing a show at Jabberjaw next month. We should all go. Trust me. I'll loan you the CD. You guys write a new song yet?"

"No," said Katy. "I guess we were too busy coming up with the name."

She looked down at her page of HTML code, and suddenly she understood Travis's obsession with technology. Within the world of computers, every problem had a solution. Creating a website might be hard, but she had no doubt that it was possible, even if it was a long drive down an unfamiliar highway. Writing a song, on the other hand, was a walk in the wilderness. You might find a beautiful clearing not on any map. You might wander around for hours and get tired and angry and bored. You might get poison ivy in unspeakable places. Katy giggled and jotted down a couple of lines. On the way out, she stopped at the student store and bought a disposable camera.

•

On Friday, Katy pulled up in front of Megan's dorm and helped load the drums into the back of Alicia's van. "This is just the ulti-mate pussy wagon, huh?" said Megan. "I'm surprised there aren't any dents in the side from women throwing themselves at it."

Nabisco Session was still in session when they arrived. At least Katy was expecting it this time. When they were done, the Laundry Room filed in and set up. Katy pulled out her camera and clicked off a few exposures. Keith, smiling and relaxed, practic-ing a scale. Travis with his hood up, clutching the microphone. Megan looking perturbed. "Travis, will you take one of me?" Katy asked, holding out the camera.

"Why?"

"Scrapbook," she lied. She posed with her guitar while he took the shot.

They played "Where Is My Mind?" and Katy messed up the riff and had to stop the song several times. "Not cool," said Megan, and her disapproval was more biting than if she'd yelled. Katy wished someone else would make a mistake, for once.

The next day, Katy took the disposable Kodak to the one-hour photo counter at the Rite Aid. While she waited, she read Rolling Stone and People cover to cover. By the time she was caught up on the Charles and Diana divorce, the film was ready, and she paid the seven dollars and slipped open the envelope. Travis, Megan, and Keith looked just as she remembered, but she didn't. She always felt a little awkward standing with the guitar, but in the photo, she looked, well, *competent*. She wore her black Lollapalooza t-shirt and a fierce expression, and her hair was a little messy, and the guitar strap between her breasts emphasized them more than she'd realized. She looked like a girl in a band.

Katy went to the computer lab and placed the photos one by one on the flatbed scanner. She renamed the files (travis.jpg), cropped them, and reduced them to what she hoped was a reasonable size in Photoshop. She fished around in her bag until she found the napkin Megan had left behind at the Stoop, the one where she'd drawn the circular door of a washing machine with THE LAUNDRY ROOM in white block letters in the center. She scanned this, too, then FTPed all the images over to the VAX.

She logged in and typed up her code, using the edge of the keyboard as a clumsy paperweight to hold open her notebook. When she was done, she loaded the page in NCSA Mosaic. Some of the formatting was weird, so she tweaked it here and there until it looked like a website.

**Travis Lee:** Vocals
**Megan Dougherty:** Drums
**Keith Lopez:** Bass
**Katy Blundell:** Guitar

*For bookings, contact* kblundell@atwood.edu

Below that was the row of photos. Katy clicked each one and watched it take over the whole window. At some point they'd have to get a picture of all four of them together, but even without that, it almost looked like the website of a real band.

Soon everyone followed Megan's lead and started calling Alicia's minivan the Pussywagon—everyone except the owner of the vehicle in question.

"I said you could borrow my car," she said, after Katy let the name slip. "I didn't say you could give it a vulgar name. You guys are terrible."

"It's a Josie and the Pussycats reference," Katy lied.

"I don't care," said Alicia. "I'm taking my keys back unless you stop saying... P-word wagon!"

This ultimatum had no effect, of course, except that after Katy relayed the story, Megan started referring to the van as The P-Word Wagon.

Megan had the Thomas Guide map book open on her lap, flipping pages as Katy drove along the 110 toward... well, she wasn't sure which neighborhood they were heading to, and she couldn't pause to think about it anyway, because she was trying to keep up with the incomprehensible local custom of driving at full speed on the freeway even in heavy traffic. Finally, Megan told her to take the exit onto Arlington, and they parked on Pico Boulevard, near their destination.

"Is this really the place?" Katy asked. The street was a row of auto parts stores, massage parlors, and print shops. A couple of blocks away in any direction, palm trees swayed like drunks loitering on street corners.

"Sure," said Megan. "It's down the block, I think." Similarly flanneled young people milled around outside the venue, whose facade was fortified with unnerving metal bars. Katy looked up at a black-and-white sign that read COFFEEHOUSE ART GALLERY, the letters pitched at random angles like shaken-up Scrabble tiles.

"Is this a fact-finding mission?" asked Travis. "Are we here to take notes on how to rock?"

"I know it's antithetical to your world view," said Megan, "but this is a fun-finding mission. While we're waiting, what was your first concert? Kiddie stuff doesn't count. I don't want to hear about how Raffi signed your *Baby Beluga* cassette."

"I'll go first," said Keith. He was wearing a slim-fitting, shiny maroon dress shirt and black jeans. He looked *edible*, thought Katy. "Frankie Goes to Hollywood, 1986."

"Okay, strong out of the gate. You were what, nine?" asked Megan.

"Thirteen," said Keith. "I was supposed to go with my best friend, but he got chicken pox the night before the show. So it was just me and my mom. I don't even remember what the venue was. It was horrible."

"Mine was INXS, 1988," said Katy. "My friend Christina's parents dropped us off, and a guy tried to sell us drugs on the way into the arena. The band looked so tiny. It was amazing."

"Travis?" said Megan.

"I've never been to a rock show," he said. "What? You're surprised by this?"

"Not, just honored to be the one to devirginize you," said Megan. "Okay, with one exception, these are good answers, but I can top you all. My parents took me to a James Taylor show in 1984. And shut up, because it fucking ruled."

"You mean the folk song guy?" said Keith. "I always get him confused with John Denver."

"That is slander," said Megan.

They filed into the club, and a heavily tattooed bouncer tore their tickets at the door. The interior was smaller than Katy had expected, and the walls were painted turquoise. Katy slipped her ticket stub into the back pocket of her jeans. The opening act was an outrageously loud industrial band that played lots of tape loops and samples, and Katy went into the bathroom to grab some toilet paper and ball it up into makeshift earplugs.

It was 11:15 when the headliner took the stage. Katy was surprised to see that the lead singer was a small woman; she'd imagined the band name was ironic, like Cinderella. She put her lips to Megan's ear and yelled at her neon blue earplug, "Is that Geraldine?"

"That's Carla," said Megan. "Pay attention."

The drummer opened with a high-tempo pickup, and the rest of the band came in all at once. When Carla began singing, Katy laughed. She'd misjudged everything: This woman's voice was enormous, at once raspy and melodic. By the time the chorus rolled around, Katy was a confirmed fan. She looked over at Travis, who was wearing the same hooded sweatshirt and intense look he always had on at practice. He swayed to the music like one of the neighborhood's palm trees.

As the band transitioned into a jangly folk tune in 3/4, Katy looked over at Megan, who nodded and mouthed, "Right?" Katy nodded back, put her hands up, and danced.

"Shotgun," called Megan after the show. As she drove down Pico, sweaty and exhausted, Katy watched Travis fall asleep on Keith's shoulder in the rear view mirror. She sighed. "Okay, what's wrong?" said Megan. "Was that not fucking explosive?"

"It was amazing," said Katy. "It's just, we're never going to be half that good, right?"

"Probably not," said Megan. "Who cares?"

"I mean, what's the point, then?"

Megan looked like she was going to punch the windshield. "Think about it this way," she said. "Do you think the Fibbers were beating themselves up during their set because they were playing Jabberjaw instead of the Hollywood Bowl?"

"Probably not," Katy admitted. Outside, the city raced past in sepia, a smear of streetlights and storefronts and the occasional glowing cigarette of a pedestrian.

"And you know what else? They're not as good as the Stone Roses, or the Pixies, or the motherfucking Beatles. So should we all just kill ourselves?" Katy didn't answer. The car was silent except for Travis's snoring. "Look, it's almost winter break, but we should play a show when we get back."

"The Forum?" said Katy.

"Very funny. I was thinking more like the Java Cave."

"Are we ready for that?"

"Are we ready to play a show in front of ten people at the dinky North Campus coffeehouse?" Megan frowned. "Actually, we're not. But unless we have something to motivate us, we'll just keep fucking around. Keith, back me up here." Katy checked the mirror. Keith had drifted off, too, and he and Travis were leaning against each other precariously. "Well, never mind. You know I'm right. Just admit it for once."

"Fine, Megan, you're a genius," said Katy. "Is that what you want?"

"I'll get us on their calendar," said Megan. "Maybe during finals week, give people a way to decompress. Trust me. Besides, there's more to a gig than practice."

"Like what?"

"Outfits."

## 18

*Salem, Oregon*
*December 1994*

"Katy, dinnertime," called Linda Blundell.

Katy had brought the red guitar with her to the airport and talked a flight attendant into letting her slip it into the first class closet. While she drank ginger ale in coach, she worried about her guitar and amused herself by imagining it giving the finger to suits in garment bags alongside it.

Now she was sitting on her bed, failing to write a new song. She flung the headphones off. "I'm busy, Mom," she yelled up the stairs. "I'll heat something up later."

"I'm not going to college," she heard Julie say.

"What?" said Katy's mom. "Of course you are."

"Not if it makes you super-bitchy."

"I heard that, Julie!" Katy screamed. "Just shut UP."

"Both of you, cool it," said Katy's mom. "My god, can't you get along for one day?"

Katy had made her parents promise not to change anything in her room, at least not during her first year away. Now, looking around at her old stuffed animals, high school yearbooks, the CDs that hadn't made the cut—Poison, Bon Jovi, Warrant, Lita Ford— she wished her mom had gutted the place. Same old room. Same old fights with her sister about nothing. On the plane she'd felt like an adult. No, better than an adult: a *musician*. A chick with a red guitar. She pretended the other passengers were whispering about her. Maybe she was a member of L7 or Throwing Muses or Letters to Cleo.

And then, upon crossing the threshold of the house where she grew up, the last three months evaporated. She had no evidence that the Laundry Room even existed. She couldn't access the website from home, and couldn't imagine trying to explain to her family what a website was, anyway. She thought about trying to call Travis to ask if he was in the same funk, but she didn't have his number and didn't know his parents' names, and there were probably a lot of Lees in Seattle.

Katy's mom came downstairs. "There's chicken soup when you're ready." She pulled Katy into a hug. "This is it, huh?" she said, nodding at the guitar. "Two hundred and ninety-seven dollars? It's beautiful. But honey, you should have asked." Linda was quiet for a moment. "Is this your rebellious moment? I kept waiting for you to turn into an obnoxious teenager like I did, but until now I thought your sister got all of those genes."

"What's she up to now?" asked Katy.

"Oh, nothing fatal," said her mom. "Staying out an hour after curfew. Listening to rap singers who curse a lot. That thing in her nose. I try to make a good show of being really upset about this stuff so she won't push it further. But we're not talking about Julie. We're talking about you. Julie I can keep an eye on. You're a thousand miles away, and you need to show some responsibility."

"Mom, please. It's not like I'm on drugs or anything. So I used the credit card. You never care about little things like this."

"I don't expect you to understand what it's like to send a kid off to college," said Linda. "But I *do* expect you to use your head. Dad and I have already cut everything out of the budget, and then we had to sit down and figure out how to come up with two hundred and ninety-seven dollars. And then on top of that, we get a notice that your financial aid is in jeopardy? We can't afford two days at that school without financial aid. It's not a little thing."

Katy started cooking up a defiant response. *If I have to get every single detail of my life exactly right to make you happy, then get used to disappointment.* In the end, though, she started to cry and leaned her head on her mother's shoulder.

"Honey, tough love isn't in my DNA. How can we fix this? Do you not like it there?"

In an instant, Katy found herself in the middle of practice, with Keith absorbed in his playing, Megan looking severe, Travis singing in that unlikely voice.

"No, I do," she said. "I'll do better. I'm sorry."

Linda pressed a fingertip against her lower lip and exhaled. "Julie won't stop talking about your band, you know. I hear her on the phone with her friends."

Katy had a hard time believing that. Guitar in hand, she followed her mother upstairs and knocked on her sister's door. "What do you want?" Julie yelled through the door.

"Just open up." Her sister opened the door. "I was wondering if you wanted to hear one of my songs," said Katy.

"I guess," said Julie. She let Katy in. They sat on the edge of Julie's bed, underneath an Ice-T poster, and Katy perched the headphones on her sister's head, with one ear exposed so she could hear Katy sing.

Katy closed her eyes, imagined the Laundry Room assembling, and played "Summer On." She sang Travis's part instead of her own, and hoped her voice wouldn't sound too thin or strained, or too much a parody of Travis's baritone. "That's probably our best one," she said.

Julie pulled off the headphones. "Not bad," she said. "Now what do I have to do to get you to leave my room?"

Later, while microwaving her soup, Katy heard Julie humming the chorus.

# WINTER

*Monday, January 2, 1995*
*17 days before the show*

"How much did you miss me?" asked Alicia. Katy climbed into the van and they sped away from Burbank airport toward Atwood.

"I missed your car a lot," said Katy. "My mom's Mazda is fine, but it's no—"

"Don't even think about it," said Alicia. "Being home is weird, right? Even when I go home for a weekend to do laundry, I feel like a baby."

Katy laughed. "I thought it was just me!" As they drove onto campus, Katy was tugged in two directions. Back in September, Atwood had felt like a temporary stopping-off point in transit to a distant country called "real life." Now, even though she still hated so many things about the place, Atwood seemed like more like home than her actual house where her mom and dad and sister lived.

She'd first experienced this existential nausea when she was eight and her family had moved to a new house. *We're staying in this weird place, but our real house is somewhere across town.* That sense of being in purgatory had lasted two weeks, and then everything seemed normal enough. Now she couldn't even remember that previous house. Maybe this was a universal feature of human psychology: *home = where you are + two weeks.*

She found Travis in his room, sitting at his computer. She decided against giving him a welcome-back hug. "Happy new year, Big T. What're you working on?" she asked.

"That is *not* going to be my new nickname," said Travis.

"Okay, what are you looking for in a nickname, then? Bono is already taken. T-Bone?"

"Probably also taken. But okay, I accept. The ladies deserve to know."

"Gross. So, T-Bone..." Katy paused. "Actually, I'm never saying that again. So what have you got for me, song-wise?"

"Not much," Travis replied. "I spent most of vacation with Trish. To the *delight* of my parents."

"Do they not like her because she's not Korean?"

"They don't like her because she exists," said Travis. "She's a distraction. 'Distraction' is my mom's favorite word. If she wrote out a list of distractions, it would be seven pages long. Video games. Girls. Music. Sports. Classes that don't end in '-ology' or '-istry.'"

"Okay, I get it," said Katy. "Want to hear something I came up with?" The guitar was back in her room, so she just opened up her notebook and sang the lyrics she'd jotted down in Alicia's van on the way to campus.

*When I go out there, I go out alone*
*And if this is home, there is no home*

"Well, that's upbeat," said Travis. "But the tune is solid. Is that the verse or the chorus?"

"I don't know yet. What do you think?"

"Hmm. I think it could work as a short chorus, maybe with a couple of repeats at the end. Hey, there's your nickname: Chorus Girl."

"That sucks, Travis."

"You started it, C.G. Okay, let me think about this a minute." He rolled a sheet of paper out of the dot-matrix printer, tore it off, and began penciling lyrics. He erased a few words and rewrote them. "What about this?"

*Return to the scene we never saw before*
*Underneath a cloudless sky you open up the door*

"It's a slow song," said Katy. "Is it okay if we have those?"

"I think that's up to the cruise director."

"Megan? Guess we'll find out on Friday."

# 20

*Wednesday, January 4*
*15 days before the show*

Wednesday after seminar, Dr. Gill approached Katy. "Ms. Blundell, I'm going for coffee. I suggest you join me." Katy slipped her notebook into her shoulder bag and followed the professor out into the sunshine. It was sixty degrees out, and Dr. Gill was wearing a blazer and a scarf. "Did you receive my note?"

"Yes," Katy admitted. "I just haven't had time to—"

"Ms. Blundell, I'll get to the point." Dr. Gill looked around. They walked past the fountain outside the social sciences building. "We have certain expectations for students in their first semester at Atwood, and at this time, you're failing to meet those expectations. I don't relish this conversation any more than you do, but as your faculty liaison, it's my responsibility to explain where you stand."

Dr. Gill opened the door to the North Campus Commons and

motioned Katy inside. The Commons was a low building that had been tacked onto the side of Broad Hall, Megan's dorm. They stepped into the main lounge, turned left, and went down the stairs into the Java Cave.

The Java Cave lived up to its name. It was dark, and the prevailing decor was shoddily reupholstered secondhand couches. Dr. Gill ordered a black coffee and said, "What would you like? It's on me."

"A vanilla latte," Katy said, then immediately regretted it, because it was twice as expensive as Dr. Gill's order and, with its lashings of milk and syrup, seemed like the kind of thing a baby would drink if babies drank coffee.

"We can go to my office for privacy or stay here if you prefer," said Dr. Gill.

"Here is fine." They sat at a wobbly table with their drinks. The Java Cave logo on their mugs had been nearly rubbed clean by years of thumbs. "If you're saying I'm a below-average student here," said Katy, "believe me, I know that."

"Ms. Blundell, that's not what I'm saying at all." Dr. Gill pulled a paper out of her briefcase and smoothed it on the tabletop. Katy stole a glance at the stage, a flat wooden box in the corner of the room, and felt a chill imagining herself standing on it. "The papers you've written for my class are superb. Your critical reasoning is far beyond what I expect from the typical first-year student. But you've also turned in a late assignment, and you've shown up late to class a number of times."

"Sorry," Katy began, but Dr. Gill was already moving on to further misdemeanors.

"According to the counseling office, you're barely pulling a 2.5 in your other classes. I haven't spoken to your professors, but I suspect their experiences would be similar to mine: When you apply yourself, you do excellent work." She looked down at the paper. "You've also shown up late for work study repeatedly, and you dropped a class. That's a major red flag in your first semester."

Katy was stunned. What else did Dr. Gill know? Katy half-expected her to say, "Your guitar skills are a C-minus, at best, and everyone knows you're into Keith Lopez."

"So what are you saying?" asked Katy.

Dr. Gill slurped her coffee and set the mug down. "Katy, this is a hard transition for a lot of people. High school was easy for you, wasn't it?" Katy nodded. "Atwood isn't easy for anyone."

"My friends don't seem to be having any trouble."

"Then you're not seeing the full picture." Dr. Gill stood up and returned with a coffee refill. "Do you have any problems you'd like to discuss with me? Family? Substance abuse? Depression?"

"No, nothing like that," said Katy. *God, I wish people would stop assuming I'm on drugs.*

"I didn't get that impression, but I have to ask." She sighed. "Based on your grades and your credit load, we're going to need to place you on academic probation. That means you'll need to maintain a minimum 3.0 average next semester."

Katy took a sip of her latte. It tasted sour. "Can I ask something? Am I the only person you're having this conversation with?"

"No, Ms. Blundell, you're not, but I'm frustrated that it's gotten to this point with you, because I know you're more than capable of doing the work. Now, I don't have to tell you that finals are coming up in less than two weeks. I understand that this campus has a way of providing endless distractions, but I suggest you focus hard on academics between now and then."

Katy looked over at the stage again. The plywood surface was marred with bits of paint and masking tape. "I understand."

# 21

*Friday, January 6*
*13 days before the show*

"We're playing a week from Thursday," said Megan. She tapped the kick drum a couple of times for emphasis. "It's just a ten-minute slot. Three songs, tops. It's basically like an open mic night."

"But that gives us, like, one more practice between now and then," said Katy. "Can we practice any other nights besides Friday?"

"I wish I could do it every night with whoever's available, but I have to study," said Megan. She gave Katy a hard stare. "You can't just let a double entendre like that go by. You always have that notebook with you, right? I'm making you keeper of the Laundry Room quote book."

Katy tried to laugh, but her head was beginning to ache. She turned to Keith and Travis. "You guys okay with this? Playing during finals week?"

Keith nodded. "Megan and I have played there before. It's really low-key." He set a tape deck on top of his amp and fiddled around with it.

Travis idly wrapped his microphone cable around his hand. "All I have to do is show up and sing some songs, right?"

"That's what it says on your business card, right?" said Megan.

"Then I can do that."

Megan went on. "Look, it's three songs, and two of them are in pretty good shape already. We can do this."

"But why does it have to be during finals week?" said Katy.

"Because it'll be good to get it over with. If we don't do it then, it'll be February. And then, shit, why not make it March? Why not play a show never?"

"I guess."

"Now, about that third song. You guys got anything, or should we work up another cover?"

"Actually," said Katy, "Travis and I wrote something earlier this week."

"Great, what's it called?"

"'There Is No Home.' How do you feel about slow songs?"

"Oh, I like slow songs," said Megan. "Without them, what would people listen to while they fuck?"

# 22

A quirk of the Atwood academic calendar was that finals were held shortly after students returned from winter break. Mid-December was one of the most laid-back times of the year, and then, in the second week of January, everyone fell into a hissing cauldron of exam prep and term papers and all-nighters: Dead Week.

Students who usually lingered for an hour over lunch or dinner would cover their plates with a sheet of foil and race back to the dorm to get their textbooks and flash cards greasy. Flash cards were huge. Anyone who seemed to have a minute of downtime would be immediately approached by a student with a deck of three-by-fives shouting, "Quiz me!" Katy quickly learned that foreign-language flash cards were the worst: She offered to help Bianca study German, but Katy's German pronunciation turned out to be worse than no help at all.

The only upside to Dead Week was the institution known as the study break. Put out a plate of cookies and a coffee percolator in an underused lounge, and the room would fill up instantly with students desperate for caffeine, calories, and an excuse to procrastinate. The religious organizations were known for throwing the best study breaks, hoping to draw stressed-out scholars into having literal come-to-Jesus moments. This was how Katy found herself eating a surprisingly good chocolate chip cookie with Keith and Travis next to a table of pamphlets from the Christian Promises group.

"Guys," said Travis. "I'm not sure where this brilliant idea is coming from, but I think we should play Christian rock."

"Shhh!" said Katy. "There are probably, like, actual Christians here."

"I'm an actual Christian," said Keith. His voice dropped to a whisper. "And these guys freak me out. Good cookies, though."

Katy laughed. "So, you guys excited about the show?"

"I will be once I survive the next few days," said Keith.

"I'm ready to rock at all times," said Travis. "Like a robot." He took a sip of coffee. "Do you think it would be unethical if I built a robotic replica of myself to send to some of my exams?"

"It depends," said Katy. "Is the robot going to go on a murderous rampage like in *Robocop*?"

"That's a really good question," said Travis. He shrugged. "Honestly, I don't know whether I'm ready to rock, because I've never rocked before."

Katy slipped her notebook out of her pocket. "Just remembered something I need to put in my English paper." She wrote down Travis's quote. "Well, anyway, I'm going to be heading to the music building most nights to practice. If you guys want to swing by, just peek into the practice rooms like creeps until you find me."

"Don't you need to study?" said Travis.

*Yes, Travis, I need to study. And learn how to play guitar like I'm not a three-year-old scraping at the thing, and try not to be a jerk to my roommate, and pick a major, and...* "I'll be fine."

Keith picked up a pamphlet from the table. "Have you heard the good news?" he said. "Travis's robot hasn't killed anyone yet."

•

The computer lab and library stayed open 24 hours during Dead Week, and the lab, in particular, was constantly full, with a long line for computers. Katy stepped into line, and even though no one was speaking, the hostility was palpable. The guy at the head of the line failed to notice that a chair had opened up, and the person behind him shoved him toward the free PC. A new sign had gone up that said ACADEMIC USE ONLY, and Katy was about to violate that edict. Would a member of the wrestling team catch her and throw her out of the lab like a club bouncer ejecting an unruly drunk?

When Katy got to the front of the line, she kept her eyes open for an empty seat and ran for it. Stress, she realized, had a *smell.* She couldn't identify all the components, but they definitely included sweat, unwashed hair, the ozone funk of computer fans, and contraband snack food.

She pulled up the Laundry Room website, then launched Page-Maker, which she'd learned while working on her high school newspaper. She pasted in Megan's logo, added the names of the band members, and wrote JAVA CAVE, 1/19/95. Then she printed a hundred copies, logged out, and nodded to the harried classics major at the front of the line.

With the flyers weighing down her bag, Katy whistled "Summer On" as she walked back to Mitchell. On the way in, she tacked up a flyer on the bulletin board in the lobby and waved at Alicia, who was sitting in the middle of their floor surrounded by a complete circle of books and papers. Alicia looked up. "Sorry, you probably want to come into your room, huh?"

"I'm good," said Katy. "Keep doing what you're doing."

She continued down the hall, where Quan and Bianca were sharing a veggie pizza. Katy looked at her watch. It was only eight forty-five. This was unheard of. "You ordered a full-price pizza?"

"Desperate times," said Bianca. "You want a slice?"

"Actually, that'd be great," said Katy. "You mind if I take two? You can totally get in on mine next time."

"We were hitting the wall anyway," said Quan. Katy thanked them, put the slices on a napkin, and took a couple of packets of red pepper flakes. She walked around the corner to Travis's room. His door was open and he was sitting at his computer, headphones on, typing up notes from his chemistry textbook. Katy crept up behind him and tapped him on the shoulder.

"Ah, look, it's Chorus Girl, trying to scare me," said Travis, draping the headphones around his neck. "You forget that my room is equipped with the most advanced surveillance technology known to engineering students and other nerds."

"Really?" said Katy.

"No, I saw your reflection in my monitor glass. But I'm flattered that you thought that was plausible. Hey, did you bring me pizza?"

"It's stolen pizza, so it doesn't count," said Katy. Travis reached for the slices, and she batted his hand away. "Hey, one's for me, mister greedy. Do you mind if I hang out and study for a while?"

"Sure." Travis reached under the bed, found a bottle of hot sauce, and put some on his pizza.

"Hey, hit me with some of that three-X," said Katy.

"It's four-X," said Travis. "Seemed appropriate to upgrade for Dead Week."

Katy laughed and put a few drops on her pizza. She glanced at the photo of Travis and his girlfriend. "So what does she see in you?"

"Other than my fourteen-inch penis?" said Travis. "I'm honestly not sure. We've been going out so long, I guess we're just good at tolerating each other's quirks."

"That makes sense," said Katy. She waited for Travis to ask her about her disappointing love life, so she could pour it all out to him, tell him that she'd never gone out with anyone for more than six months. That she had a crush on Keith and was afraid to tell him, that she loved and hated it when Nick Dimmett flirted with her. "Anyway, I made some flyers for the show. Here's your share. If you ever decide to leave your room, you can put some up."

"Ha ha," said Travis. He accepted the stack of paper. "Hey, look, that's me. Cool."

*Tuesday, January 10*
*9 days before the show*

Katy arrived at the music building and swiped her card. It was 10:30 p.m. She penciled in her name on the clipboard hanging outside one of the small practice rooms and shut herself inside. She set up her guitar and amp and ran through some scales from a beginning guitar book she'd bought at Rhombus Records. It wasn't clear to her whether scales had anything to do with playing songs, but everyone seemed to agree they were a good idea.

She ran through "Summer On" and "Where Is My Mind?" a couple of times and tinkered with "There Is No Home." The practice room was carpeted on the floor, walls, and ceiling, and the lack of echoes made her guitar sound crisp and present, and also seemed to magnify every mistake. Nobody else had shown up, and she couldn't blame them. Keith and Megan nailed everything on the first try, and Travis had probably emerged from the womb screaming the chorus from "Helter Skelter." Katy was the only one stuck in the remedial class. The rest were probably off studying, which Katy knew she should be doing, too. She thought back to Alicia's question: *Why is this so important to you?* She still didn't have an answer.

Katy's moment of despair was interrupted by music coming from one of the other rooms, and she stepped out into the hall to find its source. She wasn't surprised to find that Nabisco Session's practice was unaffected by Dead Week. It was hard to imagine Nick Dimmett or any other member of the band sitting in class taking notes on psychology or European history or women's studies. Katy slipped into the practice room and waited until the Session finished up their jam. It took eleven minutes.

The bass player set a beer can down on his amp and tilted his head toward Katy. "This one of yours, Nick?"

*Ew.* And, on the other hand, *yesssss.*

"Hey, don't mind him," said Nick. "You're that girl from Megan's band."

"Katy." She walked over to the chalkboard and found the Friday square that read MEGAN D. She erased it and wrote in THE LAUNDRY ROOM. "We have a gig coming up, and I'd appreciate it if you guys would clear out by twelve on Friday so we can set up."

"Hey, that's cool," said Nick. "I understand. Guys, keep me honest on this, okay?"

"Thanks," said Katy. "I'll get out of your way."

She turned to go, but Nick said, "Hey, what are you running from? Want to stick around for another song?"

"I shouldn't," said Katy, but Nick ignored her protests.

"You sing harmonies?" he asked.

"Sometimes."

"Cool. Steve, let her take over on the second chorus." The guitar player nodded and stepped back from the microphone. "Should be pretty straightforward," said Nick. "This one's called 'Everlasting.'"

The song started out with a languid drumbeat, and Steve started playing frilly riffs over Nick's rhythm guitar. Nick sang a verse about losing touch with a girl with sandy blonde hair, and then Steve joined him on the chorus, which went, "Woo-oooh, our love is everlasting." It took all of Katy's willpower not to laugh.

Nick was right: The song was pretty straightforward. In the second verse, he was writing a letter to the girl, describing memories of lying naked on the beach. Katy was pretty sure this lyric was lifted from another song but couldn't figure out which one. Maybe it was just lifted from the cover of a romance novel. It sounded really sandy.

Steve stepped back from the mic stand and motioned Katy over. She closed her eyes and thought about what Megan had taught her: Don't think, just sing. "Woo-oooh," she sang. "Our love is everlasting." When she opened her eyes, Nick was looking at her with a sunny grin. He nodded his head, and Steve broke into a thirty-two measure guitar solo. At the end of the solo, Nick pointed at Katy and held up three fingers. She assumed, correctly, that this meant the chorus would repeat three times, and it did. One more guitar solo, and the song was over.

"That was some good shit, Carrie," said Nick.

"Katy."

"Yeah. Guys, why don't we have a girl in the band?"

"You did," said the drummer. "Remember?"

"Oh yeah," said Nick. He narrowed his eyes.

"Well, thanks," said Katy.

Nick walked her down the hall. "You and me should hang out sometime, right? Maybe try out some more harmonies?"

Katy flashed what she hoped was her flirtiest smile. "I'm already in a band."

●

Katy was about to open the door to her room when she noticed the whiteboard read KEEPING BUSY.

"Oh, you have got to be *kidding* me," she muttered. It was the secret code they'd developed at the beginning of the year. Alicia had a boy in the room. Dead Week hookups were legendary, but Katy hadn't expected one to strike so close to home.

She lugged her gear down to the lounge, where a plate of cookie fragments on the table was the only evidence of an earlier study break. She balanced her guitar against the arm of the couch, sat down, and ran through biology flash cards until her eyelids grew heavy. She awoke to something nudging the side of her neck like a cat's paw. "What the fuck?" she said aloud. The guitar case had slumped to a 45-degree angle, and the seam at the tip was tickling her. Katy shook her head, gathered up her stuff, and trudged upstairs just in time to see Keith Lopez slinking out of her room.

Keith didn't see her. He was whistling his way single-mindedly down the hall in the opposite direction. When he was safely out of sight, Katy burst into her room and said, "What the hell, Alicia?"

Alicia was curled up on the top bunk in a way that struck Katy as smug. "What's your problem?" she said.

"You *knew* I liked Keith, and you went ahead and... how could you do that to me?"

Alicia sighed heavily. "Okay, how exactly was I supposed to know you liked Keith? Telepathically?"

"What? I *told* you..." Katy replayed the last semester in her head. Actually, she hadn't told Alicia anything. It was Keith she should be furious with... except that she hadn't gotten around to mentioning it to him, either. This was all logical, and none of it made Katy feel any less betrayed. She found herself saying, "But he's in my band!"

"And that makes him your property or something?" said Alicia. She raised a finger and pointed it at Katy. "You know what? I am so sick of hearing about your band. Every time I try to talk to you about something, you always turn it back to your band. We get it, you think you're a big rock star. Remind me again, how many hit songs have you released?"

"Fuck you!" The words seemed to catch in Katy's teeth. She slammed the door, ran across the hall to the bathroom, and started crying. She locked herself inside a stall, sat on the toilet seat, and sobbed. After a few minutes, she stopped crying and just felt stupid. She leaned her chin against her palm and studied the stall graffiti. For a good time, call the phone number of someone who probably graduated in 1987. A fading naked lady in Sharpie. The Nabisco Session logo, with "Nabisco" spelled with a K.

Katy had never cried it out in a shared bathroom before, and she assumed that someone would come along and rescue her, like in the movies. Instead, she had to listen to someone pee in the stall next door.

Was Alicia right about everything? Katy suspected she was. For reasons she couldn't articulate, Katy had been pursuing the Laundry Room with single-minded determination. But "single-minded determination" was just a nice way of saying "being a self-centered jerk," right? She thought about the photo Travis had taken of her at practice, with the hard look in her eyes. Who was that person?

She stood in front of the sink, splashed water on her face, and looked at herself in the mirror, like she'd seen people do in the movies. It didn't make her feel any better. When she got back to her room, Alicia had turned the lights out. She got into bed with her clothes on and tried to sleep.

*Wednesday, January 11*
*8 days before the show*

When Katy woke up at 8:20, Alicia had already left for class. Katy threw on a sweatshirt and went to seminar without combing her hair. After class, she walked across the campus to Megan's dorm, stopping along the way to tack up a few flyers with duct tape.

Katy knocked on Megan's open door. "Hey, sorry to be that kind of girl, but do you want go shopping?"

"I should really..." Megan began, then took a good look at Katy's face. "Fuck it, let's go. You got the keys to the Pussywagon?"

"No. Alicia and I had a fight."

"So you're grounded?"

"I don't want to push it."

"No problem. You got a little cash?" Katy nodded. "Then follow me."

They crossed the eastern border of the campus and waited at

the bus stop on Mills Avenue. "The thing is," said Megan, "room-mates are the worst. You could have Mother Teresa as your room-mate and you'd still be telling me about how she's acting like a little bitch."

"I think I was the bitch," said Katy.

"Doesn't matter. It's always the same shit. You stole my smoothie from the fridge. You left your book on the desk. You're cohabitating too often. You like the same guy as me. Am I boring you yet?"

"Don't forget 'you gave my car a dirty nickname,'" said Katy.

"Exactly," said Megan. "Other people's roommate problems are the most trivial shit in the world, but yours are Israel and Pales-tine. Which is why, a few months from now, you're going to try for a single at room draw."

"But I thought Alicia and I were going to be good friends."

"I know a lot of people who are best buds with their first-year roommate *now*," said Megan. "But not a lot who were friends *while* they were roommates. You put two strangers in a hundred square feet, you add the stress of finals, you surround them with other horny nineteen-year-olds, they'll try and shiv each other before long. It's true at San Quentin, it's true here."

A city bus pulled up, and they each dropped $1.50 in quarters into the fare box and got on. The bus was full of women, mostly in work clothes or with strollers and small children. Katy and Me-gan took a pair of seats in the articulated midsection of the bus and got off a few miles down the road. Megan led Katy to a small boutique between a produce stand and a taqueria. The awning read MARIPOSA.

"My roommate took me to this place freshman year, so I guess roommates are good for something," said Megan. "It's all secondhand, but they're picky about what they buy."

Katy paged through a rack of dresses that had apparently been sold by the ten coolest women in town. "Megan, help me out here. I'm from Salem. No one from Salem is cool."

"Yeah, and I'm from Spokane, the international fashion capital," said Megan, piling clothes over one arm. "Here, try some of these."

Katy took the fabric stack into the changing room. She pulled on a sleeveless silver blouse. Too cheerleader-y. She tried a black-and-white striped minidress. Not bad, but it was hard to imagine playing guitar in it without the hem of the skirt migrating up towards her neck. Finally she slipped into a black pencil skirt and a clingy purple t-shirt. The neck was rolled and fraying like it had been ripped out, but she figured it was supposed to be that way.

She stepped back into the store and waved her hand at Megan. "Hey. I think maybe this was a waste of time. I don't know if any of this stuff is really me. I mean, wouldn't it be more honest to just wear what I usually wear?"

Megan giggled in a very un-Meganly way. "First of all, you look fucking hot. Second, this grunge authenticity thing is bullshit. If you want to go on in jeans and a band t-shirt and let the music speak for itself, fine. That's your choice. But don't pretend it's 'honest.' We're trying to entertain people. Nirvana was so good, they could wear their regular clothes and people thought they were making a fashion statement. For the rest of us, dressing up can't hurt."

"You really think I look hot?" asked Katy.

"Well, your hair looks kind of crazy," said Megan. "But in a good way. I think. And I have a jacket that's going to look perfect with that outfit."

Katy bought it. "You ready for lunch?" she asked.

"Starving," said Megan. "You ever had *lengua?*" They went to the taqueria next door and Megan ordered them beef tongue tacos.

The meat was tender and juicy, and as long as she ignored the fact that some of the chunks had visible taste buds on them, Katy loved it. "So how do you know about all this?"

"All what?"

"Like, where the Geraldine Fibbers concert is, and the cool places to shop, and how to order tacos, and stuff?"

Megan took a big bite of her taco and chewed it before answering. "I'm glad you think of me that way," she said. "But the fact is, Atwood just has really low standards for cool. I mean, look at Keith. Classic handsome jock, right? Well, he got picked on in high school for being a brain, just like the rest of us. Around here, if you don't tuck your sweaters in, you're a fucking badass."

"What's your point?" asked Katy.

"All you have to do is put on a vintage shirt and get on stage with a guitar, and everyone at the Java Cave will think you're Courtney Love. Minus the smack habit, hopefully."

"Either that," said Katy, "or everyone will see that I'm really and truly a dork. I'm not secretly a cool kid waiting to emerge from my cocoon."

"What are you worried about? That people are going to laugh at you? Well, they're not. Because you're up there doing something they're too scared to do."

"Are people even going to show up?" asked Katy.

"I don't know," Megan admitted. "But I put up a flyer at the vintage shop." She smiled. "Put it this way. You listen to Weezer, right?"

"Sure."

"How is that guy not the biggest dork? But you totally want to fuck him, admit it."

Katy admitted it.

•

Katy waited outside the social sciences building, and when she saw Alicia emerging from her American history class, she rushed over. "Hey," said Katy. "Is it too early for a peace offering?" She held out the bag, with the gift curled up inside.

"For me?" said Alicia. She pulled out the scarf. "Oh, hey, this is nice."

"I don't know if it's something you'd actually wear, but it's me saying sorry for being such a butt."

Alicia pulled Katy in for a hug. "You really should have said something, you know. To him, or me, or, like, anyone."

"I know. But I'm happy for you, really."

"And I don't hate your band," said Alicia. "How could I? I'm going out with the hot bass player."

Katy laughed. "So will you come to our show?"

"Of course. Keith gave me his weird tape deck and asked me to record it. But I'd be there anyway."

"So we're cool?"

Alicia pressed a finger to her cheek. "Tell you what. You sign a contract pledging to refer to my car only as 'The Town and Country' and we're friends again."

*Thursday, January 12*
*7 days before the show*

Like burns and murder raps, Katy realized, sleep deprivation comes in several degrees.

First-degree sleep deprivation is when you stay up late on the phone with a friend and then have to get up for school the next morning. No big deal.

Second-degree sleep deprivation results from pulling an all-nighter. A classic high-school maneuver: Start a major project the night before it's due, stay up all night getting pale in front of the computer screen, and somehow pull it all together at 6 a.m. Go to school a conquering hero, fall asleep after lunch in biology class.

But third-degree sleep deprivation is different, the way a 9.0 earthquake is different from your sister shaking you awake. It's an affliction known mainly to new parents, prisoners of war, and musicians rehearsing for their first show just before finals.

By Thursday of Dead Week, Katy had gone full zombie. She hated her alarm clock, hated going to class, hated the sun. "How do you stand this?" she asked Alicia.

"Stand what?"

"The weather! It's like California out there *all the time.*"

"Did you not notice the return address on your acceptance letter or something?"

Katy had no response to this. She'd gone to sleep at four a.m. As she gulped a cup of coffee, ate a bowl of brand-name cereal, and staggered off to class, she was somehow buoyed to see people walking around in pajamas, looking even more bedraggled than her. She started thinking of them as the Pajama Army, and swore she'd never enlist.

Whenever she wasn't studying, or writing a paper, or answering stupid questions at the library, Katy plugged her guitar into the headphone amp and practiced the riffs from "Summer On" and "Where Is My Mind?"

She couldn't face being alone tonight inside one of the carpeted practice rooms like a mental patient, so she stopped by Travis's room. "You," said Katy. "Music building. Now. I can't practice this stuff without you."

"Wow," said Travis. "You really are scary."

# 26

*Friday, January 13*
*6 days before the show*

On Friday, the whole band met up at midnight. Nabisco Session was miraculously gone, but they'd left behind two cases worth of Budweiser cans, some lying on their sides and dripping onto the floor. Without anyone asking, Travis gathered them up and took them to the recycling bin, and returned with paper towels from the bathroom to wipe the floor.

"Okay, we need to finalize the setlist," said Megan. She wrote them up on an unused corner of the blackboard:

THERE IS NO HOME
SUMMER ON
WHERE IS MY MIND?

The list looked equal parts pathetic ("we only have three

songs") and inspiring ("we have *three songs!*"). "I think 'Summer On' is in pretty good shape," said Katy. "'There Is No Home' needs some work, right? And Megan, why didn't you warn me that 'Where Is My Mind?' is such a piece of work? Do we need a second guitar player?"

"Yeah, I've got Joey Santiago on speed dial," said Megan. "I'll ask him to come over. Alternatively, how about we practice the fucking songs?"

They ran through the set list. Katy lost her place during "Summer On," of all things, and called a time-out. Megan flung a drumstick, and it clattered across the tile floor. Travis picked it up and slapped it against his palm like he was playing the bad cop.

"Guys, please," said Keith. "Let's just get through the song."

"Shut up, Keith!" said Katy. "Oh, god, I'm sorry."

"It's cool," said Keith. He noodled around on a scale.

Katy looked to Travis for support, even though she realized at some level that she and Megan didn't have an argument worth adjudicating. But he was sitting on a plastic chair, reading a book, waiting to be called back to the mic. Travis was Switzerland in a sweatshirt.

"All right, let's take a short break," said Megan. "Then let's do 'There Is No Home.'"

They reconvened and played the song with no mishaps. "I don't know if I'm happy with that one," said Katy. "It's missing something."

"It's fine," said Megan. "The song can keep evolving after we've played it live."

"Should Katy sing lead on this one?" said Travis.

"You're crazy," said Katy.

"That's not a bad idea, Rails," said Megan.

"What did you call me?" said Travis.

"Rails, because you're skinny as one. Sorry, I've been calling you that in my head for a couple weeks. It just slipped out."

"I'll take it," said Travis. He looked at Katy. "Anyway, I think your voice might just work better on this song. I think I've been kind of trying to sing it like you anyway."

"Okay, let's try it," said Megan.

"No," said Katy.

"What's the problem?" said Keith.

"It doesn't make sense. Travis has an amazing voice. I don't. It's stupid to turn a third of our stage time over to me. It would be like if Nirvana had let the drummer sing a couple of songs."

"Fine, then fuck that idea," said Megan. Travis shrugged and sang the song again. Megan smiled. "You know, I kind of missed you assholes. You want to practice Monday?"

Katy couldn't go to sleep after rehearsal. Her head was *fizzing*. Alicia came to pick Keith up after practice, and Katy sat out on the quad for an hour with Travis and Megan, shivering while Megan defended her love of the "November Rain" video.

"You know the part where Slash is out in the field behind the church soloing like a motherfucker?" she said. "That should be you, Katy. Right now."

"Where would I plug in?"

"You think he was plugged in?" said Travis. "Those solos were entirely in his mind. That's why he's Slash and we're not."

# 27

*Monday, January 16*
*3 days before the show*

Finals were scheduled according to a complicated system. If you attended a class Monday through Friday at 8:30 a.m., for example, the final would be held Wednesday from 2 p.m. to 4 p.m. The idea was to give professors the opportunity to run a two-hour final even if their usual class period was only fifty minutes. Everybody hated this system—nobody more so than the many students every quarter who misread the chart and missed their final, a fate that was assumed to be the difference between a job at IBM and drinking wine out of a paper sack in an AM/PM parking lot.

Katy was unprepared for how completely the campus transformed between Sunday night of Dead Week and Monday of finals week. Because of the weird schedule, some students finished all their finals on Monday and left town or went home to their parents to enjoy free food and laundry service for the rest of the week.

Two of Katy's three classes didn't even *have* finals. She turned in her term papers for Dr. Watson's composition class and Professor Gill's seminar. She didn't know if they were any good, but they were done.

So the campus emptied out, and the stress dissipated like air from a balloon, and the Laundry Room started practicing more often. Nabisco Session was taking the week off, apparently, and Megan could have rescheduled practice for a less vampiric hour, but the midnight meet-ups had become a point of pride.

On Monday, Megan brought Katy a gift. "I thought this might help with 'There Is No Home,'" she said, handing Katy a yellow hunk of metal and plastic labeled CLASSIC O.D.

"Wow," said Katy. She plugged her guitar into the distortion pedal and connected the output to her amp with the extra patch cable she carried in her bag. A red LED glowed on the pedal, and Katy plucked a power chord. It was a crunchier distortion than her amp produced on its own, and when she clicked the pedal off with her foot, the notes rang clean. "Okay, I love this," she said. "Thank you."

Megan replied with a rimshot. "You owe me, C.G.," she said. She warmed up with a punk-rock beat, kick and snare on the eighth-notes.

"Keep doing that," Katy said into the mic. She stepped on the overdrive pedal and chugged through a series of power chords in time to Megan's beat. She remembered how Megan had explained that power chords don't have a third, so they aren't really major or minor chords. There was a tradeoff between power and expressiveness. Katy tried changing up the fourth chord in her sequence, switching it from a D in fifth position to an open A minor. It was an unintuitive change, and it sounded amazing when accented with Megan's double-stroke roll.

"Ah, the minor four," said Keith. "My favorite chord. Hold up a second. Katy, can I borrow a pick?" She handed him one. Megan counted off and they went back into the pattern, now joined by Keith's aggressive picking. In place of his usual fluid, walking basslines, he was just hammering the tonic on the eighth-notes, and it couldn't have been more perfect.

Travis stepped up to the mic and hummed an improvised tune into it. "Uh, maybe ignore that one," he said. He let the pattern go around again and came back in with an unexpected melody that curled around Katy's chords in odd ways. Katy looked at Megan, who was making a strange face. It wasn't just that she was working so hard bashing the drums. She looked *impressed*.

"I feel like my IQ just went down twenty points, but it was worth it," said Megan.

"You're not going to believe this, but I have a chorus idea," said Travis. He looked down at his hands. "I should probably learn to play guitar. Anyway, how's this?"

*They want to break me down*
*They want to take me down*

"Okay, give me a sec," said Katy. She fumbled around until she figured out the chords that went with Travis's vocals. Keith nodded at her. It worked. "Let's try a two-bar break before the chorus. Megan?"

Megan counted off, and they ran through the song. Katy found a minor seventh to play during the pre-chorus break. Verse, chorus, verse, chorus, and the song was over in ninety seconds.

"Can we have a song that short?" Katy asked.

"Fuck yeah, we can," said Megan. "Ever heard someone complain about a song being too short?"

"If you put that song in the same room as a Nabisco Session song, they would annihilate each other in a fiery ball," said Travis.

"Can you guys finish the lyrics for that before the show?" Megan asked.

"You think we should play it?" said Katy.

"Do I think we should play a high-energy song that'll make everyone's ass move?"

"Got it." Katy went to the chalkboard, erased THERE IS NO HOME, and wrote in TAKEDOWN.

"Is that the order you want?" said Keith.

"I don't know," said Katy. "What do you think?"

"'Summer On' is the best song," said Keith, "Put it first."

"I agree," said Megan. "Then let's put the new song second, keep the energy up. And the cover should go last. People start to zone out, we wake them up with a song they know."

Katy finished amending the list.

SUMMER ON

TAKEDOWN

WHERE IS MY MIND?

"That is a tight fucking setlist," said Megan. "Now let's see if anybody shows."

# 28

*Thursday, January 19*
*The day of the show*

"Are you The Washing Machine?" said the guy behind the espresso counter. He turned to Keith. "You're early. I'm Shane, the manager."

"The Laundry Room," said Katy.

"Right, right," said Shane, still looking at Keith. "Well, go ahead and load in. It's all acoustic acts other than you tonight, so just push your stuff toward the back. You need drinks? On the house."

Katy ordered a steamed milk with vanilla syrup. "Just the foam," she said, offering Travis a sip.

While setting up, Katy found herself pondering the question of what a rock and roll band is for, anyway. Before getting involved in one herself, she would have said that a rock band's job is to knock people on their asses with loud, awesome songs. To that end, the members of the band must spend most of their time writing songs, practicing, recording, and performing. When they weren't doing those things, the band members would enjoy ancillary benefits like making out with groupies and cashing royalty checks.

It didn't become clear to her until Thursday evening that that the actual function of a rock band is *cable management*.

Katy had already developed a new vocabulary to describe the sundry bits and pieces she was accumulating. That thing you clamp onto the neck of your guitar to raise its pitch? That, she now knew, was a capo.

But the instruments were starting to feel like mere appendages at the ends of cables. There was the cable connecting Katy's guitar to her amp, with mono ¼-inch phone plugs at each end. That was simple enough—until she added the distortion pedal, then a delay pedal, and had to wrestle two long cables and a cute little baby one with right-angle connectors, nestled between the two pedals.

Microphones required a different type of cable, with fat three-pin XLR connectors on each end, a male connector on one end and a female connector on the other. Katy found this nomenclature briefly offensive when Megan explained it, then filed it away in the "don't bother" category.

"Do we really have to hook up all this stuff every time?" asked Katy. She felt like a switchboard operator in an old romantic comedy about hilarious misunderstandings on a telephone party line.

"Only if you want us to make sound," said Megan. She whacked her snare drum. "Of course, some of us don't need amplification. Besides, as you know, setting up drums is the worst. I have like seventeen pieces here."

"You want some help?" said Katy.

"You'd do it wrong."

Shane kept interrupting them by coming over to ask Keith a question or tell him something about how the sound system was organized. "Is that guy a friend of yours?" asked Katy.

"Not at all," said Keith. "I don't think I've ever talked to him before."

"Then why—oh, I get it," said Katy. Keith looked like the leader of a band. Megan didn't.

Keith plucked a couple of notes and swung his bass around nervously. "Hey, you need to fix your cord," he said.

"Huh?"

"I forgot to mention it at practice, but if you have it dangling like that, it'll fall out."

"Put that one in the quote book," said Megan. Keith showed Katy how to route her cord into the armpit of her guitar strap so it wouldn't fall to the floor during the show. It made perfect sense, since Katy had already begun to think of her strap as just another type of cable with its own peculiar connectors. She plugged her guitar into its electronic tuner, and while adjusting the tuning peg she realized that her guitar strings were yet another set of cables, and that even Travis's vocal cords were a couple of vibrating cables. She followed this train of thought all the way down to her own DNA. *The essence of humanity is cables.* She sat down on her amp.

Travis came back from the bathroom, and Megan said, "I think Katy's freaking out."

"Are you freaking out?" asked Travis.

"No," said Katy. "There's just a lot of cables, and if anything gets unplugged, we're going to look like dipshits playing air guitar in front of all our friends."

"Right, and then we'll plug it back in and keep going," said Megan. "Jesus, Katy, finish your milk and let's get to work."

Katy found this phrase energizing. She strummed a few chords, and it sounded good. "Rails, can I tell you how much I hate it that you have nothing to set up?"

"I was doing warmups in the bathroom," said Travis.

"I bet you were," said Megan.

They pushed their amps and instruments to the back of the stage and took seats in the cafe. The sofas and tables were mostly empty. Around eight o'clock, however, Alicia came in, kissed Keith, and pulled out the chair next to Katy. "Mind if I sit here, or is this for the band only?"

"Of course you can, stupid." She put her arm around Alicia's shoulder and gave her a clumsy seated hug.

Alicia set Keith's tape deck on the table and called him over. "Does this look right?" she asked. Keith examined the dials, nodded, and kissed Alicia on the top of the head.

Shane stepped onto the stage. "We've got some great new acts tonight," he said, squinting at a handwritten sheet of paper. "Up first, the comedy stylings of Jack Jackson!"

Jack tried so hard, but most of his jokes fizzled out long before they got anywhere near a punchline. Even his cheering section, a few guys sitting down in front, had trouble faking laughs.

"Hey, if singing doesn't work out, do you think I should get into standup comedy?" said Travis. The coffee he'd been drinking before the set was apparently starting to kick in. "I have a bunch of jokes about how guys do one thing and girls do another thing. And some material about how girls with blonde hair are less intelligent than other people with different colored hair."

Katy stole a peek at her watch. Eight-twenty. The lasagna she'd eaten at dinner wasn't sitting right. She went to the bathroom and threw up. She wiped her mouth and looked at herself in the mirror. Her face was pale, and no matter how many times she adjusted her outfit, it looked like it belonged on someone else.

When Katy returned to the table, Jack Jackson had mercifully yielded the stage to a woman with an acoustic guitar singing about a bad breakup. She hunched over her guitar, but her voice was confident as she ticked off her former lover's various offenses.

Travis leaned over and whispered, "I never should have dumped her." Katy laughed into the crook of her elbow and hoped the woman didn't notice.

Everyone clapped for the singer-songwriter, and then Shane retook the stage and said, "Next up, appearing for the first time, the Laundry Room."

Katy stepped onto the stage and dragged her amp into position. The stage seemed much taller once she was on it, and she realized that the room had gone quiet. Megan didn't have a microphone, so Katy stepped up to hers. "Give us just a minute," she said. A few more people had filtered in. She saw the bearded guy from the computer lab, and Bianca from across the hall, who was mercifully wearing pants. And in the back of the room, a bearded figure in sunglasses. Nick Dimmett.

When the band members had all moved into place, Katy made eye contact with each of them. No one else looked as nervous as she felt.

The band had been so focused on rehearsing the songs that they'd never discussed who would stand where on stage. She was relieved when Travis took the front-and-center spot, but a key responsibility fell on her. "We're the Laundry Room, from the Pacific Northwest," Katy said into the microphone. "This one's called

'Summer On.'"

At the moment Megan clicked her sticks together, Katy realized that all of her practice up until this point—all of the time spent learning Nevada songs and composing riffs and learning to interpret Megan's mid-song facial expressions—was the musical equivalent of driving around a parking lot at five miles per hour. Being on stage was like taking the car out onto city streets. *You could die up here,* she thought. It was worse, in fact, because Megan had warned her never to pull over until the song was done.

So she gripped her guitar and hammered out the chords as best she could. Travis was center stage, his gray hood up, gripping the mic, singing his lungs out. Katy was so transfixed, watching him, that she forgot to sing the harmony. Her glasses slipped halfway down her nose, but she didn't have a free hand to push them up. Her fingers were sweaty against the fretboard, which made it impossible to change chords as fast as Megan's insistent drumbeat demanded, so she was dropping chords here and there, and her glasses had slipped so far down that she couldn't see her guitar anymore. Her chest was pounding, out of rhythm with the song, and she wondered whether this was what a heart attack felt like. She shot a look at Megan: *Help me.* Megan ignored her and kept playing. Katy mashed the wrong chord coming out of the chorus, wrong enough that Keith and Travis looked at each other, like, *What part of the song is this?*

By the time they reached the end of the song, Katy was dripping with sweat. She looked around for something to wipe down her face, and gave up and used her shirt. No one was clapping. She took off her glasses and set them on top of her amp, cursing the fact that she hadn't learned to play without staring at the neck of the guitar. The audience turned into a haze of blurry silhouettes, which was an improvement. "This is our first show," she said. "I want to dedicate this next song to my roommate, Alicia, for letting us borrow her car." She nodded at Megan, who launched into "Takedown."

The first thirty seconds of the song were joyful electric noise. *We're doing this,* thought Katy. Suddenly, however, it seemed like Keith and Travis were playing a different song. Had she misremembered the setlist? No, she was just horribly out of tune. Maybe without her glasses she was hitting the wrong chords?

Something flicked against Katy's right hand like an insect. It was the snapped B string of her guitar. Well, that would explain it. Katy had never broken a string before, but she understood the problem immediately: When that string broke, all of the remaining strings had to pull harder, which raised their pitch. The whole guitar was out of tune.

Katy tried to catch the eye of anyone else on stage, but without her glasses, she couldn't even tell if they were looking back. She took her hands off the guitar to pick up her glasses, which made it even worse: Her amp started feeding back in a dull, tuneless, rumble. The song ground to a halt. Katy stepped up to the mic and mumbled, "Sorry, give us a minute." Someone in the audience laughed.

Decision time. There was a pack of strings in Katy's guitar case, but she knew it would take her at least five minutes to put on a new string. And there was no way she could play "Where Is My Mind?" with a missing B string, because the whole riff was centered on the first two strings.

Katy yanked the cable out of her distortion pedal and plugged it into the tuner. While she tuned her injured guitar, she said to the band, "Can we start that one over?"

"*Fine*," said Megan through gritted teeth. "But let's play something, *now*."

Travis and Keith nodded. Katy hoisted her guitar back over her shoulder, and said to the audience, "Sorry about the interruption. Did I mention this is our first show?" She tried to make it sound sheepish, not despairing.

They started "Takedown" over, and Katy picked the chords gingerly, afraid all of the remaining strings would snap at once, like a blooming metal flower of disaster. She looked over at Travis. For a guy who never moved his feet on stage, he was a surprisingly charismatic performer. He kept his lips pressed to the mic and sang like a machine. But her guitar kept drifting out of tune.

After she'd strummed the final dissonant chord, Katy wanted to lie down and go to sleep right there on the stage. "We're the Laundry Room," she said. "Sorry." The applause was tepid. She waited to put her glasses on until after she'd coiled up her cables and tossed her guitar into its case, letting it hit the floor with a thunk of finality.

Alicia walked over to the edge of the stage. She smiled at Keith before turning back to Katy. "Not bad, for your first time."

"You don't have to lie," said Katy. Alicia rolled her eyes. Katy dismounted the stage and walked over to where Alicia had been sitting. She picked up Keith's digital tape deck, popped it open, and removed the tape.

"What are you doing?" said Keith.

"What do you think?" said Katy. "Confiscating the official record of how I ruined our show." She searched herself for a pocket, but her skirt didn't have one, so she slipped the tape into her bra. She'd never actually tried this before, and she wished there was some way to reverse the maneuver without looking ridiculous, because the plastic corners of the tape were digging into her skin.

Megan walked over. "Katy, you need to get your shit out of the way for the next act."

"Fine," said Katy. Her stomach lurched as she stepped back onto the stage. She finished coiling up her cables, and hauled her guitar and amp off to the side. Keith placed his bass tenderly into its fur-lined case.

On the other side of the stage, Travis was talking to a short woman with curly hair. "Do I know you from somewhere?" he said.

"No, um, I just wanted to say I really liked your show," said the girl. "I'm Eve." She extended her hand. Travis gave her a complicated schoolyard handshake. "Well, see you around."

"Ah, a glimpse of your future," said Megan. "Hope your girlfriend isn't the jealous type, Rails."

"Huh?" said Travis. "You think that girl was into me? You're crazy. Besides, I'm saving myself for my one true love, the woman on the Melissa's three-X bottle."

"Not the four-X?" said Megan.

"Too slutty," said Travis. "Where's the mystery?"

"What is wrong with you guys?" Katy screamed. "Are we just going to pretend that disaster didn't just happen?"

A couple of guys with acoustic guitars were standing at the edge of the stage looking nervous. Megan looked at them and nodded. "We'll get out of your way. Laundry Room, outside."

•

Standing in the courtyard, Katy could hear the folk duo's annoyingly perfect harmonies coming from the Java Cave.

"You need to pull it together," said Megan. "Fine, some things didn't go great. But the biggest problem was you acting like a pouty bitch and trying to force the audience to hate you."

"What did you call me?"

"Nothing."

"Would the two of you please stop fighting?" said Keith. "Katy, what was that 'we're from the Pacific Northwest' business? I'm from West Covina."

"Oh, shit," said Katy. "I'm sorry."

"Come on," said Megan. "Let's go back in there, clap for these earnest folk dudes, and then get a Midnight Special. Like I said, we got this one over with, now we can concentrate on the next show."

"The next show? Are you insane?" Katy looked at Travis, who was staring at his sneakers. "I ended up on academic probation for this, and I still *suck*. If you guys want to play another show, you'll have to get a real guitarist. I'm done."

"I don't fucking believe this," said Megan. "I knew you were inexperienced, but I didn't know you were literally a baby."

"This is your fault," said Katy. "You set up the show for finals week even though you knew I had to study."

"And this was all part of my master plan to engineer your downfall? Yeah, I pick one freshman every year, ruin her, and feed off her psychic energy. That's how I aced the MCAT." Megan made a fist, then relaxed it. Travis and Keith were leaning against the wall of the club, trying not to get involved. "I didn't play great either. We'll listen to the tape, learn from it, and move on."

Katy reached into her bra and pulled out the chunky cassette. "Listen to it?" The light from the courtyard lamps caught the words DIGITAL AUDIO TAPE printed on the black plastic. "A perfect recording of the worst night of my life?" She raised the tape over her head and remembered Megan's insult. *This is exactly what a baby would do.* And she didn't care. She flung the cassette against the bricks of the courtyard. Coils of black magnetic tape spilled out.

"Fine," said Keith. "This alternative stuff isn't really my music anyway."

Katy looked to Travis for some kind of support. He looked pale and wrung out, like he'd been in a fistfight. "Well, then this pouty bitch will quit wasting your time." She spun around and walked away.

# 29

Katy set her alarm for 6:45 on Monday morning. "Oh my *god*," said Alicia. "You're going to reinvent yourself as a horrible morning person, aren't you?"

New quarter, new classes. It was like Dr. Gill had said: A lot of people screw up their first semester. The Laundry Room's finals-week flameout still gave Katy a sharp pain in her stomach when she thought about it, but the timing was perfect. Now she could focus on academics. Four new classes, no distractions. She threw on her University of Oregon sweatshirt, was first in line for the Omelet Lady, and jogged to the engineering building after breakfast.

Fresh off her success building the Laundry Room website, Katy had signed up for Intro to Computer Science. She imagined the class would cover advanced HTML coding, and maybe something like the Basic and LOGO programming she played around with in middle school.

When the professor handed out the syllabus, however, it was

full of logic gates, Turing machines, regular expressions, and object-oriented design. The class had no prerequisites, and yet Katy had heard of literally nothing on the agenda.

She couldn't drop the class—*thanks for nothing, academic probation.* So she took notes during the lecture as best she could and wrote T's in the margin to denote "ask Travis about this." That is, if Travis was willing to talk to her after her tantrum at the Java Cave. Well, time to find out. After her morning classes, Katy stopped at the dining hall, built two burritos, and brought them back to Mitchell.

Katy knocked on Travis's door frame and said, "Peace offering."

"You brought me food?" said Travis. "That book about lucid dreaming is starting to pay off."

"Do you want me to pinch you?" said Katy. "Wait, did I say pinch? I meant punch."

Travis bit into his burrito. He reached under his bed for a bottle of hot sauce and shook a few drops into the burrito's interior, then passed the bottle to Katy. She waited until he was chewing to say, "So, about Thursday... I owe you an apology."

"For what?" said Travis. A chunk of rice fell from his mouth.

Well, she'd walked into that one.

"Quitting the band? Picking a fight in front of a coffeehouse full of our friends and a cute girl who wanted to get with you?"

"Well, the whole band thing was kind of a weird detour for me anyway."

"Yeah, me too. Have you talked to Megan or Keith? Are you going to keep playing with them?"

Travis shook his head. He tore a sheet of paper towel off a roll under his bed and wiped his mouth. "Nah. If you're out, I'm out. We're not going to practice without a guitar player. And I pulled a

3.8 in one of my classes. Not cool."

Katy waited for Travis to offer her a napkin. When he didn't, she glared at him while reaching around to grab her own square. "Speaking of classes, what do you know about Computer Science?"

"Now that is within my purview," said Travis. "God, I've always wanted to say 'purview.' Major life goal accomplished."

●

For two weeks, Katy poured all of the energy she'd dedicated to the Laundry Room into learning the fundamentals of computer science. She showed up at Travis's door with questions like "Can you explain the relationship between Turing machines and regular expressions?" Travis never seemed happier than when he was explaining something arcane.

Her CS professor's lectures always sounded something like, "The carburetor is kind of like a camshaft with extra distributor caps." But Travis was an excellent teacher. He explained concepts in a way that actually made sense.

"You have mismatched braces on that function," said Travis. He pointed at the screen.

"I see it," said Katy. She added a brace, and her program ran successfully, analyzing a string of text and counting the number of times the letter *A* appeared. She was too embarrassed to say it, but writing code gave her a hint of the same thrill as writing songs.

Travis showed her how to work through the program line by line to understand the logic and to spot bugs, but she already understood this one. And, to her surprise, the next assignment sounded easy. "I don't think I need you anymore," said Katy.

"Yeah, that's what all the girls say."

Without the daily study sessions, however, Katy started to lose touch with Travis again. It was weird how you could drift apart from someone who lived just around the corner.

Now that Keith was relieved of his Laundry Room duties, she and Alicia started to get along better. "It's your fault my boyfriend's not in a band," said Alicia, "but he's still hot, so I forgive you."

Katy was still worried Alicia might slip up and tell Keith about the crush, which, Katy had to admit, still flared up from time to time. She started sitting with Alicia and Keith at dinner, and they talked about class, and who was dating whom, and plans for spring break. Never the band. Why reminisce about something that had never really existed?

Megan she didn't see much at all. The collapse of the band and the gulf between North and South Campus had swallowed their friendship. They'd wave at each other sometimes on the way to class. Megan was right, as usual: If forming a band was like dating, breaking one up was just as awkward as any other breakup.

•

Katy had gotten used to finding Alicia chatting with a handsome musician in their room, but she was surprised one afternoon when the musician in question was Nick Dimmett.

He nodded at Katy. "Just who I was looking for." He was wearing a wool cap and sunglasses, and gave no indication that he was thinking about taking them off. "I caught your set at the Java Cave." Katy was pretty sure Nick was staring at her breasts while speaking, but the sunglasses made it hard to be sure, which was probably the point of wearing sunglasses indoors.

"Oh, you mean the worst night of my life?" said Katy. "Let's also reminisce about the time Kyle Cahill puked on me at the senior prom. And he wasn't even my date."

Nick smiled. "An audience will forgive more than you think," he said. "Listen, we're recording that single next weekend. I'd like you to come into the studio and lay down some vocals."

"I'm not really..." Katy began. Nick took off his sunglasses and ran a finger over the whiskers on his chin before folding the sunglasses and hanging them on the neck of his flannel shirt. "I'll think about it."

"Then I'll see you soon, hopefully." said Nick. He nodded and walked away.

"Oh my god, you know that guy?" said Alicia, who'd been pretending to study.

"Don't you already have a musician boyfriend?" said Katy.

"Can't hurt to have a backup, right?"

Nick Dimmett's car was the purest automotive extension of a human being's personality Katy could possibly imagine: A Volkswagen magic bus of 1970s vintage, paisley-painted, with the Nabisco Session logo in a circle on each side. Nick smiled when he noticed her sizing up the van. "You're going to love this part," he said. "Come here."

He hoisted her in his arms so she could see the top of the van, which boasted another instance of the logo. "In case they're watching, you know?"

Katy did not. "Totally," she said.

Nick put on a tape on the stereo and talked about Nabisco Session while they drove into the San Fernando Valley. "This studio is the real thing," he said. "Twenty-four track analog."

"Is that good?" said Katy.

"It's honest," said Nick. "I want people to hear our pure sound. Not some computer simulation."

They pulled up at the studio. Katy had imagined an imposing edifice like the Capitol Records building, but this was just the back alley of a row of warehouses. She spotted a fading sign for GLENDALE SOUND. "Can I help load in?" said Katy.

"Sure thing," said Nick. He handed her a black canvas duffel bag which seemed to contain a stiff piece of lumber.

"What's this?" Katy asked.

"The Interplanetary Transmitter. My effects rig. Come on in, I'll show you how it works."

Someone buzzed them into the studio. It was dim inside, and every surface was covered with thin maroon carpet. It looked like the music building, if it had been taken over by mad upholsterers.

Katy recognized Nabisco Session's guitarist. "Hi, Steve," she said.

He nodded at her and turned to Nick. "Thanks for showing up, dude," he said. "You warmed up? We need you in the vocal booth, like, an hour ago."

"Sorry, man." They followed Steve into a small recording studio. Cables ran everywhere. Nick stepped toward what looked like a closet on one side. "It's my time," he said. "Why don't you sit with Ryan in the control room?"

Katy looked in the direction he had indicated, and saw a harried-looking man behind a wide pane of glass. She let herself in and introduced herself. "This your first time in a studio?" asked Ryan, handing her a pair of headphones. Somehow Katy knew that if she said yes, she'd be treated to a "let me tell you all about it, little girl" lecture, so she shook her head. "Good," said Ryan. "Then you're probably more prepared than these fuckheads. But I'm just the engineer, so what do I know?"

He turned a knob on the mixing console and said into a small microphone, "Okay, this is 'Everlasting,' lead vocal, take one." He engaged the record button on a large reel-to-reel tape deck, and the intro to the song began playing in Katy's headphones. She could see Nick's face, framed in the small window of the closet door, with a large microphone hanging down in front of him. He closed his eyes when he sang.

"Not bad," said Ryan. "Give me another one." They ran through the song two more times. Nick grumbled before each take, but each time he sang, his voice was as warm and reassuring as a wool coat. Ryan turned to Katy. "All right, you're up."

Nick placed his hand against the small of Katy's back and whispered, "Good luck."

She closed herself inside. The place was literally a closet, lined with foam soundproofing material, and it reminded her of hiding among the coats during childhood games of hide and seek. She put on the headphones, the bulkiest pair she'd ever worn, and heard Ryan's voice again. "I'll give you four bars before the first chorus, okay?"

"Sure," said Katy. Her own voice echoed in her ears. Nick stood outside the booth, smiling. Katy was starting to get the idea that Nick's personal style was based on dressing for nonexistent indoor weather patterns, because today he was wearing a plaid scarf. Which looked fantastic.

The music started playing, just as Katy remembered it from practice. She sang the harmony, and it sounded pretty sweet. As she was preparing herself for the next chorus, the track cut off and Ryan's disembodied voice came back. "You're holding back. Really belt it." It was like being personally bawled out by God.

"Fine," said Katy. The song came back on, and this time she stood up straighter and took a deep yoga breath. "Wooo-oooh, our love is everlasting," she sang.

"Better," said Ryan. "Again. Feel it, okay? You love this guy. Think about who you're singing it to."

Katy rifled through her mental catalog of past boyfriends. None of them made the cut. She looked through the soundproof glass at Nick. Not quite. She closed her eyes and thought of Eddie Vedder in the "Jeremy" video. The track played. She sang—one chorus, then the second, then the third and fadeout.

"Nailed it," said Ryan. Katy was reaching for the door handle when he added, "Can you try a second harmony for me?"

"Huh?"

"One girl backing singer is fine, but two is better."

She let go of the handle and said, "Can you do two things for me?"

"Depends," said the voice.

"Can you get rid of Nick's vocal during the take?"

"Easy. What's the other thing?"

"Get rid of the actual Nick. He won't quit staring at me."

●

After Nick came back from his beer run, the whole band, plus Ryan and Katy, crammed into the control room to listen to a rough mix of the track. As the chorus approached, Katy realized she'd been holding her breath since the opening guitar riff. And then there she was—two of her, actually. Ryan had added reverb to her vocals ("so you'll sit down in the mix a little more," he explained), and even Katy had to agree that she was the perfect addition to Nabisco Session's romantic stoner jam.

Then came the three-minute guitar solo Ryan had been fast-forwarding over while she laid down her vocal tracks.

"Gentlemen?" said Ryan. "Lady?"

"Fuckin' brilliant," said Nick. It seemed like he might be experimenting with a British accent.

"No complaints," said Steve. "Can we bang out another track today?"

"I should get Katy home," said Nick. "You guys want to get started on the rhythm tracks for 'Green Revolution'?"

Katy thanked Ryan and climbed back into Nick's van. "That song was really nothing special until you came along," he said.

She smiled and rubbed the back of his fingers where they gripped the gear shift. "You never told me about the Interplanetary Transmitter."

"Why don't we stop back at my place and I'll show you."

Atwood required students to live on campus for their first two years. According to the brochure, dorm life contributed *to a tight-knit community* and *the wide-ranging academic intercourse that formed the foundation of the liberal arts.* "Yeah, right," Megan once said. "They mean you can get into a lot more trouble off-campus. If there's one thing the administration hates, it's bad publicity."

Most juniors and seniors continued to live in the dorms. The room draw process was stressful, sure, but it was a lot easier than shopping around for an apartment. Off-campus housing consisted largely of unsavory apartments passed down by graduating seniors, and this was exactly the kind of place Nick Dimmett shared with two other members of Nabisco Session.

"Nice place," said Katy. And it was, actually. Maybe Nick had cleaned it up, or maybe he and his roommates accumulated less dude detritus than she would have expected. The place was dim and smelled faintly like pot smoke. It was like Nick's corduroys in the form of an apartment. The shag carpeting looked clean enough, and everything strewn around seemed to be music-related: tapes, CDs, guitars and basses on stands, and dozens of cables. A beautiful blue amplifier leaned against one wall.

"Good eye," said Nick, noticing her interest. "That's a '68 Portaflex. It's a bass amp, but guitar sounds deadly through it. Want to plug in?"

"Can I?"

Nick flipped the amp on. "Let the tubes warm up a little." He picked up an electric guitar with a honey-colored finish that faded to black around the edges, and looked at the ceiling contemplatively while tuning it. He plugged the guitar in, played a couple of riffs, and handed it to Katy.

She threw the guitar strap over her shoulder and found a pick secreted in the usual spot under the edge of the pick guard. What to play? She tried out the riff from "Summer On," and the sound filled the entire apartment and probably beyond. Unlike Megan's small amp, this one had *bass*. Gobs of it. She strummed a chord and heard every string clearly. She walked up and down the low E string, feeling her entire body vibrate. Now Katy had two true loves: 1992-era Eddie Vedder and a 1968 Ampeg Portaflex.

"Not bad, eh?" said Nick. "That's the tone a guitar dreams of."

Katy smirked. "I think my guitar has nightmares about being back in high school without its case on."

Nick looked confused. Katy took the guitar off, set it on its stand, and stared Nick down. *There are so many reasons not to like this guy,* she thought, but her body was unconvinced, and the adrenaline from the recording session was still singing in her veins. Plus, it had been a long time since she'd kissed anyone, and she'd never kissed someone who looked like a *man*, not a high school boy. So when Nick leaned in, she kissed him back with an eagerness that surprised both of them. His beard tickled her chin. A low buzz came from the amplifier. Nick reached up the back of Katy's shirt and unhooked her bra with one hand, and they stumbled into the bedroom. When Nick climbed on top of her, she thought about the sound of that chord, playing over and over.

Nick pulled the Nabiscomobile up in front of Mitchell, and they both got out. It was sunset, and the sky was richly painted in red. Katy leaned against the van and let the last sliver of sun warm her face.

"This is going to sound weird, but the sky here is so different from back home," said Katy. "I mean, not just the weather. The sunlight is a different color, and the clouds are funny shapes. When you get any clouds, that is."

"Where's home?" said Nick. He sidled up next to her, and together they obscured the Nabisco Session logo.

"Oregon. You?"

"Marin County."

Katy knew this was in the Bay Area. "Is that where Green Day and Rancid are from?"

"No, that's the East Bay," said Nick. "Marin is up north. Mostly rich folks and hippies and rich hippies."

"So you come by it naturally?"

"Yeah. Hey, I've got to get back to the studio," he said. "I promised the guys."

"Of course," said Katy. "Well, thanks for everything today."

"Lot of fun," he said, getting into the van. He kissed her through the open window. "Lot of fun."

Katy found Alicia sitting at the desk, typing on her laptop to the strains of Tori Amos. "Hey, roomie," said Katy. She tried an impromptu dance move to the music and ended up slapping Alicia on the shoulder.

"Uh, hello to you too," said Alicia. "I'm going to meet Keith over at the party in Weller, so I'll be out of your hair in a minute."

"Can I come along?"

Alicia looked at Katy like she was trying to figure out whether this was a trap. "Of course," she said. "Mind if I ask why?"

"Are you saying I don't know how to party?"

"You want to borrow some clothes?"

Katy's eyes darted to the closet, where Alicia's two dozen dresses were lined up like P.E. students waiting to be picked by the team captains. "Yeah, that would probably be smart."

●

The DJ was wearing a black-and-white checkerboard shirt and spinning electronica. Otherwise, the scene was oddly similar to a middle school dance. A wildly dancing mass congregated near the DJ, but everyone else was standing around with beers, trying to talk over the music. The room was dark, but every time the DJ illuminated the strobe light, it was a ten frame-per-second reminder that they were just standing around in the Weller lounge.

Katy and Alicia found Keith, who was glowing in a lavender

shirt and white pants. He looked so great, Katy only thought about *Miami Vice* for a moment. "Hey, it's Katy!" he said, putting his arm around her shoulder. "So, who's dancing?"

"We'll be along in a minute," said Alicia. "Girl talk."

A siren tore through the room, and it took Katy a minute to realize it was part of the song. She wished she'd brought earplugs. She leaned in toward Alicia. It was weird to be smiling and yelling at the same time. "I can't believe you're going out with the only guy on campus who dresses better than you."

Alicia looked over at the mob of dancers. Keith was moving confidently. He looked back at Alicia and grinned. "Yeah, he's pretty amazing," she said. "At first I thought maybe he was gay, but it turns out he's just a straight guy with style. Endangered species."

"Do you love him?" said Katy. "Oh, god, that was kind of forward, huh?"

Even in the dark, it was obvious Alicia was blushing. "Yeah, I think so. I haven't told him yet, though. What's going on with you?"

Katy took a sip of water. "You know that guy Nick?"

"You mean Nick Dimmett, lead singer of Nabisco Session? That guy Nick? Yeah, I've heard of him. Spill."

Katy told Alicia everything, except for the part about the amplifier.

"That's amazing," said Alicia. "So we're both dating hot guys in bands? And you thought we had nothing in common."

•

Rhombus Records had a small section of local music, and Katy flipped through the rack until she found Nabisco Session's self-titled debut EP. Before bringing the CD up to the counter, she looked around to make sure no former members of the Laundry Room were there. Was this what buying porn felt like? On the way out, she picked up a copy of *Beat Street,* the free local music magazine.

She stopped into the bagel shop on the next block and took the CD out of its cellophane wrapper while eating a toasted sesame bagel with cream cheese. The cover featured a black-and-white close-up of Nick's face in profile. His beard at the time was a stubbly prototype of its scruffy realization, and Katy blushed, remembering how it had felt against her face... and other places. She laid the CD into her Discman and listened to the first track while finishing her bagel and completing a worksheet for meteorology class.

Despite Travis's objections, Nabisco Session wasn't so bad. Sure, the songs went on for ages, but Megan was right: The musicianship was hard to deny, and Nick's voice was soothing. There was a sort of gravelly homespun frankness to it. Not that his observations ("every day is every day") made a whole lot of sense, but couldn't you say the same for most of the bands Katy listened to? Not to mention her own lyrics.

The song devolved into alternating solos between the guitarist and drummer. Katy hadn't picked up her guitar—either of her guitars—in a couple of weeks. One of the fingertip calluses on her left hand was starting to peel around the edge, and the fingernails, which she'd kept scrupulously trimmed, were growing long. She pulled her binder out of her bag and looked over her assignments. CS: Even without studying with Travis in the last couple of days, she was keeping up. Meteorology: Worksheet done. Survey of European Literature: All caught up on the reading. History of North America to 1492 (which she'd signed up for as a sort of antidote to European literature): She probably needed to study up a little more on Aztec and Mayan political structure, but the exam was still a week off.

Sure, maybe she'd done it petulantly, but breaking away from the Laundry Room was clearly the right call. She inserted the meteorology worksheet into her binder and closed the rings with a satisfying *snap* that sounded a little like Megan's snare drum. She opened her notebook and started jotting down song ideas for a mixtape for Nick. What did he listen to when he wasn't jamming with the rest of the Nabiscos? They'd never talked about it. In fact, Katy couldn't swear that she and Nick had ever had an actual *conversation*, per se, although their time not conversing at Nick's apartment had certainly been well spent.

She ordered an everything bagel to go and walked across the quad toward Mitchell with Nabisco Session in her ears. It was a legitimately beautiful day, with none of her usual qualifiers. The sun was hanging out halfway behind a cloud in a way that reminded Katy of how she liked to sleep with one leg under the blanket on hot days. She took the path around the dining hall, through Fitz Field. The long way. Nick's music was the right soundtrack for an aimless walk.

"Best roommate ever," said Alicia, accepting the bagel. "So how are things with Beard Boy?"

"Good," said Katy. "I'm going to visit him at practice tonight. Dinner?"

•

Katy swiped her card at the music building and went inside. She recognized the song seeping under the door of the practice room, something from the EP she was carrying in her bag.

She let herself into the practice room and nodded at guitarist Steve. Nick was too absorbed in the song to notice her, so she leaned against the wall in what she hoped was a casual way and watched him sing. When the song was over, Katy said, "Hey there."

"Oh, hey," said Nick. "What's happening?"

"Nothing," said Katy. "Got some harmonies for sale. You buying?"

"Gentlemen, take five." Nick clearly relished the expression. He walked Katy out to the hall. "Listen, we're kind of busy. Maybe we'll catch up later?"

"Oh, sorry, I thought—"

Nick ran his fingertip over his beard. "Saturday... that was a lot of fun, right? Why ruin a good thing?"

"Meaning?"

"You really did a great job on that song. But it's good to let one perfect day be one perfect day, you know?" He looked at the door. "I need to get back in there. The guys think I'm a flake sometimes, but it's hard to imagine that band without me, isn't it?"

"It sure is," said Katy. On the way out of the music building, she pitched the Nabisco Session CD into the bushes.

# 32

By the time Katy got back to Mitchell, she'd already begun fitting Nick Dimmett into the "valuable experience" category. She'd never had a one-night stand or anything resembling an adversarial breakup before. She wasn't sure whether her weekend with Nick counted as either, but she was prepared to check off both boxes on the Purity Test—which would still leave her with an embarrassingly high score.

Still, the situation called for the drowning of sorrows. She would have accepted a beer if anyone had been offering, but it was Monday night, so she couldn't just wander into a party, and she and Alicia didn't keep their fridge stocked with anything stronger than Diet Pepsi. What sounded good? A deluxe quesadilla at the Stoop, the extra-greasy version with cheddar and ground beef, maybe. Travis wouldn't turn one down, and he could bring the hot sauce.

So she said hi to Alicia and continued down the hall until she was stopped by a familiar song coming from Bianca and Quan's room.

What was that tune? It was like running into a high school teacher at the supermarket: *I know you from somewhere, but... wait, Ms. Ellis, why are you here?* It didn't make any sense, but there it was: "Summer On," coming out of the boom box on Bianca and Quan's desk.

Quan was on her bed, studying, when Katy knocked on the open door. "Hey, where'd you get that?" Katy asked.

"This?" said Quan, tugging on the shoulder of her blouse. "Mariposa. You should check it out, it's—"

"No, I mean the tape."

"Oh! Alicia made a copy for me. It's her boyfriend's band, and her roommate's also—wait a second. This is your band, isn't it?"

Katy nodded. She listened to the tape. The reverb coming off her guitar had the familiar texture of the music building. Keith must have taped it sometime before the Java Cave show. And not long before, because they sounded pretty good. No, better than that. She stopped listening critically and allowed herself to get lost in the song. She was back on stage at the Java Cave, singing the chorus to "Summer On," finding Alicia's blurry face in the audience, screwing up the chords, noticing the hiss of the espresso machine, clawing desperately for the riff. But this version of "Summer On" wasn't just a pretty good first try. If she got hit on the head and the last six months vanished from memory, this would be one of her favorite songs.

"That guy has an amazing voice," said Quan. "Is he single? You playing any shows soon?"

"Nope. I mean, I don't think he's single, and we're definitely not playing any shows, sorry. I gotta go." Katy ran the rest of the way to Travis's room, threw the door open, and said, "You need to come with me, right now."

Travis was lying face-down on his bed with one arm dangling off the side. He raised his head. "Huh?"

"Were you asleep?"

"If I say yes, are you still going to kidnap me?" Katy grabbed him by the arm and pulled him into the hall. They made it back just as "Summer On" was ending. "Is that us? I gotta say, I approve."

"We need to talk to Alicia. Hey, Quan, could I borrow that tape?"

"Whatever we're doing," said Travis, "I hope it ends with frozen yogurt."

They found Alicia studying. "Hey, is your boyfriend around?"

"You think I have him stashed under the desk or something? What do you want him for, anyway?"

"Wicked, wicked things. You mind if I call him?"

"Let's see, it's ten forty-five at night, you're obviously disturbed, and you probably hate all men. How about if I call him?" She dialed the phone and, after a moment, spoke into it: "First off, this is not a booty call."

Keith arrived ten minutes later carrying a small vinyl case labeled TASCAM. He gave Alicia a kiss so involved that Katy had to look away. Alicia laughed. "Did I not make myself clear?"

"Sorry," said Keith. "You're hot. So what's up?"

"Hey," said Katy. "Is there a way to hook that thing up to the boom box?"

"Sure." He unzipped the case and found the proper cable. Katy handed him the tape, and he rewound it and pressed play. The speakers spat forth an earsplitting howl.

"Turn it down!" yelled Alicia. She and Katy reached for the

volume knob simultaneously and wrestled for it, but Keith had already paused the recording. Alicia glared at Katy. "Now you two are going to go explain to everyone in the hall that it wasn't the black chick who woke them up by blasting the stereo late at night."

"Sorry," said Katy. "Is that even a real stereotype?"

"Salem, Oregon," said Alicia, shaking her head. "But it's okay, everyone knows you're the weird loud one."

"Shall we give this another try?" said Keith. Katy turned the volume down to 1, and they listened to "Summer On" straight through.

It wasn't perfect, after all. There, in the riff before the first verse, she'd brushed her finger against the guitar string and muted a note. The harmony during the chorus wasn't quite as tight as it should have been. By the second verse, though, she could almost see the band members paying closer attention to each other. At first, each person was focused on playing their own part, but now the bits of the song fit together more closely. The unintentional whisper of feedback at the end made it sound like the song had been tucked in for bed. She'd have to figure out how to do that on purpose. Not that she was going to play that song again.

"So?" said Katy. "What do you guys think?"

"About what?" said Keith. "Are you asking me if I like the song, or...?"

"You've been in a bunch of bands, right? Is this band good or bad or what?"

"Oh, that is a dangerous question to ask a philosophy major," said Alicia. She leaned against Keith's arm. "Maybe I'll give her my answer while you're prepping your lecture on whether 'good' and 'bad' have any meaning." She turned to Katy. "This song sounds like all the alternative stuff you listen to."

The judgment fell on Katy like a pile of books. "Thanks a lot."

"I didn't mean it as a criticism," said Alicia. "I mean, you could put this song on that one radio station and it would fit right in. And I'm still not over the fact that this quiet dude from down the hall can sing like that."

"Me neither," said Katy.

"Same here," said Travis.

Alicia turned to Travis. "Imagine what you could do if you weren't singing mopey guy music."

"I recognize that as an insult," said Travis, "but I'm so invested in the mopey guy genre at this point that I have no right to complain."

Katy rifled mentally through her music collection and realized that this was her preferred genre as well. "Keith, you said this wasn't really your kind of music. Why'd you want to play with us?"

"Honestly? I feel weird whenever I'm not in a band, and I've been playing with Megan for a long time."

Alicia frowned. "Did you and her ever...?"

"Do you really want to know?" said Keith.

"Probably not. You tape any other songs?"

"Yeah, I've got 'Takedown' on here."

"Takedown" wasn't as pretty as "Summer On," but the band was warmed up and a little loose, and thanks mostly to Megan's drumming, the energy was insane, like they'd all made a pact to stick their fingers into outlets before playing the song, and fall over dead at the end.

"What is your kind of music, anyway?" said Katy.

"I love Metallica," said Keith. "The old stuff. Back in high school all my friends were other Latino kids who loved thrash metal."

Katy smiled at the thought of Keith headbanging. "Here, barely anyone listens to metal, let alone wants to play it. It's all alternative now. Including the latest Metallica."

Katy laughed. "You mean my music is the popular stuff that makes other kids feel left out now?"

"Pretty much," said Keith. "Anyway, I get the sense that you and Travis are all about songwriting, and you'll develop the technical chops as you go, right?"

"I hadn't really thought about it that way," said Katy, "but I guess so."

"Well, then," said Keith. He gestured at the speakers. "This is an early demo from some band that got really good after they played a hundred more shows. And yeah, I know it sucks when someone says you've got potential."

"We should keep going, huh?"

"As usual, that's up to Megan. If you want me to play, I'm in. Just don't expect me to run out and buy a Bush CD or something."

"Agreed," said Katy. "Alicia, I'm still mad at you for leaking this tape without asking me, but would you mind running me off a copy?"

Katy paused outside Broad Hall and turned the tape over in her hand. *TLR, practice, Jan 1995.* She buzzed Megan. "Yeah?"

"It's Katy." During the pause before Megan buzzed her in, Katy counted off thirteen quarter-notes. She held up the tape in Megan's doorway. "I brought you a copy of our song."

"Doesn't everyone have one of those by now?"

"Yeah, but this one's signed by this stupid girl who quit the band." Katy had prepared that line on the way over, but Megan didn't laugh.

"What do you want, Katy? If you think you can bring me a mix-tape and we'll have make-up sex, forget it. Too soon."

"I was heading to Rhombus and thought maybe you'd like to join me."

Megan threw her leather jacket over her shoulders. She paused to slip something in her pocket and said, "All right, let's go."

•

"Of course I listened to it," said Megan. "It was infuriating."

"Why?" said Katy. "Because of the parts where I screwed up?"

"No." They stopped at a convenience store for pineapple soda, and Megan bought a pack of tamarind candy. She offered Katy a piece, and it tasted like a Sour Patch Kid, only salty. Pretty good, actually. "Because it was like seeing my favorite character on a show get killed off."

Katy held the candy against the roof of her mouth until it hurt. "And I killed us." She looked at Megan for any sign of disagreement, but Megan just shrugged. "Well, I want to give it another try."

"Yeah, that's not going to be so simple."

"Why not?"

Megan pulled a fat envelope out of her pocket and handed it to Katy. *We are pleased to extend to you this offer of admission to the Stanford University School of Medicine.*

"Oh my god, congratulations," said Katy. "We should call you M.D. Can I hug you?" She pulled Megan in, and wondered if all drummers hugged so forcefully.

"Thanks. But do you know any rock star cardiologists? I mean *literal* rock stars?" said Megan. "Me neither. So this is probably my last chance to be in a band. And I'm not commuting from Palo Alto for practice."

"We've got a few months left before you graduate."

"Yeah, we do." They walked past Top Thai and into Rhombus Records, and automatically started flipping through the new releases while talking. The Beautiful South. Radiohead. Built to Spill. "And I have a thesis to finish, and classes."

"What are you taking?" Katy asked.

"Actually, not much," Megan admitted. "I only need three more credits to graduate, and my thesis takes up two blocks, so for my third class, I signed up for the most ridiculous thing I could find in the catalog."

"Which is?" said Katy.

"Tattoos in American Popular Culture. It's good, actually. You should take it. If you're going to be a rock star, you need to learn more about tattoos."

Katy laughed. "Does that mean we're giving the band another try?"

"Slow down." Megan scrutinized the Built to Spill CD, *There's Nothing Wrong with Love.* "I'm still really pissed at you. Not for fucking up. Everybody fucks up. For walking out. If we're going to get back together, you have to do four things for me."

"Why four?"

"Because I just pulled a number out of my ass. Number one, you have to promise me, no matter what happens, you don't quit. I fucking hate quitters. I don't care if the ghost of Cobain comes to you in the night and asks you to tour with him, you tell him to wait until June."

"Done," said Katy. "What's number two? And before you say it, I've been practicing, and I can change a string in under three minutes. Breaking strings on purpose is fun, by the way."

"It's disturbing how easy it is to imagine you trashing a hotel room." Megan handed the CD to Katy. "You know these guys? The singer looks like your friend's dad."

"What friend?"

"He looks like every white suburban dad in America. I love it when people subvert your expectations. Speaking of which, you talk to Travis?"

"Yeah, the boys are in."

"Good. So, number two, get us a gig. Like, at a real club, not some campus bullshit."

"How do I do that?"

"I don't know," said Megan. She handed Katy the latest issue of *Beat Street.* "But I bet this will help."

"Okay, what's number three?"

"Tell me what happened with you and Nick Dimmett."

"Oh, shit," said Katy. "Let's talk about that outside. This place is probably crawling with his fans."

They sat with iced coffees on the terrace outside Top Thai and Katy said, "Keith told you?"

"Of course," said Megan. "Let me tell you a story about Mr. Dimmett," she said. "A couple years ago, Nabisco Session put up a flyer looking for a drummer. Nobody had really heard of them back then, and I got in touch. I went to the audition—in our usual spot in the music room—and it seemed like it went really well. Their songs were better then, too, by the way. More focused."

"Could they be any less focused?"

"I know. So after the audition, Nick comes over, and he smiles at me, and does that thing with his eyes where he looks like he's a hundred years old but still hot." Katy laughed. "And he told me they'd be in touch, but he thought I probably had the job."

"Let me guess," said Katy. "Then you went back to his room to see his vintage poster collection or something?"

"Worse," said Megan. "They asked me to join the band. They had a show in two weeks. I worked my ass off learning their set. And Nick would always smile at me and tell me I was doing an amazing job, and I don't even think he was lying, exactly. So we play the show at this place in Pomona, and it's great. I killed it. And afterwards I went back to Nick's room."

"That sounds like a pretty good day."

"It was. And then I don't hear from Nick for a couple days. And then he leaves me a message—not even 'call me back.' A message on my fucking machine. He says they all really liked me but our musical styles didn't really mesh, and he wished me luck."

"Fuck that guy."

"Yeah. They had a new drummer and he had a new disposable woman within two weeks."

"Why didn't you mention this before?" said Katy.

"Because it's fucking humiliating. The thing that really pisses me off is, that guy could just say to women, 'Hey, I like your face. Wanna fuck?' and get away with it. But it's like he's out to prove that everyone wants to be his girlfriend."

"There's something I didn't tell you," said Katy. She told Megan about her day in the studio.

"Wow, he really pulled the full extraction on you," said Megan. "Well, you've had your learning experience. You probably didn't get any weird diseases. And you probably made that track almost worth listening to. Move on. There, that's my style of therapy. 'Get over it and move on, we've got shit to do.'"

"Makes sense to me," said Katy. "The thing is, I feel like I kind of used him, too. It's not like the guy seemed like boyfriend material."

"Do I need to repeat my motto? Get. Over. It. Write a song about it if you have to." Megan finished her coffee with a loud slurp of the straw. "I can't believe what you've done."

"What now?"

"I'm looking forward to hearing a Nabisco Session song."

"Trust me, it's terrible. Now, what's number four?"

"Shit, I forgot we were in the middle of an ultimatum. Let me think," said Megan. A smile lit up the corners of her mouth. "Okay, number four. You have to get my name tattooed on your ass. Put the G in the middle, really make them dig for it."

•

After dinner, Katy went to the computer lab. She sat at the multimedia station and poked at the mess of cables connecting the various components.

If there was one thing Katy had experience with by now, it was cables. She found a thin, beige cable, a miniature twin of the one that plugged into her guitar. It was a perfect fit for the headphone jack on her Walkman. She scanned the desktop and found an application called SoundSampler.

An hour later, she'd converted "Summer On" to a compressed audio file and uploaded it to the Laundry Room website. *Katy Blundell, queen of multimedia.* She wasn't sure which computers could *play* the songs, if any, but she had the disk space; why not use it?

Then Katy put her headphones on and wondered if she was the only person at that moment listening to the Laundry Room while walking across the campus.

She passed the Wall of Free Expression and checked it for anything new and inflammatory. At first she saw only a disappointing pastiche of perfunctory spray paint. Perhaps, Katy thought, the Wall went through an annual cycle: The boundless optimism of fall gave rise to Fuck Tornados of creativity, which dissipated under the pressure of homework and Dead Week and interpersonal jousting.

Then she saw it. At first, she dismissed it as a hallucination brought on by sleep deprivation and too much caffeine. She took off her headphones and blinked her eyes. It was still there: An anonymous artist had painted a six-foot segment of the wall in gray before adding a lively rendition of the Laundry Room logo.

Katy stepped up to the mic. "Who did it?" Cables stretched across the floor of the practice room. As much as the people in the band, it was the assemblage of equipment that gave Katy the sense that the band had never been on hiatus. "Rails, you're the one with unexpected skills. You painted the wall, right?"

"Nope," said Travis. "No visual art skills whatsoever."

"M.D.? It's your logo."

"Who's M.D.?" said Keith.

"Megan got into med school," said Katy. "Sorry, was I supposed to share?"

"Awesome," said Keith.

"That's great," said Travis. "Can you look at this rash for me? I spilled hot sauce on my arm and it's getting weird."

Katy and Keith edged toward the drum kit. "Whoa, whoa, we are NOT going to have a group hug," said Megan. "Thanks, everyone. First of all, Travis, I would gleefully violate the Hippocratic oath to avoid looking at your rash. Second, I didn't paint anything.

Do I seem like a humble person? I would have signed that shit."

"You seem like a person who desperately needs a group hug," said Katy, "but you're off the hook, because I have a new song." She set her notebook on a music stand. "This one's called 'I'm a Good Guy.' "

*Climb into my van and we'll go for a ride*
*'Cause I'm a good guy*
*Yeah, I'm a good guy*
*I'll tell you you're the only one on my mind*
*'Cause I'm a good guy*
*Yeah, I'm a good guy*
*I believe in what I say, no I wouldn't lie*
*'Cause I'm a good guy*
*Yeah, I'm a good guy*
*You and me in harmony*
*Trust me, it's all right*
*All the girls agree*
*That I'm a good guy*

By the time Katy finished demoing the song, Megan was lost in a paroxysm of giggles like Katy had never seen. "I'm sorry," said Megan. "It's a catchy song. Do you think he'll know it's about him because it's so obvious, or will he not know because he's so dumb?"

"I don't care," said Katy. "Easiest song I ever wrote. Should we give it a try?"

"Wait a minute," said Travis. "If I'm going to sing this, it means I have to put on a bad-boy persona for three minutes, right?"

"Is that a problem?"

"Look at me." Travis was wearing his usual gray sweatshirt,

slacks, and sneakers. It wasn't quite the least threatening outfit Katy could imagine, but it was in the top ten. "Hide your daughters, Rails is in town."

"Fuck yeah," said Megan. "Katy, you got lead sheets?"

"Right here." Katy passed out the photocopied lyrics and chords and watched Megan clip hers to a piece of drum hardware. "Travis, you cool on the vocal melody?"

"We're about to find out. Does anybody have a pair of sunglasses I could borrow? Shades? Isn't it weird how some words stay cool and some don't? Like, nobody ever says 'shades' anymore unless they're singing that Timbuk 3—"

"Here," said Katy. She handed Travis her sunglasses. "But they're prescription."

"Also pink," said Travis. "No problem. Part of being cool is pretending not to care what people think. I learned this from my friend and style consultant Megan, who couldn't be here tonight because she died of boredom."

"Travis, you look disturbingly like my Mexican grandmother," said Keith. "And, I mean, I love my *abuela*, so I say stick with it."

"Okay, grandma, quit making me regret allowing you back in the band," said Megan. "Let's play this shit. Two-three-four!"

The crazy thing was, even wearing Katy's pink sunglasses, even at a fighting weight of a hundred and ten, once Travis found the right degree of sneer for the song, he did seem a little menacing. The crazier thing was, even while she was playing guitar, another subroutine in Katy's brain was analyzing the song. She adjusted the riff before the final chorus on the fly, and when the song was over, she said, "Keith, I love the bassline. Megan, can you lead the song off with that fill you were doing before the chorus?"

"Like this?" Megan did the sixteenth-note crescendo thing,

and Katy came in with the opening chord progression, and it sounded just like she'd imagined it. Megan nodded. "Good call."

They played the song again, and Katy nodded at Keith and Travis when she heard them honing their parts, and sometime around the third chorus, she started to get the idea that the Laundry Room could be the biggest band in the world. After practice, before the feeling wore off, she stuffed a couple of cassettes into padded envelopes and dropped them into the outgoing mail slot.

•

Katy first saw the "Everlasting" single on the Local Interest rack at Rhombus Records. The cover was a deadly serious sepia-toned photo of Nabisco Session taken at a coastal viewpoint, with Nick Dimmett leaning against the railing, his back to the camera and head turned to the side, looking out to sea. Katy laughed, imagining the exchange between Nick and the photographer: *Can you get more of my ass in the shot?* The title stretched across the sky: "Everlasting." She flipped the CD over and read SPECIAL APPEARANCE BY KATY. No last name—definitely a dick move, but Katy decided that if no one knew that this single constituted a musical remnant of her fling with Nick, that was just as well, and at least he hadn't called her Kaylee or something. She left the single on the rack.

While she was shelving at the library, someone tapped her on the shoulder. She removed her headphones and looked up at the guy, dirty blond hair matted under a rasta cap. Maybe he was in her European Lit class? "Hey," he said, "my friend says you're the girl who sings on the Nabisco Sesh song. Are you?" Katy nodded. "Cool. You want to hang out sometime, smoke some weed?"

"Thanks, but I've got a lot of studying to do."

Everywhere she went on campus, she heard it coming out of dorm rooms and in heavy rotation on the campus radio station, which meant it played at least once an hour over the PA at the Stoop. "Whoo-oo, our love is everlasting," Katy heard herself sing, and every time it made her shake her head and laugh at how false the sentiment was. It felt as if she and Nick had once danced together at a party, and now everyone wanted to put a photo of the happy couple up on their wall.

The overnight popularity of "Everlasting" was maddening, sure, but it was predictable. Within days, though, shit got really weird.

It was easy to wave away the fact that Quan was playing "Summer On," or that the Laundry Room logo was on the Wall. Quan was Alicia's friend, and anyone could paint on the Wall—that was the whole point of the thing. Travis had probably done it while sleepwalking. Not that she had any evidence that Travis sleepwalked, but it wasn't hard to imagine him in an old-fashioned stocking cap, hands outstretched like a mummy, gripping a can of spray paint in each. She drew this image on Travis's whiteboard the next time she walked by.

A couple of days after "Everlasting" came out, Katy and Alicia were sitting at the Stoop eating quesadillas, speculating about why there was only one female Smurf, and trying to ignore the college radio station, which was playing too loud. Because of KHSK-FM's uncompromising policy of never playing any song associated with a major label, almost nobody on campus listened to the station intentionally. Katy supported this stick-it-to-the-man idea in principle, but in practice it meant they played a mix of noise music, lo-fi, imports, electronica, and hip-hop that made the fans of those genres miserable—if you liked the current song, you were almost guaranteed to hate the next one. When they did play a good tune, the DJ often forgot to announce the artist, anyway.

As clear as a smogless day, though, the DJ said, "This is Atwood's own the Laundry Room, with 'Summer On.'"

Katy pointed her finger at Alicia. "You did this somehow."

Alicia shook her head. "I can't take credit. But it sounds good, doesn't it?"

Thanks to Keith's stealthy recording skills and the fact that the practice room was designed by acoustic engineers, "Summer On" sounded as good or better than a lot of stuff they played on KHSK, which was admittedly not saying much.

After that, "Summer On" was everywhere. No one could say for sure which was the most popular song on campus that February, but it was a tight race between "Everlasting," "Summer On," and Radiohead's "High and Dry." Katy started to notice people looking at her with the same expression as that guy in the library: *Are you...?* And she wanted to tell them, "Sure, that's me, but it's not *really* me."

So who was the real Katy? She wasn't sure anymore.

•

It was impossible to overstate the importance of frozen yogurt.

In one corner of the dining hall, just past the salad bar, stood a frozen yogurt machine. It dispensed chocolate, vanilla, or swirl. Katy had seen people use this type of machine hundreds of times at Dairy Queen and Cool Temptations, but had never gotten her hands on the controls before arriving at Atwood.

To her surprise, she found that dispensing sweetened fermented milk wasn't as easy as the aproned DQ employees made it look. Once you pulled the lever past a certain point, the machine shuddered to life, quaking and groaning, and the yogurt came out *fast*. You had to guide the cup or cone with surgical precision if you wanted to realize an attractive spiral of yogurt.

Keith was known for his yogurt atrocities. He was capable of piling a haystack of yogurt onto a cone that listed perilously like the final moments of a Jenga game. "I'm not doing it on purpose!" he would protest. No one had ever witnessed the collapse of a Keith-cone, but everyone was hoping.

The yogurt machine was the most universally beloved institution on campus and widely blamed for the Freshman Fifteen, but it had certain shortcomings. It was only available when the dining hall was open, and the topping selection was meager: multicolored sprinkles, chocolate sprinkles, coconut flakes, and hijacked cereal. Katy had signed petitions calling for better toppings and 24-hour yogurt availability during Dead Week. No one knew whether their opposition was financial, nutritional, or just general dickishness, but so far the administration hadn't budged.

The cure for late-night yogurt cravings was 21 Choices, a brightly lit shop just west of campus. The S in "Choices" was, inevitably, stylized as a swirl of yogurt.

"It's weird how Butterfinger isn't a very good candy bar, but it's the best yogurt topping," said Travis. He ordered a cup of chocolate-vanilla swirl with Butterfinger, Cap'n Crunch, and hot fudge. Katy stared at him. "What? They have twenty-one choices and I took three. That's called restraint."

"What would generic Cap'n Crunch be called?" said Megan.

"It would be called a crime against humanity," said Travis.

"Cereal Captain," said Keith.

"Crunch Barrels," said Megan. "Mother Crunchfucker."

"Megan," said Travis, "you have my word that if they make a cereal called Mother Crunchfucker, I will eat it without complaining."

Katy managed a smile. Her mind had been racing all day over the news she was about to share with the band, and it was exhausting. While she made her way along the counter, she tapped her fingers against the Formica at some outrageous hardcore punk tempo.

"You know," Travis went on, "the whole reason this place exists is to sell us ten cents worth of pulverized Heath Bars for a dollar. We could get some Ziplocs and do the same thing on campus...."

"Candy bar dime bags?" said Keith. "That's actually not a terrible idea."

They paid for their yogurt and jammed themselves around a tiny red table. Katy spooned up her Oreo-topped vanilla. "Keith, is it weird for you, eating yogurt that doesn't look like it was dropped on the floor?"

"A little bit," said Keith. His strawberry-vanilla swirl was hidden under a mound of assorted chocolate shrapnel. "So, Katy, wasn't there something...?"

"Yeah, I've got some news."

"Me too," said Travis. "My rash is all better, thanks to that ointment Megan has been rubbing on it."

"You know that story about the doctor who saves lives by day and murders annoying people at night?" said Megan.

"We have a date," said Katy. "The Corona Crescent. March thirtieth. It's a Thursday."

"Nice," said Megan. "That's a serious venue. Travis, does your mom let you stay out late on school nights?"

"Your mom lets me do whatever I want," said Travis.

"Rails, you are exactly like the little brother I never had or wanted."

"You've been there?" said Katy. She unfolded an issue of Beat Street with a photo of Korn on the cover. "I just sent our demo out to places that are all-ages and book bands I've never heard of, like, let's see... Meat Circus, Jeff the Explosion, and Almighty Turd. What's the place like?"

"It's no frills," said Megan. "Big room, lots of kids."

"Bigger than Jabberjaw?"

"I think so."

"Corona?" said Keith. "That's practically Riverside."

"Yeah, it's way the fuck out in the valley," said Megan. "Are you scared of Mexicans, Lopez?"

"Terrified. No, I'm scared of road trips," said Keith. "Bad childhood memories of my brothers beating up on me in the back seat."

"You can ride with Travis," said Megan. "Travis, promise not to steal Keith's juice box?"

"Right-o," said Travis. "I'm more of a Capri Sun person anyway. Boxes are so confining."

"So it's going to be a bunch of punk kids happy to mosh to whatever's available?" said Katy. "That sounds ideal. So, we have a twenty minute spot. Maybe five songs?"

"Do we have that many?" said Keith. He pulled out a Sharpie and wrote in neat capital letters on the back of his receipt:

TAKEDOWN

SUMMER ON

I'M A GOOD GUY

## THERE IS NO HOME
## WHERE IS MY MIND?

"Hey, look at that," said Megan. "Five songs. And a month to get ready.... This could work. Not to jinx it, but we've been playing like fucking champions lately."

Even Katy had to agree. Some nights she still got the impression that Megan was patting her on the head and saying, "Not bad for a beginner," and that Keith was stoically putting in time with the only band nearby while scanning the bulletin board, looking for a flyer reading BASSIST WANTED (NO FLAKES) FOR KILLER METAL BAND. But most nights she felt like she could almost keep up.

"Are we getting paid?" asked Travis. "You guys know me. Music's okay, but I love me some dead presidents."

"Uh, I didn't—" Katy began.

"Oh, you poor naïve children," said Megan. "We're lucky they're not making us pay. A lot of places, you want to play, you put up a hundred bucks and pray to Satan you make it back out of door."

Katy decided she must look as puzzled as she felt. "What does 'out of door' mean?"

"When people pay at the door, the club takes a cut and then splits the rest among the bands. So if you bring in a bunch of people, you might make a few dead presidents, as Travis used to say on the mean streets of Mercer Island."

"Paid in full," said Travis.

"I always assumed that when I went to see a band, they were getting, like, I don't know. Five hundred bucks?" said Katy.

Megan laughed. "I don't think you-know-who even gets that much to headline Spring Fest. I made fifty bucks for a show once in high school, playing a school dance. I mean, my band did. My cut was ten. Frozen yogurt money, basically."

"So do you think we're going to be any good in Corona?" said Katy. "Unlike last time?" Megan glared at her. "Sorry. But you and Keith have played real shows before. What do we need to know?"

"Like I said, we've been sounding really tight. We should probably talk about stage patter, though."

"What do you mean?" said Katy.

"Well, think about a really good show you've been to."

"You mean James Taylor good?" said Travis.

"Exactly," said Megan. "You go to a J.T. concert, he doesn't just play songs. He tells stories, talks about why Seattle is his favorite city. And the next day he'll play Vancouver and maybe tell the same stories or different ones, but everyone in both places will feel like they were sitting on his lap for two hours."

"Ew," said Katy. "You're saying I should tell stories?"

"I'm saying you and Travis are out front, and if we leave the talking to Travis we'll get a dissertation on yogurt combinatorics. You're the glue between us and the audience." Megan lifted a spoonful of chocolate with crushed peanut butter cups. "Travis is the toppings. You're the yogurt."

Katy laughed. "That's probably the worst thing you've ever said, and you've said some *shit*."

"My point is, Travis's singing is awesome, but you're the one who can make the audience feel like we're their cool friends. Don't tell a story about how your dog ran away or anything, just talk to them like you're having a conversation."

"Is this when I'm supposed to say something modest?" said Travis. "Well, shucks, Megan, I ain't nothing special."

"Okay," said Katy, "I'll be everyone's cool friend." The idea of adding this responsibility to guitar playing and singing felt like adding an extra ounce of yogurt to a Keith-cone. But she reassured herself with the one indisputable fact about the Laundry Room: As long as Travis was singing, it was hard to pay attention to anything else. She just hoped a bunch of kids in Corona would feel the same way.

# 35

Katy carried her acoustic guitar with her to Travis's. It hadn't seen much action recently, and she felt like she was neglecting it. He was in his room, of course, wearing a Mercer Island High School Chess Club t-shirt and writing in a black-and-white composition notebook.

"Hey," said Katy. "You want to write a song? It'd be cool to have five originals for Corona."

"You want to help me memorize the structure of twenty amino acids?"

"Not really."

"Fair enough. Let's do this."

Katy strummed a couple of chords, but from the time she left her room, her mind had been in a philosophical groove. "Travis, do you believe in God?" she asked.

Travis laughed. "Those are some pretty heavy song lyrics, but sure, let's go there."

"I'm serious," said Katy.

"Why do you want to know?" said Travis. "I don't think Campus Crusade is giving out free pizza this time of year."

"Because I don't," said Katy. She poked at a pile of books with the toe of her sock. "But I know that if we sit around for an hour, we'll probably end up with something that sounds like a song, and I don't know where it comes from, and that bugs me."

Travis rearranged himself on the rug and lay on his stomach with his chin resting on his palms. "Yeah, I believe in God," he said. "But I doubt he spends his time doling out pop hooks to songwriters. I mean, a lot of amazing songs were written by real dicks."

"Sure," said Katy. She lay on her back on Travis's floor without even checking for Crunch Berry crumbs. "So you think it's all neurons getting weird with other neurons?"

"I guess so. Speaking of which, can I tell you about the crazy dream I had last night?"

"Only if nobody was naked in it."

"Nah. I was riding a giraffe through campus and people were firing paintball guns at me."

"I dare you to turn that into a song lyric," said Katy. She sat up, grabbed her guitar, and came up with a chord progression. Travis jotted in his composition book for a minute and sang:

*He stalks the hallowed grounds at a quarter past the half*
*A hot sauce splattered hero on the back of a giraffe*

"It's like one of those *Lord of the Rings* Zeppelin songs, but ten times stupider," said Katy. "More, please."

Travis grinned. "I'll have you know, you've got me writing song lyrics in my biochem notebook."

"Damn, you really are a bad boy."

*With his golden-toasted saber and his frozen aqua shield*
*Hoofbeats on the pavement, in the village and the fields*

Katy was laughing so hard her fingers wouldn't hold the chords. "Megan is going to hate this song more than she's ever hated anything."

"It's catchy, though," said Travis. "Can we give it a six-minute guitar solo?"

"If I knew how to play one, I would totally do that," said Katy. "Can we spring this on her tonight?"

"Only if we figure out a chorus." He raised his eyebrows. Katy did her thing.

•

"Remember when I told you to write a new song?" said Megan. She stood up from behind the drum kit, walked over to Travis, and put her face inches from his. "I retract that. Never write anything ever again."

Travis grinned and said, "Mission accomplished. Katy wrote the music."

"I liked it," said Keith. "Was there a part about fighting a koala?"

"Absolutely," said Katy.

Megan stood with her hands on her hips. "All right, let's play it. But you're all children."

•

The following afternoon, Katy slung her bag over her shoulder and headed to Travis's to discuss whether to rewrite the lyrics of "Giraffe." When she got to his room, he was on the phone. The rapid-fire syllables of whoever he was speaking to were audible across the room, and he occasionally responded with a word or two in Korean. She couldn't decide whether he was having an argument or whether she was unfairly interpreting the phonology of the Korean language. When he hung up the phone, however, he slumped over in his chair and groaned.

"Everything okay?" said Katy.

"Why did you do it?" said Travis. "If you'd asked me, I would have told you not to. Now I am totally fucked."

"Trav, what are you talking about?"

He did a three-sixty in the chair. "That was my mom. I thought she was calling because I got a 3.8 in O-chem, and she was, but then she started freaking out because her friend told her my name and face were on the internet, and was I in a band?"

"Oh, god. The website?" said Katy. She set her bag down and sat on the floor. "I thought only people at colleges could even see that. Is she really pissed?"

"Is she pissed that her only son is playing music with girls instead of studying? You could say that."

"Well, screw her, right?"

"No, not right!" said Travis. His cheeks were red, and he was breathing so hard that he wheezed a little. He swept his hand around in front of him. "My mom could make all of this disappear."

"Trav, you're being melodramatic," said Katy. "Do you need food? It's only a couple of hours until the Midnight Special."

"Look, I hate to admit it, but my mom is right. Being in this band, it's like trying to take a fifth class. I got a 3.8. You're on *academic probation*." He practically spat the words out.

Katy realized her foot had fallen asleep, and she shifted clumsily. She rubbed her foot, glad for the pins-and-needles sensation that was distracting enough to prevent her from crying. "I thought this was important to you."

"It doesn't matter. If my parents get another transcript like the last one, they'll force me to transfer to UW and live at home where they can keep an eye on me. I'd rather be here."

"Band or no band?"

"I guess so," said Travis. "I have to be realistic. Engineering is a real career. It's not like singing or selling hot sauce."

"Now you're just repeating crap your mom said." Katy, who couldn't recall ever wanting to punch anyone other than her sister, suddenly, desperately, wanted to punch Travis in the face. "I did this for you," she said. "Remember? You were wasting your time on music before you even met me, sitting on your butt, working on your impossible computer music project."

Travis shrugged. "I didn't say it was your fault."

"Yeah, you did," said Katy. "I'm sorry I made the website without telling you. But I'm not sorry for anything else. Do you have any idea how hard this has been for me?"

"What are you talking about?" said Travis.

"All of it. I don't know how to do *any* of this. Writing songs is so hard. I can't really play guitar. I don't know how to dress. And, news flash, I'm not even half as smart as you but I'd prefer to pass my classes, too. The only reason I wanted any of this is because..." She hugged her knees to her chest. "Forget it."

"What? What were you going to say?"

"Because I thought things might be a little nicer around here if people could hear you sing."

"Oh." Travis leaned back until his chair made an ominous creak. "Well, thanks."

"Will you at least play the Corona show with us? All you have to do is show up and sing."

He shook his head. "No, I'd have to stay up till two-thirty again tomorrow, and a bunch of other nights between now and the show, and I'd have to lie to my mom over and over, which I've never done successfully even once. You don't understand what this is like."

"You're right," said Katy. "I don't."

# 36

Katy made it halfway back to her room before she started crying. She tried to hide it, but Alicia had an overdeveloped sense of empathy. She could probably sense Katy's mood from several buildings away. As soon as Katy walked in, Alicia turned off Ace of Base and said, "What's wrong?"

"You can have Keith back," said Katy. "I think it's all over."

Alicia's shirt collar pressed uncomfortably against Katy's neck when they hugged, and she smelled like expensive perfume, but Katy stopped crying long enough to tell Alicia about Travis's desertion.

"I don't want Keith back," said Alicia. Katy looked at her quizzically. "I mean, I like that he's in a band. Your band." This started Katy crying all over again. "Okay, that came out wrong. Maybe this would be a good time to ask," Alicia continued. "Keith and Bianca and Quan and I are heading to San Diego for spring break. You want to come along?"

Without thinking about it, Katy wiped her nose on Alicia's

shoulder, just like she used to do to her mom. "Thanks, but I'll just hang around here."

"Katy, that's crazy. Nobody will be here. The dining hall's only open for one meal a day."

"I'll go to the taco place."

Alicia laughed. "I'm not letting you eat tacos by yourself for a week. What's your other friend doing? The drummer?"

"Going home to Spokane," said Katy.

"Then you're coming with us. Period."

Katy's mind immediately called up a list of objections. She'd be an awkward accessory. People would compare her to a bathing-suited Bianca, a contest no one could win. "What would we do there?"

"In San Diego? Lie around in bikinis. Get a tan for once. You may be white, but you don't have to be *that* white. Bianca's house is two blocks from the beach. You can even bring your guitar if you want."

"Okay."

"Really?" said Alicia. "You're in?"

"You don't have to sound so surprised," said Katy. "How does Keith feel about being the only boy in San Diego?"

"How does he feel about spending a week on the beach with four lovely ladies? I think he'll get over it. Now, let's choose music for the road."

•

When she called Megan after dinner to cancel practice, Katy was reminded of her first job. It was in high school, at the office of a lawyer friend of her mom's. In retrospect, it was kind of the perfect after school job: mindless filing and envelope-stuffing and occasional runs to the bank or post office, all for $7.50 an hour, which had seemed like a mind-blowing salary at the time.

One day, she had a paper due for history and tried to call in sick. "I don't think so," her boss had said. "I have court tomorrow and I need you here to get the Stoller deposition in order." Katy had never had an attempt to play hooky rebuffed in this way. She showed up to work.

"You're sick?" said Megan. "You don't sound sick. What's your bullshit?"

"Is that an expression I'm not cool enough to know, or something you just made up?"

"Come on, my thesis is driving me crazy and this tattoo class is harder than I expected. I want to hit things with sticks."

"Travis quit," said Katy. The sadness welled up again behind her eyes while she told Megan about the website and the phone call. "I didn't want to talk about it yet, but there it is."

"I think you're right to feel like he's being a dipshit," said Megan, "but he does sort of have a point."

"Can you talk to him?" said Katy. "I'm not very persuasive."

"Dude, you talked him into this in the first place. Besides, in a battle between us and Travis's mom, we're roadkill."

"So we should just let him quit?"

"Rails is a big boy," said Megan. Katy heard the sound of her fiddling with her snare drum, engaging and disengaging the metal springs. "He can make his own decisions."

"You don't seem very upset about this," said Katy.

"I just found out about it six seconds ago. I'm in denial. Did you talk to Keith?"

"No, but Alicia probably already told him."

Megan let out an exasperated groan. "Okay, let's all meet up at the Stoop at ten."

The path to North Campus was full of people heading to and from trysts and study sessions. Katy tucked her hands into the pockets of her coat and put her head down, hoping she wouldn't be pulled into an awkward conversation with someone she knew on the way to the student union. She hated pretending everything was fine. Someone flicked her on the arm with a finger. "Hey," said Megan. They walked the rest of the way in silence.

Keith was waiting for them, looking as unruffled as ever. Katy said hi and went to the counter to order a milkshake. While she waited for them to blend it up, she watched Megan and Keith talk from across the room. She couldn't really say this to them, but the way Keith and Megan were so comfortable with each other reminded Katy of her parents. They understood each other's bullshit and they were okay with it. Katy felt that way with Travis, sometimes, and she also never wanted to talk to Travis again, and she was about to burst into tears when she heard, "Large chocolate for Katy." She grabbed the overfilled styrofoam cup, leveled off the top with her spoon, and sat down.

"So what do we do?" said Keith, eyeing Katy's milkshake.

She reached into her pocket and produced two extra spoons. "I'll tell the Corona people we can't make it." said Katy. "Are we going to be in trouble?"

Megan laughed. "Yeah, it's going on our transcripts." She stole a healthy dollop of milkshake and rolled it around on her tongue in a way that was so perfectly balanced between sexy and disgusting that Katy laughed, and was then angry with herself for laughing when she was supposed to be upset.

"Hang on," said Keith. "Why do we have to cancel the show? It's not like you don't know all the vocals."

"We've had this conversation before," said Katy. "It's not complicated. Travis, singer. Me, not singer. Playing without Travis would be like, I don't know, like entering a car race without a car and just trying to run really fast."

"Well, fuck you very much," said Megan. "Let's take inventory. We've got a pretty sweet rhythm section. Our setlist is kicking ass. We've got a singer-guitarist whose voice I'm hearing all over campus on that motherfucking Nabisco Session single."

"Singing *backup*," said Katy. "Which took me about a hundred takes. Remind me how many takes we get in Corona?"

"Well, I think canceling the gig would be stupid," said Megan. "So either we convince Rails to get back in the band, or we do it as a power trio." She looked at Katy. "You promised."

"Promised what?" said Keith.

"Katy knows what I'm talking about."

She did: *No matter what happens, you don't quit.* Well, fuck. Katy thought about Travis's face while he was on the phone with his mother. He'd looked like he was in agony. "Well, I don't think we're getting him back," said Katy. "Why don't you sing?"

"Because I'm a lousy singer and I hate Phil Collins." She shoveled up the last of Katy's milkshake. "I'll sing backup. If we suck, nobody will know but a few Inland Empire kids with nose rings."

Katy gave the inside of the styrofoam cup a futile scrape. "If *we* suck? You guys never suck. You're asking for a rerun of our last show, in front of an actual crowd, without Travis to distract them from my ten thousand mistakes." She looked to Keith for support, and saw that Megan had turned toward him, too.

Keith laced his fingers and ran them over his blond hair. He looked up at the menu board for a moment like he was considering what to order. "Here's what I think. Megan, you're being unreasonable. I don't know what kind of deal you and Katy made, but forcing her to stick to it under these circumstances isn't fair."

"See?" said Katy. "I told you—"

"*However*," Keith went on. "Katy, you're just not the same guitar player you were at the Java Cave."

"That was barely a month ago!"

"Yeah, I know. But I watch you play. I have to, it's part of playing bass. You don't have to look at what you're doing or think about every chord change any more, and your riffs are getting fluid. That's a big deal."

Katy had to force the corners of her mouth down. "I don't even know if I can sing all the songs and play them at the same time. I certainly couldn't do *that* without thinking."

Megan took the opening. "Then how about this. You pick me up in the Pussywagon tomorrow, usual time. We run the set as a trio. If you want to call it off after that, I promise not to be pissy about it. Right now, we need another milkshake."

It was like Katy had developed a special bile gland with Travis's name on it. She'd think, "Hey, Travis would be interested..." and then remember the phone call, and the conversation, and then she'd be grinding her teeth and wanting to kick him in the nuts.

The fact that it was her few lines of HTML that set off the whole disaster made her feel even worse. How could someone's mom hear about a website, anyway? That would be like Katy's grandmother announcing that she was really into hip-hop.

She'd learned to keep an ear open for a question lobbed her way in CS class while working on something else, and the next day she tried to jot down as many Laundry Room lyrics as she could. She knew all the words to "Summer On" and "There Is No Home" and "I'm a Good Guy," of course, but "Giraffe" was fairly new, and Travis had improvised most of "Takedown" on the spot. She didn't sing backup on those, so she only knew the lyrics the way a fan would: a snippet extracted here and there from a lot of melodic mumbling.

She thought about asking Travis for the lyrics. He had them neatly organized in text files on his PC; Katy had seen it. But that would mean *speaking* to Travis. She'd sooner walk through the quad naked or brave steak night without hot sauce.

So Katy decided to approach the songs the way she'd always done singing along to the radio and *Friday Night Videos* and *120 Minutes:* Sing the words you know and make up the rest.

That would be good enough. She'd agreed to Megan's ultimatum: Run through the set list and see how it goes. But she was pretty sure that it wouldn't take more than one song for Megan and Keith to realize that their idea was crazy, that going on without Travis was like going on without electricity.

●

"When I said I was looking for a little backseat action, this isn't what I had in mind," said Megan. She watched Keith and Katy lug the row of seats from Alicia's van up the stairs.

"Careful of those boxes, there are shoes in there!" said Alicia. "Oh, god, stop making me yell, my throat feels like I've been singing along to Katy's music collection."

A late-season flu had barreled through campus, leaving students feverish, coughing, and almost too weak to complain. Those who hadn't succumbed yet were trading disease prevention techniques. Katy asked Megan for her recommendations. "Wash your hands and don't stick your tongue in anybody's mouth," said Megan. This advice was both effective and depressingly easy to follow.

"How come you didn't get it?" Megan asked Keith. "Are you two doing it wrong or something?"

"I had it last week," said Keith. "Remember when I couldn't stop sneezing at practice?"

"Dude," said Katy, "you sneezed like two times."

"Mmm, I promise I'll be there next time, Keithy," said Alicia. She kissed his neck. "I mean, you too, Katy."

"When you guys get to the venue," said Megan, "tell them I got grossed-out to death." They set the car seat down in the middle of the room, wedged between the bunk bed and the desk.

"All right, let's GO," said Katy. "Laundry Room world tour 1995 kicks off right now."

"Is Travis coming?" said Keith.

Katy frowned. "Not that I know of." In fact, she hadn't confirmed that anyone else from campus was making the drive.

Katy still hadn't gotten used to the idea that you could drive for hours without leaving the L.A. metropolitan area. The city was infinite, and somehow still fit in the Thomas Guide on her lap. You could probably drive off the eastern edge of the map and wrap back around to Santa Monica.

They drove through Glendora, San Dimas, Pomona, the cities clicking by like plastic digits on an old-fashioned alarm clock. "We need grease," said Megan. "Watch for an In-n-Out sign." Katy finally spotted one in Chino, and they pulled off the freeway and up to the drive-thru. When the cardboard box arrived, however, she couldn't eat. It felt like someone was sitting on her stomach.

"Try and eat a little," said Megan. She shook a French fry at Katy, who forced it down while Megan wiped her finger on the corner of map 462.

"We're not ready for this, are we?" said Katy. Even though Megan had unrolled blankets between some of the delicate metallic bits, the equipment in the back of the van rattled constantly. The kick drum heaved under its blanket like a light sleeper, revealing a corner of the Laundry Room logo Megan had painted on the Mylar drum head.

"My band teacher in high school used to say something about that," said Keith. "Every time we had a recital, someone would say, 'We're not ready.' Sometimes it was me." He fiddled with his scarf. "And he would always say the same thing: 'The best performances you've ever seen? Those people were almost ready.'"

"I don't get it," said Megan.

"I do," said Katy. "He meant even professionals get stage fright. So what?"

"No, I don't think that was it," said Keith. "I think he meant that if you feel totally ready, like you've practiced the piece to death, you're going to get lazy. Maybe you'll play sloppy. Maybe you'll just sound... robotic, I guess. You play at your best when you have to push it a little bit."

"Take this as a warning," said Megan. "Don't major in philosophy or you'll end up like Keithy here."

"I get what you're saying," said Katy. "But you know what? The worst performances you've ever seen, those people were probably also almost ready."

•

At that first practice without Travis, Katy had gone in ready to throw the game. She could see in her head how it was all going to play out. She'd stumble through a half-assed rendition of the songs that Travis's vocals brought to life. Megan would shake her head in disappointment. Even Keith would frown, shuffle his feet, wonder how much longer this awful noise would have to go on before they all accepted the truth, dissolved the band, painted over the Wall, and went back to whatever they had been doing before the Laundry Room had become this thing that bound them into a unit.

When the three-piece band assembled, however, Megan said, "Let's start with 'Summer On.'" She'd moved a boom stand next to her drum kit to give herself a vocal mic. "You sing Travis's part, I'll take yours."

"Fine," Katy muttered. Megan counted off, and Katy played the opening riff.

Once the song was underway and Katy was inside it, however, she found it impossible not to sing. Of course she knew Travis's part. She sang it the way he would have, and listened for Megan's harmony to lock in on the chorus. It wasn't like riding a bicycle; it was like discovering that her bicycle had an autopilot switch.

Afterwards, Katy was breathless and almost crying. Megan laughed. "God, I love saying 'I told you so.'"

"You don't even sound that different from him," said Keith. "Not your voice, exactly. The way you emphasize the words."

"I really hate that he's not here," said Katy.

"Hey, let's stop talking about Rails like he's dead," said Megan. "Motherfucker's two blocks away studying linear algebra. How about 'There Is No Home'?"

Keith smiled. Katy noticed—it was impossible not to notice—that he'd been honing his look. He'd always been a snappy dresser, but he was wearing a new pair of tight jeans, and tonight he'd added blue highlights to his hair. "You look radioactive," Katy had said, and the name stuck.

•

"Oh my god, what is that smell?" said Megan. "Keith, was that you?"

"Stockyards," said Katy. "Cows. Pigs. My family used to go to southern Oregon on vacation, and we drove past a lot of them."

"I can't decide if it's worse with the window up or down," said Megan. "How much farther is this place?"

"You've got the map."

"Oh. That's our exit."

Katy pulled the van into the strip mall parking lot. A small marquee with movable plastic letters read:

**CORONA CRESCENT**

MAR 29

DISASSEMBLE NO 5

CHERRY PIT

THE LAUNDRY ROOM

"Did anyone bring a camera?" said Keith.

Nobody had. It was still early, and a few kids in flannels and wool hats were milling around outside. Katy saw a skinny guy in a hooded jacket and sneakers and thought it might be Travis, until she saw his face. "C.G., Radioactive, why don't you guys go in and see what's up?" said Megan. "I'll stay and guard the shit."

Keith lived up to his moniker. He was wearing those new jeans, a pink t-shirt, and a white scarf, and he'd reapplied the blue hair dye. Katy was wearing a blue dress and boots, and she felt ridiculous walking across the suburban parking lot.

They pressed their faces to the front door and knocked, but no one answered, so they walked around the back, which also looked abandoned. A few concrete parking islands dotted the back lot, their curbs crumbling, blue paint faded, saggy palm trees dropping leaves onto old cars. Katy tried to remind herself of what Keith had said: *We're the scary ones.*

She found a door ajar and peered inside. It opened into a hallway a lot like the one at the studio where she'd recorded with Nabisco Session. A burly, balding guy with wiry black hair and a too-small Metallica shirt was carrying two massive coils of cable toward them. "Can I help you?" he said.

"We're the Laundry Room," said Katy.

"Cool," said the guy. "Ed." He sized up Keith. "You the guy?"

"I'm sorry?" said Keith.

"I heard your tape," said Ed. "We were all curious whether the guy who sings like Cobain was going look like him, too."

Katy felt her stomach turn over. Even though it made no sense, the thought rattling in her head was: *They're onto us.*

"Nah, I'm not him," Keith said. "Hey, I have the same *Kill 'Em All* shirt."

Ed smiled. "Well, you can load in through here. Your sound check's in forty-five. Good luck tonight." He lumbered off, presumably to hook up cables.

Katy and Keith knocked on the window of the van and made Megan jump.

"I think we met your future husband," said Katy. She climbed into the driver's seat.

Megan smirked. "It'd better be James Taylor."

They pulled the van around to the back and carried their gear down the hall and into the backstage area. A thick black curtain separated them from the performance space, and Katy peeked out through the break.

The room was huge and painted entirely in black. The stage was five or six feet off the ground, and a low wall had been erected between the stage and the audience. Katy recognized the setup from shows she'd been to in Portland: Security guys would stand behind the wall, ready to snatch eager crowd-surfers and herd them back into the crowd before they could reach the stage.

The walls were plastered with flyers for previous shows—at least a thousand band names. Katy wondered how many of those bands still existed, whether one of them might have become her favorite band, if she'd been here on the right night. Ed was standing in back, fiddling with the mixing board, and a couple of other guys wearing black t-shirts with STAFF printed on the back were milling around looking busy.

"You guys playing tonight?" said a voice. Katy turned around and found she was standing next to the most beautiful woman she'd ever seen, and possibly the tallest, a statuesque presence with fiery red hair. Katy nodded. "Awesome. I'm Cherry." She held out her hand, and Katy shook it. She looked around for Megan, who might have some idea what to say to this super-evolved futuristic being.

"Have you played here before?" Cherry asked.

"Uh, nope," said Katy. "What's your band?"

"Cherry Pit." Of course. "What's your instrument?"

"Guitar," said Katy. She nodded in the direction of her guitar case, then felt like an idiot for doing so. "And vocals. You?"

"Same here," said Cherry. "Well, it's time for our check. See you."

When Megan reappeared, Katy grabbed her and said, "Where were you?"

"Taking a shit," said Megan. "Thanks for asking."

"Sorry. Do you know a band called Cherry Pit?"

"Should I?"

In answer, a drumbeat filled the room. "Give me the snare," she heard Ed say.

"Megan, this is probably my stupidest question ever," said Katy, "but how do you do a sound check?"

Megan smiled. "You just do what the sound guy says. If he asks for guitar, play whatever. It's not an exam, he's just trying to make sure people can hear all the instruments. Then he'll probably ask for a song."

"What should we play?"

"'Summer On,' for sure," said Keith.

"Why?" Katy asked. "Is it especially hard to mix or something?"

"No," he said. "I just like playing it."

Katy's laugh was drowned out by Cherry saying, "Check one-two." Then the band played a song, and Cherry's voice was exactly as Katy would have predicted: a confident, sexy wail. Cherry Pit was a real band. They were older, more experienced, better-looking, and Katy would have bet a year's tuition that Cherry wasn't a recently promoted backup singer.

Megan nodded in time to the song. When it was over, she said, "Wow, not bad."

Cherry and the three predictably adorable guys who constituted the remainder of the Pit filed through the curtain. "All yours," she said.

Katy nodded. She brought her guitar and amp out onto the stage. Ed was a barely illuminated mass, miles away in the back of the room. Katy took her place at stage left and hooked up her pedals. One of the STAFF guys came over and pointed a microphone at her amp. He glanced at her and lowered her vocal mic slightly.

Katy realized, happily, that she was too busy setting up to freak out. Besides, playing for an empty room and a shaggy sound guy was no big deal. She tuned her guitar and adjusted the tone dial on her amp. Across the stage, Keith was doing the same, and he smiled at her. "M.D., you need any help?" said Katy.

"Just stay awesome," said Megan.

Ed ran them through the sound check. When he called for Katy's vocals, she said, "Check one-two," over and over until he seemed satisfied. She wondered whether everyone felt ridiculous saying that, or whether you got used to it, or developed your own intriguing sound-check mantra. Did Kim Deal say "check one-two," or did she have an understudy to do it for her?

"Okay, give me a song," said Ed. If he was still looking for Travis, he didn't mention it.

They played "Summer On," and it echoed against the walls, like they were too small to fill the large room. Plus, she couldn't hear Keith's bass, which made it hard to know if she was playing in time. "Can I get more guitar in the monitor?" said Megan.

Oh! So that's what that meant. Katy looked down at the wedge-shaped speaker next to her. "And can I get more bass, please?" They ran the song again, and Katy found it a lot easier to relax and let the song play itself. "Does it sound echoey to you guys?" she asked.

Megan laughed. "It won't when this place is full of bodies."

•

The hour between the end of sound check and the beginning of the show seemed like an interval custom-tuned to drive a nervous musician over the edge.

The club didn't have a green room, just a couch in one corner of the backstage area, and Katy leaned against one ragged arm. She distributed set lists to Megan and Keith and then busied herself twisting her finger in the loop of her boot lace. Cherry wandered through and produced a blister pack of pills. "You guys want a Xanax?"

Katy declined. She wasn't sure how she felt about drugs, exactly. Her parents never made a secret of the fact that they'd indulged in the sixties, which took away some of the illicit allure. She'd gotten drunk in high school and hated how sick she'd felt both during and after. Maybe, she concluded, drugs were like sex: She wasn't going to take a random pill from a passing stranger, even if she was the world's coolest passing stranger, but in the right context, with the right group of people? Might be nice.

Forty minutes later, however, Katy would have killed for something to calm her nerves. The worries piled up like a stack of textbooks during Dead Week. She was betraying Travis. They were going to fuck up to such a legendary degree that people would talk about it for decades. The place would be packed. The place would be empty. She double-checked the package of guitar strings stuffed into the back of her amp.

Megan put her hand on Katy's arm. "Hey," she said. "We're just going to play some songs, okay?"

The big school clock on the wall said 9:45. "Do you guys know about magic time?" said Keith.

"That's one of your worst pickup lines yet," said Megan.

"I know it," said Katy. "Drama class, right? Before you go on, you all hold hands and pray, or think good thoughts, or whatever."

Megan looked skeptical. Finally, she shrugged and said, "Oh, fine." They formed a triangle and clasped hands. Katy closed her eyes and thought about going sledding with her dad. It started as just a comforting memory, but she also realized that sledding had a lot in common with playing a show. As she remembered it, walking up the hill with her inner tube took three days, waiting in line at the top took three hours, and sliding back down took three nanoseconds. So it was with playing songs: You rehearse for weeks, drive fifty miles to the venue, spend hours sound-checking and plugging and unplugging and just sitting around, and then with any luck you make it through the set with no musical disasters.

Keith tilted his head toward the curtain. "Is anyone even out there?"

Megan peeked. "Yeah, one or two people. Shall we?"

•

The Crescent was a sea of flannels and ripped jeans, girls with big earrings and tight sweaters and Doc Martens and army jackets borrowed from nearby boys. It's not that Katy was expecting a round of applause when she followed Keith and Megan onto the stage, but she was greeted with the characteristic pre-show sound of kids talking about whatever they damn well pleased, shouting over the club's mix CD. It didn't sound any different from the stage than it did in the audience. She scanned the crowd in vain for anyone she knew until her eyes finally alighted on Cherry, standing far off to stage left.

Katy placed the set list on the floor next to the mic stand, threw the guitar strap over her shoulder, and turned the volume knob up to ten. She double-checked the elastic band holding her glasses against her face. Ed nodded at them from the soundboard. The song playing over the PA stopped abruptly.

Years later, Katy could remember not only which song was playing—Screaming Trees, "Bed of Roses"—but the exact moment in the song where the needle came off the record. The house lights clicked off, and a row of stage lights came on, blinding like L.A. daylight. Katy waited a moment, thinking Ed must have hit the INCINERATE button by mistake, but Megan was hissing at her, "Now!" No wonder so many people wore sunglasses on stage.

Katy's lips brushed against the head of the mic. "We're the Laundry Room, from Los Angeles, California." She heard her own voice talking back at her from the monitor, and it sounded a lot more brash and confident than she felt. Megan was already on the third beat of the count-off. Katy raised her pick and dug into the opening riff of "Summer On." Note-for-note, perfect. She sang the first verse through a half-smile, then stepped on the distortion pedal and Megan joined in for the chorus.

*Summer on, summer on*
*We will all summer on*

The crowd was pulsing, bodies smashing together with live-for-ever recklessness, and Katy caught a glimpse of the red spray of Cherry's hair fanning out in the strobe light as she danced.

They finished the song and Katy mumbled, "Thank you." Her stomach roiled. Maybe she should have eaten more. But she remembered what Megan had said: This was a conversation. "Everybody having a good night?" she asked, and the answer was two hundred layers of that high whistle that sounds ridiculous if you make it by yourself but delicious with enough sweaty compatriots. She caught the eye of a boy in the front row who couldn't have been more than fifteen. "You mind if we play something loud?" The boy roared in approval.

The Laundry Room pummeled its way through "Takedown." Katy tried to wipe the sweat off her face, but it just kept rolling down. She really felt Travis's absence on this one, the meaty growl he brought to the vocals, and she tried to imagine him standing in her place, both hands on the microphone, face half-hidden by his gray fleece hood.

They segued into "There Is No Home" and "Giraffe," and then she looked at the set list and, somehow, amazingly, there was only one song left. "Thanks so much for coming out tonight," said Katy. "This is Keith on bass. Megan on drums. Cherry Pit is up next, and they're incredible. My name is Katy, and this is our last song."

It wasn't until they finished "I'm a Good Guy" that Katy saw the guy himself standing in the back, smoking a cigarette.

# SPRING

"You ready to talk about the show?" asked Alicia.

Katy must have dozed off. She raised her head and looked around at the white sand obscured by hundreds of beach towels and beachgoers of every skin color—all displaying as much skin as possible. Katy, in her dark blue bikini, was no exception. A hundred yards down the beach, a rowdy volleyball game was underway. Every Beach Boys song was true, and this California thing was not so bad.

Three days had passed since Corona, but it was already hard to believe any of it had happened. The scene at the Crescent that night was repeated a thousand times over at suburban clubs across the country. Some unknown young band takes the stage to play its first show, does a decent job, makes an ungainly mass of kids slam into each other and sing along by the second chorus of their best songs.

Just a typical Thursday night. So why did it feel like the most important thing that had ever happened?

Katy's memory of the show, she found, had been sliced up into discrete units, like the digital samples making up a CD. The hum of her amplifier between songs. The nod from Megan after they nailed "Summer On." The way the faces in the crowd only occasionally clicked into focus, all with a familiar expression that she recognized from her own life: the face of a person completely checked into the music.

"It was the best night of my life," said Katy. "And kind of the worst."

"Because I couldn't make it? I hear you. I'll be there for the next one, promise, unless Keith gives me rabies."

"I don't think there's going to be a next one."

Alicia pouted. "Oh, come on."

Katy sat up and looked out at the water's edge, where Keith was wrestling with a Boogie Board. "You just want to see him do his rock star thing."

"Hey, that's not fair. I mean, of course I do. But I also want to see my roommate kick butt. Also, you obviously want to play again."

"Not without... never mind."

"Oh, so you can't even say his name now? For what it's worth, I think he wanted to come to the show."

"Really?"

"Yeah, he was talking about it at dinner, maybe fishing for a ride. But I think maybe he was afraid to see you play without him."

Katy thought about this. "Afraid we'd be bad or good?"

"If it were me," said Alicia, "I'd be kicking myself either way. So why'd he quit, anyway?"

"You know," said Katy. "Strict mom. Homework. Outside his comfort zone, I guess."

"Not because he's totally into you and he couldn't stand having you dangle it in his face anymore?"

"What the hell are you talking about?"

Alicia rolled her eyes. "Oh, you can't be serious."

"He has a girlfriend. And... you're being ridiculous. Travis and I are friends. Were friends." The images rolled in like waves. Travis offering unsolicited opinions of every CD at Rhombus Records. The way the hood of his sweatshirt fell over his eyes. Arguing about cereal. "I don't know."

"So who are you into?" Katy's eyes automatically went to Keith and his magical abs. He waved at them and yelled, "Come on in!"

"You still can't have that one," said Alicia.

"I know." Katy stared out at the water. The ocean, when she thought about it, was a very weird thing. Huge and dangerous and full of things that wanted to sting and bite you, but still so alluring it was impossible to stay away. The ocean was a bad boyfriend. Maybe there was a song in that.

"The thing is," said Katy, "after what happened with Nick, I feel like I don't trust my judgment about guys. At least I haven't been bringing anyone back to the room, right? Maybe next year I'll make your life interesting."

"You're already interesting," said Alicia. "Which is nice way of saying 'crazy.' But I still love you. Let's get our feet wet."

They splashed into the water, where Keith gave Alicia an impromptu bodyboarding lesson and offered Katy the next one. As alluring as that sounded, Katy was already drifting away, looking around for a peaceful spot amid the salty mosh pit of the Pacific.

•

Alicia dropped Katy back on campus on Friday before heading home to Palos Verdes to introduce Keith to her parents. "You going to be okay?" Alicia asked.

"Of course," said Katy. "No offense, but some time to myself would be great."

A deserted campus offered Katy the rare pleasure of blasting KROQ at unsociable volumes with her door open. The playlist was so repetitive that Katy became clairvoyant: That Elastica song would always be followed by Better Than Ezra's "Good" or Live's "Lightning Crashes." So she went down to the dorm lounge to eat Cheez-Its and watch the O.J. trial. How could murder be so boring? She squirmed on the couch, unable to find a comfortable position for her sunburned shoulders.

Fine. She gave up on the justice system, put on some sunscreen, and took her acoustic out to the quad. The only audience was a dozen funky-smelling trees. She picked a blade of grass, braced it between her thumbs, and blew a dissonant blast, a trick she'd learned at camp.

"That was kind of metal," said a familiar voice. She opened her eyes and saw Nick Dimmett standing over her.

"What do you want, Nick?" She didn't get up. "What are you even doing here?"

"Taking care of a couple things on campus," he said. He set down a black duffel bag and lay down next to Katy, using the battered duffel as a pillow. It clanked, kind of like Megan's drum hardware, but more hollow, like he was carrying tin cans.

"Thanks," said Katy. "Now, do you mind? I'm not in the mood for company."

"Funny you should mention that," said Nick. "Here's the thing, Katy. I'm a senior. This fall the Session will probably be playing

KROQ Acoustic Christmas, and the Laundry Hamper, well, you guys can start figuring out what you're good at."

"What are you talking about?" Getting angry felt surprisingly good; at least it was different from lonely.

"Spring Fest is coming up next month," said Nick. "Ben Harper, Nabisco Session. We've got this girl Alison doing backing vocals, and she's the greatest. Are you guys playing?"

"I don't know yet."

She felt Nick smile next to her. "Don't get me wrong. I like you guys. You have a lot of potential. Maybe next year."

Katy set her guitar down. She knew the words were futile as soon as she started forming them, but couldn't help it. "You saw us out in Corona. That wasn't potential, we—"

"Hey, relax," said Nick. He stood and slung the duffel over his shoulder. "We played that place a couple times, early on. Bunch of suburban kids with nowhere else to go. And you get up there with a guitar and that body?" He turned to go. "Of course they loved your set."

Katy waited until Nick was out of sight before playing a snarling rendition of "I'm a Good Guy." While she packed up, she glanced at the Wall. The Laundry Room logo was gone.

•

The rumor was true: The frozen yogurt machine was left unguarded during spring break. Katy filled two cups, rushed back to the dorm, and turned right, into Mitchell II.

Travis's door was open. She'd scoped it out earlier, walking down the hall in socks until she could see the door ajar and hear music spilling from overly loud headphones.

She knocked. Travis slipped his headphones off, and she heard a few bars of "Negative Creep" before he hit pause and said, "What's up?"

"Just the Foam started a new chain. It's called Just the Yo. All yogurt, no toppings."

"Seriously?"

"Seriously? Yes, Travis, the fake espresso place you invented has a spinoff. You think we should invest?" She set the bowls on the floor and held up a pair of spoons. "Seriously, I brought you yogurt. With toppings."

Travis got off the bed, compared the two bowls of vanilla yogurt, and took the one with chocolate sprinkles, just like Katy knew he was going to. "You're right," he said. "Just the Yo wouldn't make it into a weird lumpy pile like this."

"Yeah, Keith would never make it past the interview." Katy sat beside him on the floor, leaning against the side of the bed. "What have you been up to this week, anyway?"

"Studying. Eating a lot of Thai food. The gym is open and I've been shooting hoops."

"Yeah, right."

"I'm serious, actually. I'm not going to try out for the team, but I could probably beat Shaq at free throws. Let me know if you want to play HORSE sometime."

"You're on," said Katy. She twirled a spoonful of yogurt, which had softened to the perfect consistency and was starting to pick up a patchwork of colorful stains from the Fruity Pebbles. "So are we going to talk about the show or what?"

"Is that why you're here?"

"I don't know."

Travis fiddled with the cable of his headphones, which had

coiled itself into a spaghetti-like mass. "You ever wonder why there aren't vanilla sprinkles? I mean, a bunch of white sprinkles on chocolate—"

"Dude. I'm trying to talk to you. Are you pissed at me for playing the show?"

He slid down a little. "Yeah. But that seems illogical, because you only did it because I quit. It's like if I stole your wallet and then got mad at you for not buying me lunch. Hey, pick a CD."

Travis's wooden CD rack had room for two hundred discs and was currently home to about a hundred and fifty. The last few discs on each shelf had toppled over into rough piles. Katy had inspected and borrowed from Travis's collection dozens of times, and she could only find two things wrong with it: He took terrible care of his jewel cases and liner notes, and he didn't have enough albums by female artists. Actually, she remembered, she'd called his collection "testosterone-infested," then retracted the comment after realizing that her own collection was probably no better.

She flipped through the rack and pulled out *Siamese Dream.* "Okay?"

Travis nodded. "I approve. When I get tired of that album, you can bury me." He handed over the Discman, and Katy swapped out the discs and plugged in the multimedia speakers. While she hunted for the *Bleach* case, the initial plucks of "Cherub Rock" came on. Travis slid down until he was on the floor, staring up at the ceiling. "The thing is," he said, "I really wanted to be at that show. And at the same time I didn't. Having two feelings at once really sucks. Having *any* feelings seems like kind of... an unnecessary feature."

"What are you talking about?"

Travis tapped out the beat on the floor. "Like, this song. It's great, right? I mean, look at your face. And after this we could listen to 'Violet' and 'Kashmir' and 'I Wanna Be Adored,' and it'll make us feel good for a minute or two, but I'm surrounded by great songs, and I still feel like shit a lot of the time."

Katy's neck tensed up. "Travis, I didn't know that."

"Doesn't everybody? Sorry, I guess I'm wearing my I HEART FEELINGS shirt today."

Katy knew he was being sarcastic but couldn't help looking anyway. The Pixies' *Trompe Le Monde* cover art was peeking out from the zipper on his jacket. She leaned against the edge of his desk. "So then why'd you join the band in the first place?"

"Because you wouldn't take no for an answer." Katy threw a soggy Fruity Pebble at him. Travis picked it off his shirt and ate it. "Why do you think? Because I got to hang out with cool people and sing songs. And it made me happy, and also miserable."

"Miserable how?"

"Remember the Java Cave?"

"Still trying to forget."

"Yeah, me too." Travis whistled along with the guitar riff. "After the show, you seemed *ruined*. People say empathy is great, but it sucks. Seeing you like that made me feel like garbage."

"It wasn't your fault," said Katy.

"I know. But it still felt like it was. And with you and Megan there was always some kind of emotional martial arts battle going on. I mean, being Asian, I'm naturally good at all martial arts. Just not that one."

"Are you saying girls are too emotional to be in a band?"

"No, I'm saying *I'm* too emotional to be in a band. Like when Trish and I broke up—"

"Wait, you broke up? When did this happen?"

"Couple months ago. She said she thought generic cereals were pretty much the same as the real thing, and I dropped her like a bowl of Lucky Stars." He looked down at his lap. "Actually, she broke up with me. It wasn't a surprise. Things were weird over break."

Katy looked over at Travis's desk. The photo of him with Trish was missing. "Travis, it's bad enough that you didn't talk to me about this, but you didn't even write a song about it? Like, about how bitches are always up in your grill or something?"

"Like an N.W.A song?" said Travis. "Now, that's an interesting challenge. I mean, I was born gangsta, straight up, south side of Seattle. I've got the melanin. It's quite possible I can rap." He dropped a few lines from "Straight Outta Compton" and looked at Katy's appalled expression. "It's also possible I can't."

"Travis, if I let you back in the band, will you promise never to do that again?"

"You can't put a lid on this flavor."

Katy followed Travis's gaze to the ceiling. You could see where a former occupant's glow-in-the-dark stars had been painted over. "You want to hear about the show or what?" she said. She walked him through it, minute by minute. "A kid came up to me afterwards and asked if we wrote those songs."

"What did you tell him?"

"I said I wrote them with my friend." The last chord of the song rang out, and Katy sat back down next to Travis on the floor. She smoothed her skirt out over her thighs.

"I thought it would be really simple," said Travis. "Like, I didn't exactly *want* to quit the band, but once I did, I was like, cool, now I can go back to doing my usual stuff. Keep my head down. Be mysterious and captivating."

"How's that going?"

"Terrible. Especially since people won't stop playing our tape. Some girl asked me at lunch if I would sing a song. So I sang 'Happy Birthday.' She didn't think it was very funny."

"Hey, shut up a minute." "Soma" was Katy's favorite Smashing Pumpkins song. She'd read that Billy Corgan had recorded over forty guitar tracks, and at the time she hadn't understood what that meant. Now she imagined herself in the studio, trying guitar lines over and over, layering them until she'd created something that sounded like a message picked up from a planet where they'd figured everything out. "Rails, it's just one more show. We can show Nabisco Session's fans what a good song sounds like. What do you say?"

"Asking me during this song is totally unfair. You could convince me to drive Nabisco Session's tour bus." He pressed his tongue between his lips like he did when he was really pondering something. "Could you get us more yogurt? I'll call my mom while you're gone. Tell her I joined Slag."

# 39

Travis was welcomed back with a conquering-hero cheer. "Thanks, everyone," he said. "Before we play any music, I've prepared a few remarks." He took a few folded sheets of paper out of his pocket and looked around. Megan looked horrified. "You know I'm not serious, right? These are lyric sheets. I forgot half the songs."

"Well, that's encouraging," said Megan. "So how did Katy convince you to come back?" She made an obscene gesture.

"Megan, Jesus!" said Katy. She pulled the flyer out of her bag. They were all over campus, so she figured stealing just one wouldn't reduce attendance.

**SPRING FEST**

SATURDAY APRIL 29

FITZ FIELD

BEN HARPER

NABISCO SESSION

THE LAUNDRY ROOM
CHERRY PIT
AND MORE!
BEER (21+)

"How'd you convince them to let us play, huh?"

"Truckloads of blowjobs." Megan spun a drumstick between her fingers. "Actually, the SBA events coordinator is a friend of mine. But she already knew who we were. Also, she had to book them, but she's not a huge Nabisco Session fan, and I told her we might play a song about a certain member of that band."

If Katy had to give one piece of advice to an up-and-coming band, it would be: Break up often. She hadn't realized the extent to which Travis's departure had improved her guitar skills. Megan was right: Having to sing and play at the same time on every song meant she had to play every chord on autopilot—no cheating and peeking at the fretboard. Now that Travis had returned, it was like getting her legs back after a sack race. Megan joined in on the "Summer On" harmonies, and the song tightened up until it felt like a smooth stone she could put in her pocket and carry around.

Megan sat up straight and wiped sweat off her forehead. "Rails, how does it feel to be back?"

"Normal," he replied.

•

Katy and Alicia found seats in an upper row of the auditorium a few minutes before *Back to the Future* started. Every Thursday, Katy's meteorology lecture hall was converted into a makeshift movie theater showing eighties classics, sometimes preceded by

Looney Tunes shorts.

"Hey, I wanted to ask you something," said Alicia. She handed Katy a twist of red licorice. "You want to room together again next year? I know you probably have your eye on a single, but if we went in on room draw together we could maybe get a place on north campus, and it's closer to—"

Katy dug her teeth into the Red Vine. "Of course I do. I hope they have more closet space up north, though, because I'm planning to buy sixteen pairs of shoes over the summer."

"You are not."

"Would you believe one pair?"

As Alicia pondered this, Katy settled into her seat. Somehow, the school year was almost over. Everything these days was prefixed with "final." This was the final Thursday night movie of the school year. Soon she'd eat her final omelet, work her final shift at the library, take her final final.

"Earth to Katy," said Alicia. "You guys ready for the show on Saturday?"

"I think so. You ready to get rocked?"

"I'm not going to dignify that with a response. But yeah, it's not entirely uncool that my boyfriend and my roommate are both famous rock stars."

"We are not!" Katy said it automatically, but when she thought about it, it was sort of true. Sure, no one beyond Atwood knew about the Laundry Room, but here on campus, it was hard to find someone who couldn't sing at least the chorus of "Summer On." And for the past nine months, Atwood College had been Katy's entire world. "By the way, thanks for painting our logo on the Wall."

Alicia laughed. "How'd you know?"

"You threw a can of spray paint in the wastebasket. If you'd just take out the trash more often, you would have gotten away with it."

The two guys in front of them who looked like they'd come straight from a hacky sack session were talking during the Sylvester and Tweety cartoon. Katy wasn't listening in, exactly, but it was hard to miss the words "Nabisco Session" and "tour" and "canceled." She smiled at the idea, even though she hadn't heard that Nabisco Session was planning a tour.

"Yeah," said one of the guys. "Ben Harper, too. They're heading out on the road with Dave Matthews and Rusted Root. You wanna line up for tickets with me?"

Katy leaned forward. "What are you guys talking about?"

"Spring Fest," said the guy. "It's canceled."

•

By the time Katy got to Broad Hall, Megan had already heard. "Okay," said Katy. "Let's pretend I already called Nick Dimmett every swear word in six languages, and figure out how we're going to book another show. Could we play Bricker Auditorium?"

"What are you talking about?" said Megan. "Dead Week starts on Monday. Even if we could put together another show, which we can't, nobody would show up. And as much as I'd love to help you build a Nick Dimmett piñata, you would have done the same thing in his place, and you know it."

Katy felt her stomach turn to jelly. "But you always know how to fix stuff."

"Well, I don't know how to fix this. But hey, we played a good show in Corona. Next year you and Travis can—"

"Next year?" Katy picked up a drumstick, then let it clatter to the floor. "You and Keith are graduating. Travis and I aren't going to become an acoustic duo next year. We're going to go back to being stupid, normal, boring—"

"Hey, Pity Katy is back! I sure missed her."

"Shut up."

"Look, I'm pissed too, but we tried. Let's at least have one last practice tomorrow, okay?"

•

The music room. Practice.

During "I'm a Good Guy," Katy broke a string. "I got it!" she yelled. Megan and Keith traded solos while she sat on the floor, fished a high E string out of its paper envelope, and had her guitar back in action in two minutes. Battlefield surgery. Megan mouthed "two, three, four" and Katy stepped on the distortion pedal and finished out the song.

Travis had taken to wandering the room during the verses of "There Is No Home" and reappearing at the mic just when he was needed. It made Katy nervous, but no more so than when he stood motionless, staring at her, until his part rolled around.

Tonight he was so intrigued by a stack of small blue vinyl boxes that he missed his cue. "Travis, you're in a band, remember?" said Megan.

"Hey, can I try something?" said Travis. He opened one of the boxes and removed a glockenspiel and a pair of small mallets. "Hang on." He stacked a couple of cardboard boxes next to his mic stand, set the small xylophone on top, and adjusted the microphone until it was pointing at the metal bars. "Okay, from the top."

Travis plunked out an inspired riff on the first try. As they finished out the song, Katy laughed: The glockenspiel refrain that turned "There Is No Home" into a complete, perfect song was the result of Travis's inability to stand still for even one single minute.

"You know what's weird about this place?" said Katy.

"A lot of things," said Keith. "Many of which are in this room."

"True. But specifically, it's weird that this version of Atwood is never going to exist again."

"Guys, Katy is sounding like me again," said Travis. "Did you plug my cable into her amp by mistake or something?"

Megan snorted. "I am not even going to touch that one."

Katy strummed an F major, which seemed like a good getting-attention kind of chord. "I mean, a couple weeks from now, a quarter of everyone on campus is going to graduate, including half of us. And four years from now, nobody here now will be left except professors and dining hall workers and Nick Dimmett's buddies on the five-year-plan. But it'll be pretty much the same around here. Probably some other band will be in here trying to write a song. Doesn't that seem crazy? It's like the world is ending and no one really cares."

"Like the U2 song," said Keith. "'Until the End of the World.' Serious bassline on that track."

"Oh, you mean unequivocally the best U2 song?" said Travis. "I approve."

Katy nodded. "Yeah, I think it's my favorite, too."

"You idiots," said Megan. "Ever heard of Sunday Bloody Motherfucking Sunday?"

"I know the 'End of the World' riff," said Katy. "You want to give it a try?"

Travis offered to run over to Mitchell and grab the CD. When he got back, Katy plugged the Discman into her amp and they all listened to the song together. Keith played the bass intro. "Does that sound right?" said Keith. "Megan?"

Megan tried out the drumbeat, and when Keith came back in, it was a believable approximation of the opening groove. Megan hit the sixteenth-notes of the fill, and Katy brought it together with the spiky guitar riff. Then it all fell apart when they tried to transition to the verse. "Shit, guys," she said. "This song is *hard*."

"You know what's an easier song?" said Megan. "Sunday—"

Keith interrupted her. "Let's try it again."

Katy knew it made no sense at all for the Laundry Room to spend ninety minutes on their last night as a band learning to play a U2 song. But when they finished nailing down the arrangement and Travis's voice soared over it, it seemed like time well spent. Just to needle Megan, Katy capped off the song with the opening riff of "Sunday Bloody Sunday."

"Look at me ignoring that," said Megan. "Now, can we play 'Takedown' one more time before we officially put this band on the funeral pyre? And let's play it fast."

The Laundry Room broke up one minute and seven seconds later.

Katy's mom loved reminding her that she had been a terrible baby. She'd wake up ten times every night, usually screaming. She spit up constantly. "And then we had Julie and realized babies are just like that," her mom had explained. "We could laugh at it instead of feeling like we were doing everything wrong."

Katy had filed this under the huge category of "annoying things parents say that you're expected to just nod along with." But she was reminded of it during spring Dead Week. It was still a blur of flash cards and twenty-page papers, late nights and study breaks, frozen yogurt and milkshakes. This time around, though, it didn't feel like she was being stretched on a medieval torture device. Sure, partly this was because she was no longer trying to juggle academics and music. But the work itself seemed easier, too, like she'd formed a special set of muscles last time around, and this time she just had to dust them off and give them some exercise. Katy was going to pass her finals, and she knew it.

She took her meteorology final on Wednesday afternoon, and

with that, her first year of college was over. It wasn't that she was expecting to be greeted by a victory party outside the science building, but the way the school year just fizzled out was unexpectedly depressing. She walked past the Wall. A couple of maintenance workers were painting it a neutral gray, to be defaced again in the fall after a few months of lying fallow. It was hot out, and the white glare of the L.A. sun fell across her eyes in the most piercing way. Plant aromas and smog filled the air. The world was ending.

It hadn't really sunk in yet that Keith and Megan weren't going to be back next year, even though she and Travis were planning to stick around until Sunday for commencement. It was hard to imagine Atwood College had existed before Megan arrived to dole out hard-edged advice. Katy wondered whether the mantle would pass to her. Maybe some confused first-year would show up at her room next year so she could say, "You want to be in a band, huh? I've been there. Here's the straight shit."

*But what do I know?* Katy thought. The Laundry Room had played two whole shows, and never a good show with the full lineup. They left behind one recording, barely even demo quality. Katy had gone from a novice guitar player to an advanced beginner with a couple of rock and roll outfits in her closet. None of this added up to much of anything or qualified her to give advice. *Another classic Katy Blundell dead-end.*

That evening, Katy went to the computer lab to check her email.

**From:** amukherjee@grinnell.edu
**Subject:** Your song

Hello, Laundry Room. A friend sent me the link
to your song Summer On, and it got me through
some really hard times this spring. Are you guys
touring? My friends and I would definitely drive to
Des Moines or Iowa City to see your show.

Yours truly,
Asha Mukherjee
Grinnell College, Class of '97

Katy thought of this message as Number One. Ten years later, it would still be in her inbox.

She whistled the chorus to "Summer On" on the way to the Wednesday night physics department study break. Travis was taking his physics final in the morning, and she knew he'd be there, not least because they were holding it in Mitchell Lounge. She found him doctoring a bowl of salsa with Four-X. "Whoa there, buddy," she said. "You sure you know what you're doing?"

"Chem final was this morning. This is just a simple titration problem." He offered Katy a chip. She dipped, and sure enough, bland supermarket salsa plus dangerously spicy hot sauce equaled salsa nirvana.

Alicia came over holding a chocolate-chip cookie. "I can't believe we're done," she said. Katy gave her a high-five which transformed into a clumsy fingers-clasped handshake and then a hug.

"Sorry you never got to see us play," said Katy. "For real, I mean."

"It's okay," said Alicia. "Maybe Keith will bust out a bass solo at commencement. Hey, are you listening to me?"

"Sorry." Katy's eyes were taking in the room. Mitchell Lounge was about twenty by thirty feet, with plenty of electrical outlets along the baseboard. "Hey, I gotta run. You up for taking a drive on Friday?"

*Thursday, May 11, 1995*

Mitchell Lounge had nothing resembling a stage, so they just set up along one wall with a couple of mic stands liberated from the music building. When the last plug was nestled in its jack and she'd changed the nine-volt battery in her distortion pedal, Katy smiled at the red glow of the LED and walked over to where the rest of the band was huddled in the corner. "Okay, I think we're good," said Megan. "Set lists?"

Katy handed them out.

THERE IS NO HOME

TAKEDOWN

I'M A GOOD GUY

SUMMER ON

UNTIL THE END OF THE WORLD

They'd put out the word in the morning that the Laundry Room would play a show to celebrate the end of finals. By that point, no one was left on campus but graduating seniors, a few confused-looking family members who were in town for commencement, and people stuck with a Thursday final. Atwood was so tiny, however, that even in its depopulated state, rumors got around, and Katy counted seventeen people in the audience. Most were seniors Katy didn't know, but Bianca was there, and she recognized a couple of Megan's friends. Alicia was sitting in front with Keith's DAT recorder. "Who's that old guy?" Katy whispered, pointing out a slim fiftyish man with gray hair and a camera hanging from a strap around his neck.

"Dude, that's my dad," said Megan.

"I see the resemblance now," said Katy. The sky was darkening, and a few raindrops pelted the windows behind them. "So, before we start, I just want to say." She rubbed her eye like it itched. "Keith. Megan. Thanks for letting me join your band."

Keith nodded. "A while ago I said this wasn't my kind of music. I don't know what I was thinking. I'm so proud to be part of this band."

"Rails?" said Megan. "You look like you have something to say, too."

"Oh," said Travis. "Well, I want to say thanks to Katy." He looked down at his hands. "This has been a really weird year. I don't know how to give a speech. Someone else go."

"Jeez, my turn?" said Megan. "C.G., what you said is totally backwards. This is your band, dumbass. Thanks for letting us be in it."

Katy took a deep breath. "We should get out there before everyone leaves to follow the Nabisco Session tour." The others laughed. "You're my best friends and I love you. Now let's make some fucking noise."

They clasped hands in a circle. "What did I tell you guys about group—" said Megan, but it was too late.

Alicia was in the driver's seat, for once, in full command of the minivan as they hurtled down the 210 through the San Fernando Valley. The law stated that you automatically get the shotgun position when your significant other is driving, so Keith was sitting in front. Katy and Megan claimed the middle seat, and Travis was asleep in the back, twisted up in the seatbelt like a cardboard box sealed with duct tape.

"That's where we turned off for the Corona show, isn't it?" said Katy.

"You mean the Best Show Ever?" said Alicia. "The one nobody saw?"

"That's the one," said Katy. "Radioactive, remember the kid who wouldn't stop crowd-surfing?"

"Stop calling him that!" said Alicia. "You know, I played an amazing solo concert in—" She glanced at a highway sign. "—Rancho Cucamonga last week. Sorry you guys couldn't make it. Johnny Depp was at the show, and I won two Grammys."

At Redlands, the highway merged with the 10 freeway. In Salem, the freeway had always been called "I-5." Here, every skin color, nationality, and accent was part of the cultural quilt, but saying "I-10" rather than "the 10" would brand you as an interloper. Where did these linguistic oddities come from? Katy decided it probably had something to do with the fact that Salem had two freeways and L.A. had a fractal patchwork of state routes and US highways and interstates.

"How far are we from campus?" Katy asked.

"I don't know," said Alicia. "Seventy miles?"

As she said it, the urbanized area ended, and they were in the desert. Noise barriers, billboards, malls, and cookie-cutter houses were replaced by sagebrush and barrel cactuses. Katy laughed.

"Yes?" said Megan.

"It's just so... stereotypical," said Katy. "Like a cartoon of a desert. Hey, look, there's one!" She pointed at a low tree with spindly limbs, bent over like it was photographed in the middle of its aerobic routine.

"Hey, that's crazy," said Travis. He unrolled himself from the seat belt and sat up. "Do you think we can find the place where they did the photo shoot for the album?"

"I assume so," said Katy. "Isn't it probably marked, like Jim Morrison's grave?"

The sign for Joshua Tree National Park came into view. Alicia handed over five dollars at the admission booth, and they continued down a two-lane road into the park. Now the trees were everywhere, hundreds of them, like skinny-fingered arm wrestlers. Could you call this a forest? Katy wasn't sure. In the Northwest, forests were always green, towering, with a carpet-soft floor.

Travis pulled the wrinkled insert from the U2 CD out of his

pocket and held it up to the back window of the van, truing the edge against the heating elements of the rear defroster. "I'm not seeing it," he said. "You'd think those guys would be too busy to drive very far into the park."

"Hand it over," said Megan. "Rails, there's only one tree in this picture. It's probably trick photography. They shot the picture in front of a blue screen in Dublin, and The Edge saw a magazine with a tree on it while he was waiting for the dentist, and boom. Classic album."

"Maybe," said Travis. "Hey, why do only two of them have nicknames, anyway? Do you think it sucks being the other guys? Or, wait, maybe it's better being those guys, because nobody even remembers what they look like, but they still have billions of dollars and groupies. Let me know if you see them, because I have a lot of questions."

"Speaking as one of the 'other guys' in this band," said Megan, "I want my share of the billions and hotties. Keith? What do you think?"

"I don't know," said Keith. "It's too pretty out here to think."

"Well, look at it this way," said Katy. "All four of us have nicknames, so we're either a hundred percent better than U2, or a hundred percent worse."

Alicia parked the van in a lot near a cluster of huge, flat rocks, and they pulled the backpacks and sleeping bags out of the car. Katy found the sunblock in the pocket of her backpack and rubbed some onto her cheeks and shoulders and legs. When she looked up, she saw Megan and Travis doing the same. Alicia shook her head. "God, you Northwest people."

"Do you think it's okay if I leave my guitar in the van for now?" said Katy.

"It's only the acoustic," said Megan. "A bunch of hippies might borrow it, but other than that I wouldn't worry."

They explored the low brush lands, hiking between massive rocks and stands of Joshua trees. Travis speculated loudly about the possibility of rattlesnakes, and Katy screamed when she saw something dart out from behind a rock. It turned out to be a jack-rabbit, with comical Bugs Bunny ears.

At sunset, they unrolled the sleeping bags on top of a rock and had a dinner of assorted semi-perishables scavenged from the dining hall and 7-Eleven. Katy clicked on her black Mag-Lite. "Hey, Travis, I'm going to grab my guitar. Come with?"

"Do you really need help with that?"

Megan flicked him on the arm. "The rattlesnake venom's not going to suck itself out."

"Thanks a lot, M.D.," said Katy. "Do they teach that in med school?"

Travis was uncharacteristically quiet on the way to the car, but it was a comfortable silence. Katy popped the hatch of the minivan and grabbed the handle of her guitar case. "Hey, Trav," she said. "My parents are talking about a family trip to Seattle this summer. You want to go to a show? I hear Nabisco Session is on tour. Or we could see some of that mopey-guy music you're into."

"Sure thing," said Travis. Katy couldn't see his face in the darkness, but it sounded like he was smiling. "Meet me at Just the Foam."

When they got back to the rock, the meaty part of the sunset had settled in, a riotous patchwork of red and pink and gold behind the silhouettes of rangy, twisted trees. Alicia whispered something to Keith, who said, "We're going to take a walk. Anyone else want to come?" Everyone picked up on his tone: They weren't invited.

Katy took out her acoustic. She strummed a G chord and winced. *How does a guitar get so far out of tune just sitting around in its case?* She tuned up and said, "Requests?"

"Freebird," said Travis.

"Ignoring. Hey, do you know all the words to 'I Am the Resurrection'?"

"Was I alive in 1990?"

"Great, let's do this," said Katy. She and Travis sang in unison until they got to the guitar solo, at which point the song fell apart spectacularly. Megan gave them a slow clap, and Katy segued into "There Is No Home," with Megan and Travis joining in on harmonies during the chorus.

"Shoulda brought my Glock," said Travis. Katy gave him a quizzical look. "You know, my glockenspiel."

The sunset had faded to dark gray streaks, and even though the sky was still dusky, stars you could never see in L.A. had come out. Megan took an Altoids box out of her backpack, opened it, and fiddled with something between her fingers. Katy was thinking she could really go for a mint when Megan said, "I'm going to smoke a joint. If you care to join me, great. If not, that's cool. This is not a peer pressure moment." She flicked a lighter, and a dot of burning leaves glowed in the darkness.

Katy accepted the joint and inhaled. The smoke tasted better than it smelled, with a sweet, almost cotton-candy note. She passed the joint to Travis, who looked at it quizzically. "Don't worry, your mom's not here," said Megan. He brought the joint to his lips.

It was getting cold out, and Katy pulled on her U of O sweatshirt and unfolded her sleeping bag across her legs. She looked up at the sky. When she was ten, Katy's parents took her and Julie camping in central Oregon in late August, just before school started. None of them realized until the first night that their trip corresponded with a particularly exuberant display of the Perseid meteor shower. She'd asked her parents to explain, over and over, what meteors were and whether one was going to land on their tent.

But she'd never seen this many stars. When a jet of light streaked across the sky, it seemed *inevitable*. Even though Katy knew meteors and stars were completely different phenomena—one the size of a pebble, the other larger than everything she'd ever known put together and multiplied by a billion—it seemed like the shooting star must have been an actual star that said, "Look at me! I'm going for it!"

In other words, Katy was pretty fucking high. "Rails, do you know constellations?" she said.

"Only the big famous ones," said Travis. "The Bono and Edge constellations, not the other guys. That's Venus over there." If he was pointing, Katy couldn't see his finger in the dark. "People used to call it the Evening Star, because people were dumb."

The joint went around again. "I think the guy with the glasses is cute," said Megan.

"Which guy with which glasses?" said Katy.

"From U2."

"Oh yeah. Which one is he?"

"I don't know, the bassist or the drummer or something," said Megan. "The glockenspiel player."

"They should name constellations for bands," said Katy. "Wouldn't it be great if our descendants took their kids out in the backyard and said, like, 'See those four stars over there? That one's called the Beatles.'"

"The Blur constellation just looks like a blur," said Travis, giggling.

Katy reached out her hand and Megan set the joint gently across her fingers. She took a drag and passed it to Travis, then fumbled with the zipper on her sleeping bag, closing herself inside. "What was it like on campus when he died?" said Katy. "Cobain, I mean."

Travis got into his own sleeping bag and lay down next to Katy, his head at her feet. "The dorms didn't have ethernet yet, just dialup," he said. "So I was at the lab, reading alt.music.alternative. Usually that group gets like a hundred messages a day, but I logged on and there were seventeen hundred. And they were all saying the same thing. Mostly people were just posting the news over and over, stuff they heard on the radio, like it wasn't real until they said it themselves."

"I was in my room, listening to KROQ," said Megan. She was still sitting up, but she'd arranged one of her fraying drum blankets over her lap. She stubbed out the tail end of the joint. "It seemed like an April Fool's joke. Like, he'd tried to kill himself before, and it didn't work, so this must be another one of his crazy pranks. But then I headed out to the quad, and a lot of people looked like shit, so we just blew off classes, and people brought out boom boxes and acoustic guitars, and we hung out and talked about our favorite songs. That's where I first met Travis."

"Oh, that's right," said Travis. "I was really upset, and I felt like no one could possibly understand, because people usually don't understand what I'm feeling, and also it seemed weird to be upset about some guy I never met. Illogical. And then it turned out a bunch of people felt the same way. I still don't really get it."

"Did people paint the wall?" said Katy.

Megan laughed. "The whole thing was one big memorial. The art was fucking abominable, but it seemed important at the time. What about you? What was it like in Salem?"

"Miserable," said Katy. "I heard about it on the local TV news, and like you said, Travis, the newscasters seemed confused that anyone would care. I wanted to go to the memorial in Seattle, but my parents weren't about to let me skip school and drive two hundred miles. So my friend Christina and I went to Ranch Records in downtown Salem. People mostly just seemed stunned. If I'd known how to write songs then, I probably would have written something really sappy."

"I'd like to hear that song," said Megan. She took a deep breath. "I want to tell you guys about something I never talk about."

"Okay," said Katy. Somehow even more stars had come out, and the sky reminded her of the unpopped kernels in a spent bowl of popcorn.

Megan sat up. "Two years ago, my sister Maya died in a car crash. She was in high school, and—well, the details aren't important. The point is, I was here and she was there, and then all of a sudden she was dead. And after that, my family pretty much fell apart. My parents split up, and none of us really wanted to talk to each other anymore, because it was too painful."

"I'm sorry," said Katy. She sat up and looked out into the night, hoping to catch the silhouette of a Joshua tree, but it was too dark to see anything. "Does Keith know?"

"Yeah. Let me finish. I think people can respond to something like that in a lot of different ways, and my way was to try and avoid caring that much about anyone ever again. It's not like I was a touchy-feely person even before it happened, but I decided that the only way to live in a world where that kind of thing could happen was to be a cold, hard bitch who didn't give a fuck about anyone."

"That's what I would have done," said Travis.

Megan kicked him through his sleeping bag. "I still wanted to play music, because I liked how hard it is to think about anything else while you're doing it. Other than that, my plan was to study, not make friends, and go be a doctor. And before you ask, I was already planning on med school before Maya died. I'm not *that* much of a cliché." She sat up and looked around. Katy nodded to show she was still listening.

"Anyway," Megan went on, "you're both high, so I'm going to spell this out like you're babies: I love you guys. Don't make me regret it, okay?" Katy and Travis wrapped their arms around Megan in a clumsy, stoned hug, and they all collapsed, giggling, onto the rock.

The glowing beam of a flashlight announced the return of a happy and disheveled Keith and Alicia. "What in the world?" said Keith. He sniffed the air. "Aha."

•

In the night, Katy woke up and checked the glowing hands of her watch. Two-ten. Her face was freezing, but the rest of her body was warm, and the contrast wasn't unpleasant. She looked up at the sky. The stars had shifted. Her sleeping bag was wedged in among all the others, and before she fell back to sleep, she picked out the four stars of the Laundry Room constellation.

# ACKNOWLEDGMENTS

Hey, you read this book all the way to the acknowledgments! (Or flipped directly to the acknowledgments, which is a weird thing to do unless you're my mom. Hi Mom!)

Everyone below deserves the utmost thanks. I mention this so I don't have to keep writing the words "thank you" until they sound like gibberish.

Yeah, I know every author says it. But seriously, the fact that Molly Wizenberg and Laurie Amster-Burton's names are relegated to the back of this book is a travesty. Each of them had to talk me through multiple freakouts when it seemed like the book was broken (true) and couldn't be fixed (untrue). They contributed many of the best ideas and best lines in the book.

Jennie Shortridge was one of the first people to whom I admitted that I had an idea for a novel. In exchange for coffee, she told me everything she knows about novel writing. Which is a lot, since she's published five, most of them bestsellers.

Becky Selengut, Jen Chiu, Erica Kim, Christine Inzer, Jane Vail, and Iris Amster-Burton read drafts on short notice and nudged me in the right direction.

Maya Rock did the developmental edit. Cathy Yardley helped

with plot. Elayne Morgan did the line edit and final proofread. Writing a book? Please hire all of them.

Liza Daly and Neil deMause helped craft the Kickstarter campaign text. CL Smith (goonwrite.com) designed the cover.

Denise Sakaki designed the Laundry Room logo.

My agent, Michael Bourret of Dystel, Goderich, and Bourret, put in a ton of work on this project in exchange for absolutely nothing. Michael, I'll try to write something with commercial appeal someday.

Jaan Uhelszki gave me my first music writing job, at Addicted to Noise magazine, in 1995.

*Our Secret Better Lives* is based in part on my experience playing in a number of marginal rock bands. Thank you to my former bandmates Adam Cadre, Liza Daly, Herbert Bergel, Kip Fagan, Heidi Schreck, Truman, Kenji Baugham, Karen Reagan, Bryan Fry, Ryan Thomson, and Peerapong Tantamjarik.

Steve Krolikowski came up with "Just the Foam," and I totally bought it. Check out his band Repeater. Colin Hay is responsible for the idea of "almost ready." If you ever have a chance to see a concert by Hay, who is the founder and lead singer of Men At Work ("I come from a land down under..."), don't miss it.

Molly Wizenberg and I co-host a podcast called Spilled Milk, and without our industrious and delightful producer Abby Cerquitella, we wouldn't have time to write books or do anything else.

While I was working on this book, Foo Fighters released an EP called *Songs from the Laundry Room*. A happy coincidence, I swear.

This book would not exist without two remarkable songs.

1. **"Oregon Girl," by Someone Still Loves You Boris Yeltsin.** Yes, this is the most unwieldy band name you've ever heard. Fans call them SSLYBY, which isn't really helpful, because how do you

pronounce that? Anyway, "Oregon Girl" is a lovable stuffed animal of a song, but it isn't told from the perspective of the titular girl. So I was like, hmm. By the way, SSLYBY seem like super nice guys, and they're great in concert.

**2. "Where They Go Back to School But Get Depressed," by The Loud Family.** I'm just now noticing that one of these songs has an easy-to-remember name but the band name is impossible, and the other…. This song begins with the line: "And will this be our second chance / Our secret better lives?" It's a song about going back to college as an adult with the goal of doing everything better this time around, and finding that, of course, it doesn't work that way. (I guess this is also sort of the plot of the Rodney Dangerfield movie *Back to School*.)

"Where They Go Back to School…" was written by Scott Miller, who put out album after brilliant album with his bands Game Theory and The Loud Family in the 80s and 90s. It's hard enough to write a perfect straightforward pop song like "Oregon Girl." Scott was perfectly capable of writing that kind of song (see "The Red Baron" or "Crypto-Sicko"), but mostly he wrote weird songs, with intellectual lyrics and melodies that veer off in unexpected directions. He wrote an eight-minute epic about the Heaven's Gate cult ("Sister Sleep") and a meditation on songwriting with lyrics based on The Tempest and Dr. Strangelove ("Motion of Ariel"). These are bad ideas for songs, but they're insanely catchy, moving, and timeless.

Most of Scott's music is available on your favorite service, and I encourage you to seek it out. *Our Secret Better Lives* is about that feeling you get at the moment a song changes your life, and no songwriter has had that effect on me more times than Scott.

Scott Miller died in 2013. This book is dedicated to him.

*Our Secret Better Lives* was brought to life by 114 backers on Kickstarter, including Abby Cerquitella, Allyn Adell Humphreys, Amanda Powter, Amber Andersen, Amy Koester, Amy Plank, Amy Reece, Andrea Frabotta, Angie S., Anita Crotty, Anita Verna Crofts, Beth Hilleke, Betsy Turner, Blair Feehan, Brad Mohr, Bridgette Lee, Bruce and Susan, Caroline Cummins, Chris, Christine Inzer, Christopher Glenn, Connie Fahling, Constance, Dan Pashman, Dan Shiovitz, Danielle Kramer, Darsa Morrow, Daryn Nakhuda, David Glasser, Dawn Wright, Denise Sakaki, Doug Jones, E Carr, Emily Short, Emily Voigtlander, Evelyn Buell, Gail Ringsage, Gemma Docherty, James Turnbull, James Whetzel, Jason Truesdell, Jennifer and Greg Barnes, Jess Severe, Jessica Prunty, Jim Naureckas, Jim Sterling, Jonathan Blask, Judah Morford, Judy and Richard Amster, Julie Kodama, Justin de Vesine, Kairu Yao, Katharine Bond, Katherine Malloy, Kathleen Burton McDade, Katie Panciera, Katy Foreman, Katya Schapiro, Kieran Holzhauer, Kirsten Burt, Kristin Nelson, Laura Buell, Lauren Dykstra, Lauren Kingston, Liza Daly, Lizz "L7" Zitron, m3, Marcia Hunt Goldberg, Matt Cline, Megan DeBell, Megan Tortora, Melissa DeWild, Michael Burton, Michael Fessler, Michael Zwirn, Mike & Lizette Lee, Milagros L. Wilson, Molly Wizenberg, Momi, Neil Graham, Nozlee Samadzadeh, Phillip Harris, Rachel Balota, Randy Saldinger & Kevin Kelley, Rebecca Braverman, Rebekah Denn, Rebel Powell, ribblefizz, Richard E. Morrison, Robin McWaters, Ryan "Whammy Bard" Thomson, Sarah Evangelista, Sarah Pedlow, Sharyn November, Shigeru, Stacy Cowley, Stephen Gibbon, Steve Nicholson, Storme Winfield, Sue Trowbridge, Susan MacCulloch, Susann Rutledge, Suzanne Kraft, The Laney Family, Virginia Mead, Wendy Burton, and Whitney Brandt-Hiatt.

Special thanks to Allen Garvin.

Finally, I've put together a Spotify playlist featuring some of the songs that inspired this book: *http://spoti.fi/2fhwCWZ*

# ABOUT THE AUTHOR

Matthew Amster-Burton is the author of five books, including *Pretty Good Number One: An American Family Eats Tokyo,* which was an international bestseller. He cohosts the hit comedy podcast Spilled Milk. Matthew lives with his family in Seattle.

CPSIA information can be obtained
at www.ICGtesting.com
Printed in the USA
LVOW03s0128260717
542657LV00002B/227/P